PRAISE FOR
LAY FIGURES

"*Lay Figures* is a richly imagined novel set in Depression-era Saint John, where the vivid world of artists comes to life, their loves and losses shaping what they create. With war changing the destinies of those around her, the young writer Elizabeth MacKinnon searches for a subject that will allow her to realize her potential. Her exploration of what inspires art, for herself and for others, makes for a very compelling read."

    –**Anne Simpson, author of** *Speechless*

"*Lay Figures* is beautifully written. Blagrave's prose flows easily and is full of robust descriptions of both the cityscape and land-scape…[his] descriptions are evocative and vivid, enveloping readers in sensory language…. Above all, *Lay Figures* provides a fascinating look into what Blagrave rightly labels 'the under-sung city of Saint John….' A captivating commentary on art and creation, love, lust, and betrayal, social disparity, and the cultural history of the Maritime region."

    –**The Miramichi Reader**

"*Lay Figures* is a rich, satisfying, and enormously entertaining reading experience. [It] presents the lucky reader with both the glamour and the grit of art making while staying true to the plain, very unromantic fact that artists are not born, they are made…. Vivid, evocative, well-written, and beautiful."

    –**Arabella magazine**

"Novels about the lives of artists rarely get it right. Mark Blagrave's *Lay Figures* is a rich, enormously entertaining exception. Like Atwood's *Cat's Eye* or Corbeil's *In the Wings*, *Lay Figures* presents the lucky reader with both the glamour and the grit of art making. The questions and challenges faced by Blagrave's artists are eternal, and more vital today than ever. Saint John is Canada's Atlantis: a once thriving cultural hub whose contributions to Canada and the world are too often forgotten. *Lay Figures* brings the era and the city that was back to vibrant, sexy life."

—RM Vaughan, poet, essayist, and author of *Bright Eyed*

"Just as great pressure creates diamonds, the Great Depression squeezes some ambitious, cosmopolitan artists back into their hometown. WWII looms and Saint John, with its contrast of old-money gentility and proletarian grit, seems an unlikely place to create art that will shine in the world outside. But the artists find that the city ignites their talents in ways that Paris, New York, and Chicago didn't. A bohemian procession of writers, models, actors, directors, and artisans are drawn to the energy that radiates from the studios, where the artists work, socialize, engage in sexual intrigues, and—with urgency and without apology—argue the purpose of art in a world where commerce and war rule. In Elizabeth, Mark Blagrave places the perfect participant/observer in the centre of this turbulent cast of characters."

—Costas Halavrezos, host of the *Book Me!* podcast

"Mark Blagrave is a superb stylist, and his novel *Lay Figures* is an intoxicating love letter to a salty Maritime city and its misfit community of poets and painters and dreamers."

—Mark Anthony Jarman, author of *Knife Party at the Hotel Europa*

PRAISE FOR SILVER SALTS

~

"Blagrave's book has captured a series of stills in historic Saint John and spread a fine dusting of silver on an ordinary life starring one Lillie Dempster that will not fade to black for some time in the minds of readers…. Rendered in splendid detail, the city of Saint John—as much as Lillie—is the central character of the novel. Blagrave effectively creates a film montage of early Saint John—its streets and businesses, bars and bootleggers, and above all its temperament."
　–New Brunswick Telegraph-Journal

"Enormously entertaining novel…. Blagrave skillfully weaves fact and fiction…an engaging tale of excess and exploitation."
　–The Fiddlehead

"True to its time, it is a slice of film life, a you-are-there invasion of cinema in its infancy."
　–The Sun Times

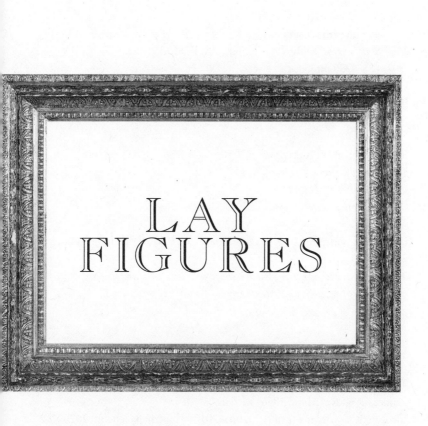

LAY
FIGURES

Vagrant Press is an imprint of
Nimbus Publishing Limited
3660 Strawberry Hill Street, Halifax, NS, B3K 5A9
(902) 455-4286 nimbus.ca

Printed and bound in Canada
NB1402

Editor: Bethany Gibson
Editor for the press: Whitney Moran
Copy editor: Kate Juniper
Design: Jenn Embree

Cover design inspired by *Wood Lay Figure with a Mirror* by John Bulloch Souter

This story is a work of fiction. Names, characters, incidents, and places, including organizations and institutions, either are the product of the author's imagination or are used fictitiously.

Library and Archives Canada Cataloguing in Publication

Title: Lay figures / Mark Blagrave.
Names: Blagrave, Mark, 1956- author.
Identifiers: Canadiana (print) 20200162012 | Canadiana (ebook) 20200162020 | ISBN 9781771088329 (softcover) | ISBN 9781771088336 (HTML)
Classification: LCC PS8603.L296 L39 2020 | DDC C813/.6—dc23

Canadä Canada Council Conseil des arts
for the Arts du Canada

Nimbus Publishing acknowledges the financial support for its publishing activities from the Government of Canada, the Canada Council for the Arts, and from the Province of Nova Scotia. We are pleased to work in partnership with the Province of Nova Scotia to develop and promote our creative industries for the benefit of all Nova Scotians.

LAY FIGURES

MARK BLAGRAVE

Vagrant
PRESS

ONE

FALL 1941

"YOU WON'T BE ABLE TO WASH IT OFF. SMASHING THE WALLS would be the only solution, I'm afraid. The pigment is part of the plaster, you see."

The landlord stops scrubbing, short of breath, sweating even in his singlet, and most likely overdue for his lunch. I don't think he wants a lesson in fresco painting, but there would be no point in his slapping a careless coat or two of paint over the work.

"It's a calcium-based colour you see, and it bonds into the plaster as it dries. Quite permanent. It will just come back to the surface if you paint it over."

I am not sure this is true, but I am frustrated with William, and, after only a few minutes looking at it, I would like to see it utterly and irretrievably destroyed.

The landlord and I stare at the grotesque figures leering out from the plaster, which cover every inch of the four walls and one corner of the ceiling. I wonder what *he* is seeing in them.

"Why couldn't he have painted on canvas like an ordinary person?" he grumbles, dropping his brush into the bucket.

"An ordinary person?"

"Or worked in a factory and left my walls alone."

I am about to say that he did work in a factory, twice, actually, but decide I don't owe the man anything, neither explanation nor excuse. More importantly, I don't want him realizing how well I knew William and prying into things I am trying to forget. He might try to hold me responsible, come after me for the damages (as he sees them). Better he should be left thinking we were simply neighbours in his cheerful dump of a building, strangers who might have nodded on the stairs or begged one another to ask their friends to keep the noise down on a Saturday night. I am grateful that, as far as I can see, William has not included my face in the mural. The landlord could not possibly make any connection. He has only invited me in to view his problem because he heard me on the stairs.

"His rent was paid up. That's something. But it's not going to cover the expense of getting rid of this."

"I heard he joined up. Enlisted in the air force." Perhaps stirring the patriot in the man might stifle the complainer. He can simply consider destroying William's mural his contribution to the war effort this week.

"What a fellow like him is going to do for the air force, I'll never know."

"A fellow like him?"

"You know, an artist." He lisps the word, raising one shoulder, crooking his elbow, and letting his wrist flop: the universal symbol for *pansy*.

As it happens, I do know artists. Especially this artist. I expect William will shoot down more Germans than any career officer. He has never done anything by halves. "Right."

"You know of anybody who might be interested in this place? I'll put the sign out, but it's always good if we can get somebody a tenant can vouch for. Somebody more like you."

If I didn't know better, I would think he was flirting. "I'll keep my ears open." I cringe at the stupidity of the expression. Keeping one's ears un*covered* would be more accurate, but odd. Unstopped?

The man does not seem to share my concerns. "Much obliged. Why he couldn't have gone and rented himself a studio…." He takes my elbow, pulls the door closed behind us, and begins creaking down the stairs away from me. I can smell the boiled cabbage in his immediate future.

Staring at the outside of William's locked apartment door, its abstract shapes of flaked paint a sharp contrast to the painstakingly drawn figures teeming over the walls inside, I think I should try to find Henry. If anyone knows why William decided to cover the walls of his apartment with indelible images and then leave, Henry will. Everyone tells him everything—and what they don't, he finds out anyway.

The cat yowls from behind the door of my flat. I can hear it as I climb from the landing below. It needs to be fed. In a manoeuver practiced over thirty months, I unlock my door and sweep with my foot as I enter, to make sure it doesn't escape. William used to tease me about keeping it indoors, made all the predictable jokes about the metaphor of the locked-up kitty. Only he didn't use the word *kitty*.

I drop a mound of mashed chicken liver on a saucer. William used to badger me about that, too. He said the cat ate better than most people we knew. It didn't matter to him that the butcher slipped me the chicken livers for free on a Saturday when he hadn't found buyers for them that week. You couldn't win that kind of economic argument with William. The inequity he could see in front of him was what troubled him, not the background factors that might actually explain it. I listen to the cat's motor purring as it vacuums up the liver, enjoying it much more than any person I know would. If William were still around I would descend the stairs and cross the hall to make exactly that point. My typewriter dares me to join it across the room and get some work done. Instead I grab my coat and leave the flat, nudging the cat away with my foot as I close the door.

Princess Street is deserted, probably thanks to the rain. I glimpse the back of the Capitol across the street and consider going to see a film (it doesn't matter what, anything to get lost in), but there is no change in my pockets. And I should be saving every penny. I head west toward the harbour and down the hill to Prince William Street, where I decide to break into William's studio. Seeing his apartment makes me wonder what other bizarre legacies he may have left.

Henry Ward is on the landing outside the studio when I arrive. He claims he has been waiting for me to appear. We don't speak much right away. Henry is a wonderful hugger and I need that first.

"You've seen it then?" he asks, finally. "He was obviously a bit off the rails. We knew that, of course…his behaviour the last few months."

"I could kill him. Why leave something like that behind, something nobody can do anything with? The apartment's unrentable as long as it's there. The walls will have to be torn back to the lath. He has to have known that."

"What did you think of it, though?"

"I didn't get a really good look, but I could see it was strong. Miserable, and mean, I'm afraid. All that allegory…if that's what it is. Did you know?"

"I saw it last week. He was too drunk to care much, but he obviously didn't want anyone knowing what he was up to."

"He would have already known he was leaving when he started painting it. The walls were bare a few weeks ago. At the birthday."

The birthday. We were all invited for a drink, which turned into several. It was the last time William had let me into his flat, and not many days before we stopped speaking altogether. Someone had produced a bottle of sparkling wine (I don't think it was champagne) and the cork had bounced off the plaster, leaving a small nick. Henry had commented on how odd it was that a painter's flat should have no art on the walls. Emil Bojilov (who must have been the one to pop the cork) suggested that the newly nicked wall was now a sculpture, or at least sculpturesque. William, who liked Emil but could never allow that a potter might actually have an informed aesthetic opinion, said it was just a shitty bare wall that had been made even shittier by accident. That had led to a debate on the relative merits of intentional and aleatoric art making, which remained unresolved as always.

"He could have chosen to do something portable. Something that could outlast his lease. But I suppose that was his point, really, wasn't it? About the fragility of what we make?"

"I think so," I say, more to fill the air than because I have an answer.

"He was very upset about losing the post office commission." Henry does not say anything about William's losing me, if that is even what happened. "It's nothing like the cartoons for the post office mural, though, is it? The bright colours, all those classical figures…I'd never have imagined William was that interested in mythology."

"I really didn't get that good a look, Henry."

We hug again in the silence that follows, and then Henry asks: "Ready?"

"No. But let's go ahead."

We don't have to break in. Henry has been holding the key the whole time, I realize now. It has to be put in just so or the lock sticks. When I had a key I sometimes fumbled with it for fifteen minutes. Henry demonstrates the knack on the very first try.

Turpentine and linseed oil. All painters' studios smell of them, but the exact mixture in William's, combined with the scents of dust and booze and sweat, has always held unique associations for me, from the first time I entered this room.

I had only just started living on my own when I bumped into Suzanne Pickard on Prince William Street that day and she insisted I follow her here. She was modelling for him then. They were lovers, too, though they did everything they could to keep the two dynamics separate in those days.

An unfinished canvas of one of William's newsboys is the first thing Henry turns around in the abandoned studio. Newsboys make cheap models, though not as cheap as friends.

"I can't believe he didn't sell this one," he says.

"Master McPhee," I say, recalling the boy's name from the one time we met. "He would have had to finish it to sell it."

Not finishing it was William's way of paying respect to the model. The newsboy had been found in Market Slip not long after his second sitting for the picture. It was not clear whether he had fallen in the harbour and frozen to death before he could drown, or frozen to death and then rolled in. The coroner did not spend a lot of time on cases like his.

I count out five studies of Suzanne as Henry turns the paintings one by one to face the room, as if he is playing solitaire or telling a fortune. You can read in the studies their brief history: model to lover-model to model again. A thoroughly worked charcoal sketch, head and shoulders only, stands beside two much rougher full-body portraits that are frankly, exuberantly, pornographic. Like something Egon Schiele might have done. There is a sketch that reeks of Modigliani and one with a whiff of Degas.

But it's the sixth one that really interests Henry. "Do you recognize it?"

"It's Suzanne again. But as what? As Daphne, I think. Those leaves on her hands."

"Obviously it's Suzanne, but where have you seen it before?"

Of course. The mural.

We start flipping through the dozens of canvases and boards with new purpose, hoping to piece together how the mural came to be—thinking that if we can trace William's process we will understand better what he was trying to say as he covered his apartment walls. Frank Gray is recognizable in a smudged charcoal sketch, crowned in laurels that William can only have meant ironically for his arch rival. Movina Sudorfsky is caught on kraft paper, her dancer's body still, her face an intricate patchwork of rounded beach stones. Next to it is a tiny oil study of Reuben Weiss holding Movina's pug in what looks like a peaceful pose until you notice the startled look in his eyes. We can find nothing of Henry, and nothing of me, though I know William has not sold anything for months. Perhaps he painted over.

After fifteen minutes of shuffling and reshuffling the contents of the studio, Henry bounds across the room and throws open a window. We both need air.

"God, I love that view," he sighs.

The studio is only two flights up from Prince William Street, but the city's dramatic topography thrusts it about six stories above the harbour. I look across the grey water to the Carleton shore, the steeple of St. George's, the Martello Tower with Partridge Island below it.

"William always worked with his back to the windows. Said they were too distracting. If he hadn't needed the light, I think he would have boarded them over. He did paint the harbour once or twice, of course, as a change of pace, but he never painted it from inside here."

"No. This place was for painting the figure, for serious portraiture. The real stuff, I mean, not this recent banal caricature." Henry waves dismissively at the rows of studies we have lined up along the walls behind us, and then returns to looking out the window. "I think we should photograph it."

"The mural? I told the landlord he would have to smash it."

"For posterity."

"How in hell did he get all that work done in his apartment without my knowing?"

"Who did he want to find it?" Henry asks. "Apart from the landlord, obviously."

We wait for Tuesday evening before we break into William's vacated apartment, because the landlord goes out every Tuesday evening. I don't know why I assumed that Henry would have a key. It is only after we have made the plan that he tells me he doesn't.

"I don't think the lock is particularly good," Henry says. "They never are in these old places. There are lots of gaps, and dry rot. It doesn't take much to get in if you are determined."

Living in the same building with the same kind of lock, I don't find this very reassuring, but I know it will be helpful for our purpose.

I feel a pang of sympathy for the landlord who will now have to repair the doorframe too. Henry is able to wedge a screwdriver into the crack to pry the strike plate away from the wood.

The screws barely resist. Then he uses the end of the screwdriver to chip away the wood in front of the mortise. The still-extended bolt slides out from the lock body through the broken frame when he swings the door towards us.

"What if the door had swung inwards?" I ask as he pockets the screwdriver. "Isn't that more usual?"

"Lucky for us."

I stop Henry as he reaches for the light switch. "Won't that draw attention?"

"The landlord is out, you said. Who else would care? If anyone is attracted to the light we'll tell them we're William's friends, come to clear out his things. That's the truth. A version of the truth."

The single bare bulb on the ceiling does little to dispel the gloom and even less to illuminate the walls. The painting must have been done mostly during the day, unless William brought in special lights. We start on the south wall, allowing our pupils a minute to dilate. There is Suzanne: in *port de bras*, midway between fourth and fifth positions, her hands and forearms sprouting twigs and leaves.

"Did he see Suzanne as a victim?" I ask Henry. "I mean, it's ultimately disrespectful to Daphne, isn't it? Daphne was raped. I don't think Suzanne was raped. Frank is certainly not a rapist."

"William always saw things his own way. Larger, exaggerated. You of all people know that. He didn't draw sharp lines between things the way many of us do. What Frank might call a ritual of seduction, William might see as rape. Especially given the way things always were between them, the tensions, the competition. Unless...."

"What?"

"Unless we are starting from the wrong end."

"Of the room?" I turn myself a half revolution clockwise.

"Of the relationship. What if we start from Frank here as Apollo? Those laurels."

"Oh. That makes sense. It's a dig, then. Frank crowned with laurels he didn't deserve."

"Or something a little deeper," says Henry. "William always scorned Frank's measured approach, his cool calculation. He loved to mock it. When he wasn't bawling me out for choosing to teach painting instead of doing it," he added.

"And so he paints Frank as Apollo, the Greeks' cold calculating god. And the Daphne portrait just flows out of that because of Suzanne's involvement with Frank. Collateral damage."

Henry squints around the room, "It would make sense then for William to be Dionysus but I don't see that anywhere, do you? Just a minute. There he is."

I am not ready to look at William yet. "Apollo was Leto's son, right?"

"I think so. You're the literary one."

"Does that help us with Movina here?" I run my hand over William's depiction of what can only be Niobe. The cold plaster of the wall enhances the illusion that she has turned to stone. Movina's tears are so perfectly executed I half expect my fingers to get wet. "Niobe mocked Leto, didn't she? Something about how blessed she was with her seven sons and seven daughters, while Leto had only two children: Apollo and Diana."

"And so Leto got her children to kill Niobe's seven sons. I remember that part, but none of their names."

"And then, although she was devastated, Niobe was foolish enough to boast that, while she had lost her sons, she still had seven *daughters*. With predictable consequences. But Movina has no children. That we know of."

"She would certainly not have kept them secret. Movina doesn't know the meaning of the word. We're being too literal, I think."

Henry turns back to Daphne and Apollo. "But is there something to be made out of Frank as Apollo killing Movina's happiness? Maybe when he broke off their affair?"

"Or is William simply trying to say that even if Movina turned to stone she would still find a way to be an emotional maelstrom?" I sound arch, but I am not prepared to accept responsibility for Movina's grief at Frank throwing her over for me.

It crosses my mind that we may be trying too hard to wring meaning out of it all.

Then we locate poor Reuben Weiss. It is the bloodiest depiction of Actaeon either of us has ever seen, which is saying quite a lot. His body is divided among the dripping mouths of a pack of six hounds. His head lies on the ground. For all its grim realism, his face is oddly formalized, fixed. Still recognizable as Reuben, it is also the mask of Tragedy. There is perhaps something of the marionette in it, too.

"I'm surprised the hounds don't have human faces."

"I don't suppose he thought it necessary," is all that Henry says. "Shall we get to it? Is there enough light?"

Henry has unpacked his camera, the Gandolfi. He unfolds his tripod, screws the camera on, and begins fiddling with the bellows. I have been counting on this total absorption for what I need to do. I sidle over to the sideboard and lean my right elbow on top, while my left hand slides the uppermost drawer out three inches—just enough to allow me to feel around. It seems empty, so I slide it out further to be sure I can reach right to the back. William could have pushed the pages I am looking for back there.

If Henry hears the drawer he has decided to ignore it. There is nothing there, and nothing in the other either.

"Can you help me? I could use a second pair of eyes to make sure I've managed the best framing. It's a big work for a small room. I don't want to miss any of it."

It is hard to make out much on the viewfinder's ground glass in this dim light. That the image is upside down doesn't help, but learning to see differently is one thing I have managed over the past few years. Still, it is slower work than I would have imagined. I have little experience of proper cameras and Henry is very painstaking.

Each framing takes ages, and the film plate has to be changed for each shot. That the clock on William's mantel has run down doesn't help. Every time I look over, I think for a second that time is actually standing still.

When we arrive at the birth of Adonis, I can tell that Henry is quite uncomfortable at what he sees. The cue for William's crude visual pun is there in Ovid, of course, one of the half-dozen-odd stories about incest, in which, for seducing her father, Myrrha is turned to a myrtle plant, and from her arborified womb Adonis is born. The infant Adonis in the mural is clearly William. It is one of several appearances he makes on the walls, in various guises. Myrrha has been reduced to a single, giant, and intimately rendered anatomical feature, sprouting a wild growth of twigs and leaves. A bush-bush, Suzanne would say. The effect is undeniably erotic, if grotesque. Henry doesn't ask me to check his framing of this section.

When we have moved the camera through all three-hundred-and-sixty degrees, Henry asks out of the blue: "Did you find it?"

"I don't know what you mean. We should hurry and pack up now. I don't know how long the landlord's poker night goes. I suppose it depends on his luck."

"And you've had none? Could I help you look? Or is it something unmentionable?" Henry giggles like a twelve-year-old.

I consider telling him I am looking for a corset and riding crop just to see his reaction. "It's papers, the carbon copies of that manuscript I was working on for a while. Those social sketches. Trivial stuff. I've destroyed the original and was hoping to finish the job here, but I can't find the copies."

I had given them to William in a series of installments over a period of nearly two years. I didn't know why I felt he needed to see what I was writing moment by moment. Maybe I just wanted to give him proof that I *was* writing. The first batch was produced early in September 1939, when he was still with Suzanne. At that point, with the war beginning, what I was writing may have had something to do with a fear of extinction. As time went on, I think I wrote and shared the sketches to show that I was there, that all of us were there, in that place and time.

William said that was only because I hadn't yet found anything bigger and more worthwhile to write about.

TWO

SUMMER & FALL 1938

THE FIRST TIME I SAW WILLIAM UPHAM WAS ABOUT THREE weeks before I moved into the flat upstairs from him on Princess Street.

There was a party in Rothesay, given by friends of my parents in their enormous clapboard house overlooking the river. The river is the Kennebecasis, tributary to the Saint John. It starts in the hills of Albert County, crosses the farmlands of Kings County, and meets the larger river, just north of the city proper, above the Reversing Falls. While all the water runs down toward Saint John, the wealth and power tend to run in the opposite direction. To escape up the Kennebecasis to Rothesay is to leave behind the fog, but it is also to render the city out of mind because out of sight. It is easy, in Rothesay, to forget about the tall smokestacks and the stooped workers of Saint John, which makes it easier on the conscience to profit from them.

I was only just back from a year on my own in London and already feeling stupefied by life outside a city. The people my parents introduced me to in Rothesay inevitably asked about my golf, or tennis, or did I sail. Nobody asked if I was a poet, and it wasn't the kind of thing I felt comfortable just declaring. I wasn't ashamed of it, and neither were my parents, thank god. I suppose I was ashamed of talking about myself—something to do with how I was brought up, no doubt.

It was different at university. There, I didn't need to tell people what I was. They knew, or at least they thought they did, by what I wore and what I read, by whom I went around with. Or they read my work in the student newspaper. Later, in London, nobody really cared. Everybody was something, but there were so many everybodies that nobody bothered keeping track. I missed that anonymity within a week of returning to my parents' house in Rothesay. I longed for any of my father's other postings, any one of the cities we had lived in since the Great War ended, and I resented the army for plunking him down now in New Brunswick.

Attending parties with my mother had always demanded vigilance. By the end of an evening, she would either have entranced the entire drawing room or she would be throwing up in the powder room. We never knew which it would be, though my father assured me things were going better and that I should just try to enjoy myself for a change.

The guest list was eclectic in terms of age and station, but I was immediately doubtful that it included the unshaven young man with paint beneath his fingernails whom I noticed almost immediately. *Someone must have brought him out from Saint John*, I thought, *told him the Crosbys wouldn't mind one more bohemian in the house.* And they didn't appear to, even when he stood on a coffee table and began making a speech about the Spanish Civil War.

I knew about the war mostly because of Hemingway. I had not been able to persuade myself to like the man's writing; I supposed I might like it more if I were a man myself. But you couldn't help admiring his courage. I didn't understand the issues of the war any better than anyone else I knew, but I was fairly sure the young man on the coffee table had things horribly muddled.

"If we stand idly by and do nothing to help eradicate the Loyalist threat, Spain will become the puppet of Mussolini and Hitler. General Franco needs our support. *Viva la* revolution!"

Just before he toppled off the table he raised a glass of red wine, and I felt like he was looking straight at me, then through me. Miraculously, he did not spill a drop. Mrs. Crosby might have found her tolerance too severely taxed by a stain on her carpet. I felt a hand placed lightly on my shoulder and turned away from the spectacle.

"My friend is a little drunk. And he's a better painter than he is a student of international affairs, or the Spanish language. I don't think we've met. Frank Gray."

He was everything the other young man was not: combed, clean-shaven, square-jawed, fair-haired, and well turned out. I could well imagine the Crosbys inviting him.

"Elizabeth MacKinnon." I didn't hold out my hand. Ladies usually didn't. "As in the painter Frank Gray?" My parents had one of his portraits, an oil of a young woman dressed implausibly in every imaginable shade of blue. The painting was a little old-fashioned, I always thought, but beautifully executed. It could stand with the better-known Impressionists—that's what my father always liked to claim. I had long since stopped trying to debate with him the need to compare it to anything.

"Guilty." Mr. Gray, who had two glasses in his hands, offered me one.

"What is it?" I asked before accepting.

"It's called a Bronx. Equal parts gin and Italian and French vermouths. Oh, and a little orange juice."

I wished I could make clever cocktail party banter—say that I preferred Manhattan to the Bronx and did he have any rye?—

but I suspected he had actually been to New York and might quickly exhaust my pretended knowledge.

"Sounds delicious."

The juniper scent of gin always returns me to my childhood: my father reading me a story and tucking me in. My mother, whom I cannot recall being present at those early bedtimes, never smelled of gin. It was only in the last few years that I had discovered that vodka does not smell. That was my mother's genius, how she'd managed to fool everyone for as long as she did.

"I think I'll stick to wine, though."

If Frank Gray was disappointed, he didn't show it. He simply nodded and held the glass out at arm's length, where it was taken by a tall woman who had glided up beside us. She had a perfect chignon and the refined features to go with it.

"Frank, darling, who is your charming friend?"

I couldn't tell right away whether she was a jealous amour or simply playing a part.

"Try it a little softer on the *r* in *charming*, I think, Suzanne," said Frank, cutting off my escape route as he did. "This is Suzanne Pickard. She's working up for an audition. Noel Coward. For the Little Theatre." When I looked puzzled, he explained: "You know, community players...devoted amateur thespians who try to garden this cultural wasteland while carrying on the most baroque romantic intrigues. What is the play again, Suzanne, *Naughty Pine*?"

"*Fumed Oak*, you beast. I didn't catch your name."

"Elizabeth. MacKinnon." I held out my hand, but she was looking anxiously across the room.

"We had better get young William back to the city before he says or does something *we* will regret. I'll bring the car around if you can manoeuver him to the door. A pleasure to meet you, Miss MacKinnon. Chaahhm'd." And she pirouetted and strode into the hallway.

"Can you give me a hand? An arm would be better actually." Frank did not wait for me to answer, simply grabbed me by the elbow and steered me toward the scruffy young man who was now chipmunking the scallops wrapped in bacon, while continuing to hold forth. Nobody was listening. I had seen it before, the practiced overlooking of the awkward drunk. Rothesay society was proving to be as good at it as any I had seen in Paris, London, or Bombay, though no better. I wished I could think of a Cowardesque aside to toss to Frank Gray as we flanked the still-chattering man called William and helped him out the front door.

Suzanne Pickard had the Packard waiting, though there was some trouble with the passenger door.

"Don't throw up on us, William," Frank muttered. I had been worrying about exactly that, which motivation helped me to get the stubborn latch to work at last.

"Ta-ta," crooned Suzanne as she let out the clutch, and I was left on the gravel driveway, waving as I might to longtime friends embarking on a transatlantic crossing and leaving me stranded at home. As I let my hand drop, I decided I would do everything I could to move to Saint John. Any city was better than none.

That night I dreamed of Frank Gray: his bright blue eyes and chiselled nose, the shock of blond hair swept back off his broad forehead, his strong hand on my elbow. But it was the booze-and-sweat scent of the dark rumpled man called William that I had decided not to wash off my hands.

I was determined to love my apartment in Saint John from the moment I moved in, and it was everything I had hoped for. There was no hot water except on Saturdays, the flocked wallpaper was peeling in a pattern that defied logic but encouraged speculation, and there was a rust stain in the sink that resembled a cameo of Keats I had seen somewhere in London. There was no point in fussing about cleaning the place, and nobody to whom I had to be responsible. It was not, strictly speaking, a garret, but I was convinced I could do my best work there.

Persuading my parents that I needed a flat in the city had not been difficult. I had raised the possibility the day after the Crosbys' party, reminding them of how I had fended for myself unscathed for a whole year in one of the largest cities in the world; surely, I would be safe in one of the smallest. I would be only a dozen miles away from them, and flats were cheap, times being what they were. The small inheritance I had from my father's unmarried sister could be stretched to cover a couple of years' rent if I wanted. My mother had read Mrs. Woolf's essay a decade before and quoted bits back to us about rooms of one's own. Perhaps she had always secretly pined for one. My father, who was the first person to protest he knew nothing about art, nevertheless granted that a certain amount of *la vie bohème* was probably *de rigueur* for a poet. It was the most French I had heard him speak since we were posted to Paris when I was a very little girl.

My first discovery, as I sat at the desk that I had created by balancing an old tongue-and-groove pine door across a pair of tea crates, was that the old building made noises that I had to investigate. They weren't sinister, but I would need to score them in to what I could then dismiss as the obbligato of everyday life so that I could listen, undistracted, to my muse. I began to suspect, too, that certain arrangements of furniture (what little I had) might be more conducive to creation than others. And so I spent my first week as a dedicated full-time writer with a place of her own checking the radiators, wondering when the mice (I hoped it was only mice) would finally scratch right through the wall, and moving the chairs around. Fortunately, nobody I knew was around to ask me how the poetry was coming along.

I wondered briefly about getting a pet. Perhaps another beating heart about the place would be a help. But pets, I knew, required feeding and watering and bathrooming; and the point of this exercise was to relieve myself of all responsibilities outside my writing, not to add to them.

By week two, I felt I really needed to produce something. Anything. I thought of a cartoon I'd seen somewhere, maybe in *The New Yorker*, in which one man (of course it *would* be a man) is saying to another man, 'I am a writer' and is then challenged to prove it. 'Go on,' says the second man, handing him a pen, 'write something.' I began to taunt myself like the man in the cartoon. What good is a poet who doesn't produce poetry? Is she even a poet? And if I am not a poet, who am I?

The long poem I wanted to write had seemed so pregnant with possibilities when the idea first came to me after the Crosbys' party. Something about chance encounters and imagined futures. But when I tried to put words around it—lines and feet and rhymes—it slipped away. I tried to locate the exact spot behind my eyes, between my ears, where the poetry lived, thinking if I could just locate it, I could write something worthwhile.

In my procrastination my own reflection became a distraction—a clear sign that things were growing dire, since I had never thought of myself as worth looking at before. If my hair were two or three shades redder, I always thought, it might be arresting. If my eyes were not washed-out hazel, they might be worth diving into (although the diver might still come to grief on the reef that is my nose). As a child I had wished that it would take shape, would cease to look like a daub of clay in the middle of my round face. By the time I was twelve, the fairies had heard me and implanted a spine of bone that rose sharply up off an increasingly oval-drawn face. At the same time, they erased the freckles I had loathed as a child but would have welcomed as a woman. Faced with a blank page in an empty apartment, however, I started to find my own face fascinating. I would catch myself looking for it in the kettle, the wall sconces, the glass in the picture frames. If I detected the hint of a blemish, it would drive me away from my desk and into the ill-lit bathroom and an actual mirror. Indulging my vanity, a fault I had never believed mine, became a very viable substitute for creative activity.

So I developed a discipline of turning the pictures to the wall and putting the kettle away in a cupboard when I wanted to write. I wrapped my head in a kerchief and removed the little bit of make-up I allowed myself. I even bathed before I sat down at the desk, in case my body's familiar smells reminded me of who I was and tied me down when I needed to soar, to be someone else. The blank page still stared back at me.

The idea of a new typewriter was quickly set aside—the small inheritance could not provide the money for that. And they all looked pretty much alike anyway. For a few days, I put the old machine away in a drawer and sat instead with pen poised, but I missed the outward sign of being a modern writer, probably all the more so in the absence of any of the inward grace, so the typewriter was restored to its rightful place on the desk. And my dry spell went on.

❧

I had only been living on my own for a month when I bumped into Suzanne Pickard on Prince William Street. She was bar-relling down the Princess Street hill without looking as she rounded the corner and knocked all of my parcels into the street. We dodged cars and other pedestrians as she helped me gather up the torn brown-paper bundles that contained the raw ingredients for my suppers for the week. I was full of apologies even though the mishap was clearly her fault. She didn't once say anything like sorry; she just kept swooping and picking until everything was back in my arms. Only then did she actually look at my face.

"Say. You're that girl from the party, the dreary party in Rothesay."

"Guilty," I chirped, trying to sound like one of Noel Coward's heroines.

"What are you doing right now?"

I was about to point out what I would have thought was the obvious: that I was going home with my (now) tattered parcels.

"You need to come with me. There's something I want you to see. And some*one* you should see, too. I was just on my way. It's just along here."

By then, she had taken hold of my elbow, tightly crooked to prevent any further loss of parcels, and was steering me along the uneven sidewalk towards a doorway fifty feet down the street. "Don't you love this city? The substance, the solidity? All these funny little shop fronts vying for your attention right this minute, distracting you. But then you just look up at the upper storeys and it's another era altogether, sixty years ago and more—timeless somehow."

The black paint on the wide wooden doorframe had peeled in regular bands about an inch wide, and there was a jet of what might have been soot or simply the grime of the ages on the brick above the door, but the doorknob was gleaming brass with a delicate motif of geometric figures stamped into it. The floor inside was marble, an arc etched into it where the door had scraped it, probably for decades, and caked in dirt everywhere else.

"It's up two flights, William's studio. You can leave your parcels down here if you want. There's not much traffic in the building, and we know pretty well everyone, so if something goes missing we'll find out who took it and draw and quarter them."

I said I would be fine carrying the lot up two flights. Then I asked if William was William from the party. I didn't mention that I had discovered he lived down one flight of stairs from my new apartment.

"Of course. Didn't I explain? I'm late for a sitting. Well, it's not really a sitting. That implies that he is making the painting *for* me, doesn't it? And he isn't. Not by a mile. It's a painting *of* me, to sell. So he can eat. So *we* can eat, actually. He's good that way, about sharing the money he gets."

She paused at the first landing. I tried not to show my relief at the moment's rest; the stairs seemed steeper than normal and the noses of the treads were badly worn, so I had to take extra care. But then she was off again. By the time we reached the open door of the studio she had removed her hat and coat and was starting to unbutton her blouse.

"Sorry, darling, to be late! I bumped into Elizabeth here and she got me talking." She disappeared behind a screen, discarded clothes flying high to land, draped, over the top. I stood, unsure of whether to shut the door.

William Upham looked me up and down, trying, I suppose, to figure out where he had seen me before, if he had seen me before. He was less dishevelled than the last time we met. His dark hair was swept back now, and he must have shaved, since there was only a blue shadow on his cheeks. His face seemed even more narrow than before. His eyes were nearly black, with surprisingly little contrast between iris and pupil, and they looked right through me.

I wanted to deny having held up Suzanne, who, by her own admission, was already late when she bumped into me, but I was prevented from excusing myself as recognition dawned in him.

"The beauty from the country club party. Hello again."

"It wasn't a country club—"

"Of course not. Have you modelled before?"

"What? No. I mean, I am not here to model. And I haven't. Modelled before." I had never given a moment's thought to modelling. Suzanne immediately reminded me why that was when she swept out from behind the screen utterly naked. *Nude*, I learned to call it in the weeks to come. Her breasts, I was surprised to see, hung quite low. You could see the red lines from her bra's efforts to hold them up. Her nipples were hard and brown and the areolae wide, so that the effect was like two miniature chestnuts, each on a pool of chocolate. She held her right hand cupped in front of her belly in what I thought must be an attempt to hide her pubic hair. *From him or from me*, I wondered.

"Ta-da," she crowed as she suddenly whisked the hand away.

"Fabulous." William did not sound very enthusiastic.

"It's henna. Isn't it marvellous? It's thousands of years old and I'm just finding out about it now. Why is that? Cleopatra probably used it. Brightens the old bush up, wouldn't you say? What do *you* think, Elizabeth?"

"Goodness," was the best I could manage out loud. I didn't even take off my underpants at night until I had my nightie tugged well down over my hips. This exuberant display, the ease with which she was talking about her private parts—the very idea of her dying herself down there—all left me speechless.

William saved me from having to try to venture an informed opinion by barking: "Shall we get to work? We're behind schedule already."

Suzanne, her hopes of rave reviews dashed, slinked across the dusty hardwood floor to seat herself on a torn armchair, which seemed to have leaked as much stuffing as was left inside. It was raised on a six-inch plinth of rough plywood, like a sad throne.

"Same as yesterday?" she asked, and William nodded. I couldn't take my eyes off the hennaed patch between her legs, but when I glanced over at William's easel he was working on her face. "What do you do with yourself, Elizabeth?"

"Mouth closed, please, Suzanne." Then after a moment, he asked me the same. "What *do* you do with yourself, Elizabeth?"

"I've just moved into town, actually. A few weeks ago. From Rothesay. My family is there. We haven't been there long. My father's in the military," I added. I didn't want them to think I came from money. Then I was afraid I was making too much mention of family. "I was away for almost a year. In London." I could feel the burn in my cheeks that always came with talking about myself. The embarrassment was doubled now by the experience of sitting in a room with a naked woman and a man who was openly looking at her. It didn't help that I was still wearing my hat and coat and clutching my parcels.

"I'll take New York over London any day." The way he spat out the word *London*, I suspected this was meant to be insulting rather than simply a statement of preference.

"Because you've never been to London, William. He thinks London is a museum. New York is the only place for an artist these days. Right, William?"

I expected him to ask her to stop speaking, but when I looked over he was painting her belly, so I supposed it didn't matter anymore that her mouth was moving.

"What were you doing in London? Going to finishing school?" This was definitely meant to be insulting.

"I am a poet," I said. I might as well; I couldn't blush any more deeply than I already was.

"Like Wordsworth? Not much money in poetry these days, is there?"

"And a novelist." It felt positively dangerous to say this out loud. I liked it. "I plan to write a novel one day. I met Mrs. Woolf."

"I'd love to go to London," Suzanne cooed as she raised her hands above her head to give herself a little stretch. I could see the faint shadow of stubble in her armpits. No henna treatment there.

"Oh, *do* take a break, Suzanne. You must be getting cramped after sitting for all of two goddamn minutes."

"I thought you were working on my thighs. They haven't moved."

William said nothing.

"He hates that I can tell where he's looking, what he's painting, at any given minute. It breaks the contract, he thinks: the unspoken agreement that he is not looking and I am not on display. Or is it simply about control, William?"

"Suzanne loves to chatter. Half the time I don't think she even listens to herself."

It was like listening to an old married couple bickering over their bowls of soup. Only they weren't old. And she was naked.

"I should go."

"Nonsense. You've only just arrived. Take off your coat. Put those parcels down. Tell us about your poetry." He looked up from his canvas and fixed me in his gaze.

"It's not really something I like to talk about." I put the parcels down nonetheless.

"Write us a poem then."

"What?"

"I'm working," growled William, "and Suzanne's working… after a fashion, and when she's not taking breaks. You should work too. Write something."

I always carried my notebook in my purse, so I took it out, licked the end of my pencil, and furrowed my brow in a desperate attempt to look like a serious writer.

"Don't let this beast boss you around, Elizabeth. You can't simply tell a poet to start a poem, can you? It's ridiculous."

But by the time I had pulled off my hat and shrugged out of my coat I found I was already scribbling much more easily than I had been in my own working space. There was something about the energy in the room—the vigour with which William was painting, Suzanne's generous display—that made me want to channel it, to capture it, or at least match it, with words. What Suzanne had said about the contract between them interested me as a central idea I might be able to do something with…. What did it mean to be looked at? What she was giving, what he was taking, could it be measured? Which of them owned her image?

I became engrossed in my notebook, but not so engrossed that I missed it when Suzanne changed pose or when William threw a brush aside to try something else.

It was hard to tell how much time had passed when I heard a shuffling on the stairs. I wished then I had shut the door. A small round face peered around the doorframe: a boy no older than eleven, although he had the sloped shoulders of an old man.

"Master McPhee. One moment," William grumbled, apparently as unfazed as Suzanne was by the eyeful the boy was getting. She reached languidly for a robe, pivoted on her right foot as she stood, and wrapped herself, presenting, finally, a clothed back to the boy as he crossed the threshold.

I was ridiculously relieved when William told Master McPhee to keep his cap and coat just as they were. What had I imagined?

I waited for someone to introduce us, and when nobody made a move in that direction I said my name and held out my hand. The boy looked at it as if I were offering him a stinking fish. Then he loped over to sit in the armchair where a moment before Suzanne's bare behind had been planted. I wondered whether he could feel her warmth.

It was several minutes before Suzanne emerged once more from behind the screen. She clearly took more care dressing than undressing. William set aside the canvas he had been working on, mercifully turning it to the wall so the boy didn't have to gaze on the copy, having already seen the radiant original. Then he retrieved, from a jumbled pile, a canvas on which I could already see, emerging, a portrait of Master McPhee.

"They're newsboys, mainly," Suzanne told me as we shut the studio door behind us and started down the stairs. "They work for almost nothing. William loves their jaded innocence. That's what he calls it. I think he overreaches, don't you?"

Suzanne was also responsible for introducing me to Henry. One evening a few days after our first meeting, we bumped into one another again on Prince William Street. She assumed we were both headed for Henry's. When I told her I did not know any Henrys, she said it didn't matter, that he'd be delighted. "Besides," she said, "I saw how your eyes lit up in William's studio. You have to see some others."

I needed a break from my own four peeling walls and silent typewriter, so I agreed to tag along. The building, a block south of William's, was cleaner but no grander. There were people everywhere as soon as we went through the street door. Half a dozen were sitting on the first flight of stairs, and more on the second. Some were smoking; most had glasses in their hands. We had to turn sideways to get past. I was quite sure that one of the men had a good look up my skirt, but when the expected wolf whistle didn't follow, I decided his interest was purely aesthetic.

Just inside the studio door, beside a brightly painted box that I would later learn was a marionette theatre, a birdlike woman was gesticulating wildly, as though readying herself for flight. I thought she might cuff Suzanne as we swept past her towards a table strewn with straw-bottomed wine bottles and an array of mismatched tumblers. Suzanne poured us each a glass.

"Shouldn't we try to find the host?" I asked. It didn't feel right drinking the man's wine before I had met him.

"Oh, we'll bump into him eventually. Don't worry. He's very hospitable, loves to have people here, especially new people. He'll be thrilled with you. You'll make a wonderful addition to his collection."

"His collection?"

"You'll see."

The contrast between William's studio and Henry's was so striking that I wondered whether it was fair to use the same word to describe them. Henry's studio, Suzanne had whispered to me on the way up the stairs, was also his living quarters, which certainly might account for some of the difference, but it was more than that. The grand piano, the art on the walls (none of it by Henry, I was told), the mahogany dining table, Henry's four-poster nestled discreetly behind a Japanese screen—all provided the unmistakable hallmarks of an apartment. But there was also a corner fitted up with an easel and model's throne, its floor daubed with paint. It looked more like a stage set than a work site, I thought. Everything was too perfectly arranged; even the spills looked contrived. It was hard to imagine that art was actually made there.

That wasn't a fair assessment, I learned quite quickly. The art of conversation was the true business of Henry's studio. He had an obvious and irrepressible talent for putting the right people together, the brightest people, the most creative, and just starting the ball rolling.

The birdlike woman had raised her voice and it sailed across the room. "The marionette is the actor purged of ego and ignited by pure form! This is not *puppet plays*, for heaven's sake! This is *art*! With a capital *A*!"

Suzanne had already tossed back a glass of wine and was pouring a second. "You need to meet Bea Johnstone. She's a poet too. Right now she's all hopped up on marionette theatre though. Thinks wooden actors are better than the real thing. Henry has a lot of people excited about his dolls. Don't call them dolls, by the way."

"Suzanne."

"Henry!"

He appeared out of thin air: this tall balding figure with piercing blue eyes and a hawk's nose. It was impossible to tell his age. "We haven't seen you here for weeks."

"Days. But thank you."

"Where have you been keeping yourself?" He turned his gaze on me. "Will you introduce me?"

"Henry, this is my friend Elizabeth."

"Libby," I said, partly on a whim, "call me Libby," and I held out my hand. I'd always liked the sound of it, wished someone had thought to use it as a nickname for me. This seemed as good a time as any to make the change.

I couldn't tell whether his kissing my hand was a genuinely courtly or an utterly ironic gesture. "We must get you some wine, Libby."

I pointed out that I still had half a glass, thank you, but he poured more into it anyway.

"Tell me about you," he crooned as he steered me towards an overstuffed chintz-covered sofa whose occupants scattered as we approached. Suzanne hung back. Once seated with Henry, I could no longer see her, and I felt suddenly adrift. "Are you new to Saint John?"

"I suppose. Not entirely. That is, I have been here before. Plenty of times. But I have recently taken an apartment. On Princess Street."

"Aha. Joining *la vie bohème*. But you are not a painter. Your fingernails are too clean. And not a sculptor or a potter because you *have* fingernails. You can't be a dancer or an actress or Suzanne would not have befriended you. She hates rivals. Who can blame her? A novelist?"

"A poet for now. Perhaps a novelist. One day."

"You make it sound like an evolution, a metamorphosis. The lowly caterpillar poet leaves all that behind to become a butterfly novelist. My friend Bea Johnstone would not thank you for that. That's Bea over there, beside the marionette theatre."

"Suzanne pointed her out."

"Would you like an introduction? Or perhaps you have come to meet *different* kinds of artists."

"I came because Suzanne scooped me up off the street, I'm afraid."

If he was disappointed, he didn't show it. "Then it is sheer chance! Pure happenstance that you are here! Not pure, I suppose, but nevertheless, you might just as easily not have arrived. At least not today—I am certain you would have found your way to us eventually. All the truly interesting people do. Perhaps you would like to meet my marionettes. Suzanne calls them my dolls, I know. She thinks I mind. I do."

He steered me then across the room to where Bea Johnstone was brandishing a wooden figure for anyone nearby to admire. She was holding forth about its roots in Javanese *wayang kulit* puppetry, although the further she went into detail, the less compelling her case seemed. The wayang, she said, were essentially flat: fashioned of hide that was stretched, dried, etched, and painted. By contrast, the marionette she was holding was obviously wood and very carefully carved in three dimensions. She went on to describe how the Javanese tradition favoured shadow play, and how the figures were controlled by a rod and sticks from below. More like puppets than marionettes, she acknowledged, but the essence was the same, she insisted. I wondered how that was possible, but was not yet comfortable enough with these new people to argue.

"Henry. Thank god." Miss Johnstone shifted rapidly from lecturer to acolyte, passing the wooden figure to him. "I am afraid I have gotten his strings all tangled, poor dear. I was trying a walking manoeuvre and I must have done something wrong. It looked quite good for just a moment, and then this." She appeared to be having trouble extricating her right hand from the strings, but I wondered whether she simply wanted an excuse to hold the marionette, and therefore Henry's attention, a moment longer. If so, it worked.

"Bea, dear, there is no knot that cannot be untied."

She giggled as though he had just made a crack about her maidenhead. Which perhaps he had.

"I want you to meet my new friend, Libby."

But Bea Johnstone was not to be distracted. "I should stick to the Sicilian style."

Henry translated for my benefit. "The Sicilian marionettes have a rod rammed right up through their body and head, and a single string for one hand."

I could not tell whether this was more coded banter or a sincere effort to include me. Its effect, in any case, was to force Bea to acknowledge my presence.

She offered her hand jerkily, quite in the manner of a marionette. "Welcome, Libby." Then she continued the gag by subsiding to the floor in a series of beautifully articulated moves, as if her strings had·been cut one by one. Her head remained erect at the end, until someone called out "Snip!" and it fell to one side. Three or four people who had been watching applauded.

There was a sudden commotion behind us, and whispers of *He's here* ricocheted around the room.

"Ah. Frank! Thank you for bringing our special guest." Henry briskly folded the marionette's legs and posted it through the proscenium opening of the miniature theatre as he made his way to the door.

I recognized Frank Gray from the party in Rothesay, but I had never seen the man with him. It seemed that none of the other guests had ever seen him either, but that he was why they had all come that night.

"My dears," Henry addressed the room at large after clapping for attention, "may I introduce Mr. Reuben Weiss."

The guest of honour was a foot shorter than Henry, with hair as thick and dark as Henry's was wispy and fair, and dark circles under his eyes that matched the dark shadow of his beard.

"He's a refugee." Suzanne had appeared beside me and whispered this in my ear. "From Germany. You know."

I did know. My father's military position had meant that our household always took a keen interest in world affairs. Around the breakfast table, we had discussed with horror the accounts creeping out of Nazi Germany.

"Not a homosexual, at least I don't think so, or a gypsy. The other." I was surprised that Suzanne, who could talk so freely about her private parts, could not bring herself to say the word *Jew*.

"I understand." My mind turned to the horrors of Kristallnacht, of which I knew a little from the admittedly meagre accounts that had made it into the press, but Suzanne had already begun to penetrate the knot of people surrounding Mr. Weiss, holding out her glass of wine as though she had poured it especially for him.

I felt a hand on my elbow. "Like moths to his flame. Poor man. I am sure he would value a little peace after all he has been through to get here. Not to mention before." As she said this, Bea

Johnstone steered me back to the sofa where I had sat only a few minutes before with Henry. "There will be plenty of time to get to know poor Mr. Weiss when the others move on to the next flower. Oh, listen to me! Flames and flowers, moths and bees. Where do *you* stand on mixed metaphors? Let's talk about you."

As it turned out, we talked very little of me, but I didn't mind. By the end of the evening, the rest of which I spent on the chintz-covered sofa with Bea, I had agreed to consider auditioning for a role in the Little Theatre, to think about attending a workshop on marionettes, and to meet her every Tuesday to drink tea and discuss poetry. She had also undertaken to arrange a visit for me to Frank Gray's studio.

"It's so interesting to see how other people work, don't you think? And where."

I started spending nearly every afternoon at William's studio with Suzanne. When I was in the room with them, I scribbled furiously: images; phrases that seemed to bristle with tension and brilliance when I wrote them down; and even, twice, a fully formed couplet, although I ended up erasing them both. But when I got the notes all back to the apartment and set myself to shaping them, they were only so much cold porridge. I would tear the sheets from my notebook and stare at my typewriter, daring it to make a meaningful contribution, to earn its keep.

I began to resent the easy road that painters of the figure seemed to have. Landscape painters had an easy time, too, I supposed, though I didn't know any of those. William had Suzanne right in front of him when he painted. Subject and expression inhabited the same space. There was a tangible and immediate connection between them. I knew he worked on his canvases between sittings, too, but even then he was working on something that was already embodied. I imagined the roughest sketch must bring rushing back to him the warm presence of her flesh, even if they were not lovers. One day I would work up the nerve to ask him. In the meantime, I could only envy him the immediacy, the embodiment.

Sometimes, when I heard someone in the hall outside my apartment, I would clatter away on the keys, producing a ding every five seconds and then loudly returning the carriage. If they had knocked I would have let them in and then made a show of removing the page from the roller with a flourish and stuffing it in a drawer, muttering that it was a very early draft, not ready for anyone to look at yet. Not ready, indeed: *asdf ghjk ljelwjqi.*

My first Tuesday conversation about poetry with Bea proved less helpful to my own work than I had hoped. Although she was taking a break from verse to work on a play for Henry's marionettes, she had no trouble talking about past successes as if they were current achievements. She had managed to place poems in a handful of small American magazines (there were no such outlets in Canada, she said) and had even found a publisher to put out a chapbook.

When I asked her whether she had ever felt she had nothing to write about, she spit her mouthful of tea back into her cup. "There's always something to write about. Look around you. Look inside you."

"I have. I do." My eyes smarted and my voice cracked.

"Finding the right *words*, now *that* is often a problem." She laughed. I was about to tell her I supposed that was what I had meant. "And then getting them in the right order," she continued, "That's a bitch too. You'll be fine, Libby. Everybody has dry spells."

But I didn't know that I would be fine, and I was not sure I could count a dry spell until after I'd published a lot more work than a few poems in my university newspaper.

It was Suzanne who finally helped me turn a corner. We had bought a bottle of wine and taken it back to my place after one of her modelling sessions with William. Two glasses in, I told her I was thinking of giving up the apartment and going back to Rothesay. I surprised myself when I said it, but I didn't wish it back.

"What, and leave all this behind?" she giggled, pointing at the buffalo-shaped water stain on the ceiling and the crumbling plaster icing above the door. "What's wrong, sweetie?"

And so I told her about my doubts, about how I believed that a writer writes, and, if she doesn't, then she isn't a writer anymore.

"I am a dancer."

"Right."

"Do you see me dancing right now?"

I wondered whether it was significant that she had not identified herself as an actor for this argument. Was she acting now? "No."

"But I have danced (*j'ai dansé*) and I will dance (*je danserai*)."

"That's the problem. I can't tell for sure that I will write again."

"You scribble away in William's studio. Are you writing grocery lists?"

"I thought I was writing something about looking and being looked at, about the nature of inspiration. But I can't get a shape around it. And then I think about what's going on in the world, all the awful things that happened to that Reuben Weiss fellow and thousands like him, and I think I should be writing something *committed*, something about the way the world is right now, the terrible things that are starting to happen in Europe, the poverty and hunger I see on the streets even here."

"Because you think you can fix them? Isn't that a bit—?"

"Naïve?"

"Arrogant, I was going to say. Just do something with what you write in those notebooks."

"I've tried. Nothing comes. I try to make something out of the notes and nothing happens."

"Stop trying so hard." She poured the rest of the wine.

"What?"

"Maybe the notes *are* the poems. Or maybe they don't need to be poems. Maybe they're something else."

"They have no form."

"They have a form. Just not one you are used to, not one you are expecting. Type them up just as you have written them down. You'll see."

"They are just what comes to me in the moment."

"Exactly. Why can't that be poetry?"

I was pretty sure she was wrong, but the next day I tried it. The clacking of the typewriter was reassuring. I felt that anyone passing by would think, *Yes, a writer lives there.* When I had covered five pages I stopped to look them over. It wasn't poetry. I had been right about Suzanne being wrong about that. But it was definitely something—something worth working on.

THREE

WINTER 1939

ON MY FIRST VISIT TO HIS STUDIO, FRANK GRAY GREETED ME as if we were old friends.

"Libby!" he exclaimed when Bea ushered me in one Tuesday after our weekly tea and poetry.

I was delighted that the nickname was catching on. At the same time, I was a little taken aback by the instant intimacy it seemed to afford people I barely knew. I had only met Frank briefly at the Crosbys' party and had not exchanged more than a few words with him at Henry's in the months between. On the other hand, William, whom I thought I was getting to know quite well, continued to call me Elizabeth.

Suzanne was on the throne, which was a much finer affair than the one at William's studio. It had all its stuffing, and a rich blue brocade covering. She threw Bea and me a little wave with the fingers of her right hand, the palm of which stayed as stock-still as the rest of her body. I could tell immediately that modelling for Frank involved none of the freeform restlessness she experienced modelling for William. I didn't think that the art being made was necessarily any more serious here, but the process clearly was.

"Have you been in a painter's studio before, Libby?"

I didn't think I had been gawking at Suzanne's nakedness or at his paints or easel, so I suspected that something else had prompted Frank's question. Perhaps it was a way to get me to admit to my nearly daily visits to William's studio. I had heard the two men were bitterly jealous of one another, that they competed in everything, and that likely included workplaces.

"Oh, the odd time, I suppose. Yours is magnificent, truly lovely." I hoped the compliment would distract him from probing further into what I might mean by 'the odd time.' In fact, I had probably been in William's studio with Suzanne more than fifty times by then.

"Oh my god, I can't believe I didn't see it right away! I absolutely *love* the choice of book!" exclaimed Bea. A thin volume bound in blue boards dangled from Suzanne's left hand. Her index and middle fingers straddled the spine while her thumb appeared to be holding her place. The effect was as if she had just left off reading. I had seen something similar in the Tate.

"*Un petit hommage*," said Frank, blowing her a theatrical kiss.

Bea explained. "Last year, I wrote a poem about Frank at work in his studio. At least that was the surface narrative. The actual meaning of the poem was something else, of course, something about inspiration and truly seeing."

Bea was describing essentially what I had been trying to do with my notes about William and Suzanne at William's studio. "Frank promised to return the compliment by including something of my work in one of his. That's my chapbook, that slim volume in Suzanne's exquisite hand. But Frank is having a little fun with us. Observe the pose. What are we to interpret? Has the woman in the painting been moved by my poetry to the languid state we see her in? Or is it something else that has put her in this daze? Something else a woman might do for herself in private?"

I had thought I was becoming quite sophisticated about what went on in artists' studios and the kinds of things my new friends talked about, but I could feel my cheeks burning. I expected Suzanne to shout something in response, to fling the book across the room at Bea's head, but she simply maintained the pose, sitting on, as though none of us was even in the room. I admired the discipline. Or the worldliness. Or both.

Bea leaned in closer. "Why should the viewer have to choose between forms of self-pleasure? What do you think, Libby?"

I was spared almost certainly making a fool of myself by a rustling of fabric and jangling of bracelets that heralded the arrival of Movina Sudorfsky. She whirled into the room, a dervish of shawls and bandannas, heading straight for Frank and planting a long kiss on his lips, claiming her territory in this room of women in case there should be any doubt. Suzanne might as well have been a piece of the furniture for all the notice that she took of her, but Movina greeted Bea warmly and appeared curious about me. Curious and a little wary.

Although we had never been introduced, I knew a few things about Movina from my new friends and what I had been able to observe. Whenever she came to Henry's she was always in performance mode, just as she seemed to be now: deliberately two-dimensional and larger than life, like an image on a movie screen rather than a person, she seemed to picture everyone else in the room as those round *o*'s that were meant to stand for audience heads in cartoons and futurist sketches.

I had heard Suzanne wonder whether Movina was actually what Movina claimed to be. The stories of her escape from Russia were almost too hair-raising, her accent a little too thick for someone who claimed to have been in North America for fifteen years, first in New York and then Saint John.

"And why had she fetched up in Saint John at all," William had added. The émigré community could not be described as large. But perhaps that was it. There was nobody to call her bluff.

"Madame Sudorfsky," Bea said, "this is Libby MacKinnon."

"You must call me Movina, darling Miss MacKinnon. Madame is for my dancers. You are not my dancers." As if to prove I did not have the mettle to be one of her dancers, she pumped my hand, waggling my arm until I was afraid it would come away at the shoulder. I thought of one of Henry's broken marionettes.

"Movina, darling, we are trying to work here." There was an edge to Frank's voice that I had not heard before. He sounded more like William for a moment.

"You and the *model* are trying to work, but these two ladies are here to be entertained. I will boil some tea." In a whoosh and a jingle she was gone again, presumably to some kind of common kitchen down the hall.

"The *model*. Did you hear that? As though she doesn't know my name." Suzanne had by then broken pose and was scratching her left breast. "Bitch. Sorry, Frank." Frank put down his brush.

"Careful with my book, Suzanne," said Bea. "There aren't that many copies around."

I had heard a little about the book from Henry, who had described the poetry as deliciously and wickedly erotic but obscure enough to avoid censorship or scandal.

Suzanne retrieved the book from the floor where she had let it fall and held it in her armpit while she lit a cigarette. Although I had seen her do it at William's dozens of times, it still fascinated me, the ease with which she could go about ordinary habitual tasks while stark naked in the presence of others. That and the way her breasts changed shape when she inhaled.

Bea took the book from Suzanne and handed it to me. "In case you haven't seen it," she said. It was impossible to tell whether this was genuine modesty on her part or a subtle form of shaming that amounted to 'Why haven't you bought yourself a copy?' I took it eagerly, hoping to signal at once both the awareness of what a treasure I held and my earnest intention to buy one of my own, even if I had no idea how or where I might be able to do so.

This charade didn't help me with the next step, however, which was knowing whether to leaf appreciatively through the book, admiring its design and the obvious effort that went into producing it, or whether to start reading carefully from the first poem onward. I decided it would be antisocial to hunker down as though I were going to read the whole thing right there, and insulting, too, to suggest that a volume of poetry, no matter how slim, could be read in a single sitting. I riffled the pages, opened the book at random and glanced at the leaves before me, running my fingers over the words. This was apparently the right decision because, after less than two minutes, Bea lifted it out of my hands and returned it to the dais beside the throne.

The painting session clearly ended, Frank went off to help Movina with the tea.

"She'd have a fit if she thought he was in here with me standing around smoking and naked," Suzanne giggled. "He is only allowed to relax with one of his models—her. With the rest of us, it has to be business only. That's the only way she'll tolerate it. The funny thing is that nobody has ever seen a single painting he's done of her, while his pictures of the rest of us hang all over the city." Suzanne trailed off as the ash from her cigarette fell in her lap and she had to brush it away.

"Movina is very territorial, is true," said Bea, putting on the accent with a cruel grin. "But she has been very good for Frank."

"He did tend to get a little distracted, sometimes, with his models. The Russian *vifey* has scotched that." Suzanne smirked.

"He has to be particularly careful with Suzanne," Bea volunteered.

I thought she must mean that the two had been lovers in the past, but Suzanne quickly set the record straight. "That bitch has no reason to be jealous of me. Frank and I were never interested in one another that way. She just never liked me, from the moment she got off the boat or whatever she got off of. Her broomstick, I would say, except I think she's still on that."

"Suzanne's pash for Martha Graham meant they were doomed from the start. Can you imagine an odder basis for a rivalry?" Bea had then to explain to me that Movina taught classical ballet—Russian ballet, in fact, a method called Vaganova—followed by the essential differences between that and the Italian method. Mercifully, Suzanne grew bored and broke in.

"I'd better put something on before they get back with the tea. There's no point in pissing her off. She'll only take it out on poor Frank." With this, she scooped up the robe that had been carefully arranged so as to appear casually discarded, shrugged it over her shoulders, wrapped it not quite tightly enough for complete modesty, and tied a neat bow in front.

Frank and Movina had the Bojilovs in tow when they returned a minute later. Apparently they had been visiting someone who lived on the top floor and Movina had caught them coming down the stairs and invited them for tea. I doubted that Frank would be able to return to painting again that day, or that Suzanne would ever finish reading the book of poetry. But then that was the point of the painting, I supposed.

Emil and Marijke had had a session with Henry and the marionettes that morning, and Bea was eager to hear all about it. She was writing a version of the Phaethon story for which they were crafting the figures and the chariot. The use of pottery rather than wood was a departure for Henry and it seemed there had been some surprises. At the rehearsal that day, two of the four winged horses had collided, and their glaze chipped off. Now Marijke pleaded with Bea to alter the script, to reconsider the behaviour of the horses, but Bea scoffed at the idea. When had medium ever dictated content, she wanted to know. Besides, their unruliness was crucial to the story. It was myth, she said. The elements of myth don't change.

"Phaethon has to be doomed to failure from the beginning. We have to know he cannot possibly handle what he has begged to take on. He's no Icarus. With Icarus, we have a little hope that his father's ingenuity might pay off. Phaethon is just a reckless teenager hopped up on testosterone wanting to borrow the family Packard. We have to know that the Packard is un-driveable. The horses are the Packard," she added when the Bojilovs looked dumbly at her.

"We'll try some other finishes, harder ones," sighed Emil. "And perhaps Henry can manage to have the horses give each other just a little bit wider berths."

With that settled, we all took tea. Movina, who had been more silent than I had ever seen her throughout the conversation about the marionettes, returned to performance mode and we were regaled once more with what Suzanne would later insist were new and unlikely tales of escape from Russia, these ones all involving unruly horses. Bea and I excused ourselves as soon as we had downed one cup. Frank's studio was bigger and cleaner than William's, but I had decided there was nothing I needed to learn there.

My walks around the city in the early winter of 1939 were not wholly procrastination. It is true that they kept me from my typewriter, but they also provided me with new things to write about when I did get back to it.

I felt I needed a change from the subjects I'd been working on, and from William's studio. Watching William look at Suzanne—seeing how he translated those looks onto canvas, observing how she allowed herself to be looked at, what she wanted him to see—all of this was fascinating. I envied what I saw, and wanted my writing to capture the essence of that relationship between artist and model, even if I knew by then that Bea had already published something very similar. But I had not been able to work out my own position in it all. I watched both of them closely, but it felt like only Suzanne looked back at me. William looked through me sometimes, but never at me. I was invisible to him, it seemed. That shouldn't have bothered me, but it did.

Walking was a way of trying out a different working space, and at the same time finding new things to look at and write about. There was always some small chance glimpse into a stranger's world. Never the full picture, just enough dots for me to join, enough ice for me to sketch out the berg below. A woman, glimpsed through a window, might set her clock facedown on the mantel at the same hour every day. What did that mean? A small boy one day carried a bulging sack that squiggled and meowed as he headed tearfully for the harbour. What parent could have ordered him to do that? I never allowed myself to stop moving my feet. Standing still would make what I was doing seem like peeping. And I did not want to learn too much; it might spoil my writer's game of filling in the large blanks in these strangers' lives.

The buildings had stories asking to be constructed, too. The glossy red door of one house must be a retaliatory response to the sober black of its neighbour. A grand entry hall, glimpsed through its original tall windows, had been carved up and ceiled in, or exterior wooden stairways had been grafted on. Why had the owners been driven to subdivide? I never stopped long in front of any one house, preferring the rolling diorama.

Saint John is a city of hills, and a winter walker takes her life in her hands. The threat of the pitched and icy sidewalks raised my heart rate, put blood in my cheeks. It wasn't exactly the flush of inspiration I was looking for, but it would have to do while I waited.

I tried to walk a different route every day, tracing imaginary letters within the grid that was so carefully laid out on the peninsula below Union Street. One particular day, I had begun by working on a huge outlined block letter *T*, along Canterbury to Duke, left on Duke, then right on Germain, left again on Queen up to Queen Square, and left on Charlotte. Then I walked Charlotte all the way to Union and followed it west. *I must be heading for the station*, I thought, but then at the top of the hill I veered toward Long Wharf. This happened all the time: what started out as a deliberate route metamorphosed into something else, controlled by something unseen. Bea said once it was like automatic writing. I told her I had never tried that and she admitted that she hadn't either and maybe we should experiment together sometime. Most days, where I ended up had no particular significance that I could divine. Some days I hoped that if I looked at a map later I would discover that I had after all written something clever with my steps. But I could never make anything out. This particular day, however, it became clear why I had been guided to the wharf.

William didn't see me at first, and I broke my rule by standing still to observe him. I told myself this was all right because he was himself so obviously observing. It was obvious to me, anyway, though most people probably wouldn't have noticed. He had gone out of his way to avoid notice: the brim of his hat was snapped down low over his eyes and he had positioned himself in a loading doorway, taking advantage of the shadow cast by an enormous concrete pier. I followed the angle of his hat to determine what he was looking at.

They were what my mother would call rough men. Unshaven, *unwashed*, she would say, their huge upper bodies out of proportion with the rest. Longshoremen most of them, but there was a knot of casual lookers-on as well, men too old or too weak or too unlucky to be hired on. Unemployed, they came to watch the others work, their open spectatorship the exact opposite of William's furtive stance. As I watched him, I could see that he had a small red notebook in his left hand and a stub of a pencil in his right. Each time one of the longshoremen looked as if he might be looking his way, William palmed the pencil and made a show of examining his fingernails. I was not convinced that this gesture would be any more welcomed by the men than the sketching, but I supposed he knew what he was doing, had done this before.

"What are *you* looking at, sister?" It was one of the lookers-on. He had a cigarette and blew a cloud of smoke towards me. It was time to move along. I cursed myself for breaking my rule. "Looking for a fella? Is that it? You're about ten years too late. One time, this use'ta be the spot. Problem is, we ain't got no dough. And you ain't gonna give it away for free. Not in that coat and this ecaw-nuh-mee." His mates laughed as if he were Noel Coward. I could hear the ripples of their mirth, punctuated by the sound of my hurried heels clopping, as I ran half the way up Smythe Street.

And then the ice got me. My feet went out. I seemed to pause for a second in the air before gravity reasserted itself. My coat cushioned my tailbone and elbow, but nothing could prevent the wind being knocked out of me. I sat for a moment, trying to catch my breath, and then William was there.

"You look like you could use some help."

"I'm fine. Thank you. Just winded. Well, all right, I could use a hand. It's very slippery. Are you following me?"

"I was going to ask you the same thing."

"I go for walks. It helps me think." I began to brush myself off.

"Around there? I doubt it."

"The walking or the thinking?"

"Both. You blew my cover."

"I'd have thought I provided a distraction."

"I couldn't stay. Not once they could see I was there, thanks to you."

"Why not just ask if you could sketch them? Why the cloak and dagger?"

"Respect, I think. Compassion."

"You're not that bad a painter, surely?" It was the kind of flirty teasing thing I thought Suzanne might say to him.

"For their lot in life," he continued, ignoring my joke, "for the hand they've been dealt. It can't be right for me to turn all of that into a painting that I can sell for money. Why should *their* poverty help put food on *my* table?"

"You could pay them. Give them something in return for what you are taking from them."

"I can't afford to pay. And it's not that simple. I am who I am. They are who they are. What gives me the right to treat them as subjects for my work?"

"You think it's condescending? But if you capture their condition, if you say something important about the way things are for them, maybe something will change."

"You *are* new to all of this, aren't you?"

"It's good to have hope," I said then, suspecting that I was simply confirming his assessment of me.

"I can paint them, but I am not one of them. What does that make me?"

"An artist. It makes you an artist." It seemed so obvious to me, but he grimaced.

"What does Lear say? You'd know the line. 'Take physic, pomp. Expose thyself to feel what wretches feel.' How can I accomplish that? I produce my paintings of these men in the studio, you know. I make the working sketches down by the docks where they work, but then I go back to my comfortable studio to recreate what I saw."

"With models? *Unpaid* models, I suppose, since you're so broke."

"I use lay figures."

"What's that?"

"You know, those little wooden model people with lots of joints. You can make them do anything almost, bend them how you want. I only have the one, actually. I have to move him around in different poses."

"Can I see your sketches?"

He tore three sheets roughly from the red notebook in his hand and passed them to me. By then we were ambling along Water Street. The wind off the harbour made my eyes blurry with tears, but I stopped walking so I could give the sketches my full attention.

What he had recorded was nothing like what I had expected. I had supposed I would see a tiny version of the scene that had been spread out before us. Instead, the sheets were covered in abstract directional lines and scribbled notes. Here and there were some thumbnail sketches of a recognizable detail: the line of a chin, the crook of an elbow, the way a trouser leg fell over a boot. But there was nothing that suggested what I would call an actual picture. Evidently, what he did was more complicated than I had thought. I handed the pages back.

"Would you like a drink? Not at the studio. I live quite near actually," he offered.

"I know. It's funny, actually. I live upstairs."

"And you didn't think to mention it all these months? What would Mr. Freud say?"

His apartment was larger than mine, and on the opposite side of the building. The walls of all three rooms were bare, which lent an air of asceticism, but there was lots of furniture—too much furniture: tables made out of tea crates and orange crates, armchairs with gashed upholstery oozing flecked grey stuffing that either came from or was destined for a mouse nest. Amongst it, though, were some valuable pieces of the kind one might find in Rothesay: mahogany, definitely not Victorian, earlier and sparer. Possibly United Empire Loyalist...not the Spanish kind about which he had been so confused that first time I saw him.

"I have rye and rye," he announced. I had followed him into the kitchen, where he was pouring a generous tot into one jam jar while grabbing a second. I nodded and he poured again, wiping the rim of the jar with his cuff just before he passed it over. I suspected that he wanted me to cringe, to be disgusted by the squalour, so I did my best to pretend that I drank rye out of filthy old bits of glassware every day. I coughed when the rye burned the back of my throat and hoped he would blame that on the spirits and not the vessel.

"I don't entertain a lot. Not like Henry."

Through the open bedroom door I could see a satin chemise crumpled on the rumpled sheets. It was one I had seen Suzanne shed in the studio a week earlier. *I suppose it all depends on how you define entertaining*, I thought. The image of William and Suzanne wrestling on the bed in the next room made me feel suddenly very self-conscious. So I asked the first thing that came into my head that didn't involve sex: "What brought you back to Saint John? From New York, I mean."

"Money. As in, the absence of. There's a depression on, though maybe you hadn't heard about that in Rothesay."

It was an unfair thing for him to say. I wanted to remind him that my family only rented in Rothesay, and they had only been there for two years. They were far from belonging. I looked into my jar of rye.

"It's the same story for most of us, I guess. This is not an easy time to be an artist. Everybody has to settle, to make ends meet. Bea has the nursery school to keep her solvent. Henry teaches, although it's hard to know how long that will support him. Half the proceeds go directly into the gas tank to get him to his various little jobs around the province."

"But you devote all your time to painting. You and Frank."

"Yes. But we are obliged to do it here. Not in New York. Not in Chicago."

"You have done what you can to make it like one of those cities, though. The visual art, the music, the theatre. Besides, if you can do what you love, does it matter where you are? And think about what an amazing coincidence it is that you should all fetch up here at the same time, from all the places you've been studying and working."

"Broke."

"But not starving." I regretted it the minute it left my lips. It was too harsh, too self-righteous, too close to his feelings of guilt about the longshoremen. "I'm sorry. I have no right."

"You don't. But you are right nevertheless. I get by. How's the poetry going?"

I knew he was hoping to poke a nerve in return. "I've been very productive," I lied. "The move to the city has been wonderful."

"Lots of opportunities to walk around and think. Spy on people."

"Something like that."

"What does papa think?"

"About?"

"His little girl living all alone in the big city."

"Saint John is hardly a big city."

"The den of iniquity, then."

"That either. My parents want me to be happy. Being here makes me happy."

"For now."

"I suppose. Happiness is always for now, isn't it?"

"Do you ever feel worthless?"

"Goodness. That's quite a thing to ask."

"It's a very easy thing to ask. It's quite a hard thing to answer truthfully. Do you ever think to yourself that writing—that poetry—might be worthless? In a place where people are out of work, where some people—whole families—are hardly able to eat, do you ever wonder what's the goddam good of poetry?" He looked through me again.

I had wondered exactly that dozens of times since moving in upstairs.

"I wonder that about painting all the time," he said.

"And so you skulk about in the shadows, making sketches of longshoremen."

"Or maybe I knew you'd happen along, watching me." He reached for me then. I got close enough to smell the rye on his lips before I broke away.

"Suzanne is my friend."

"Mine too."

"I am not that kind of girl." I hated myself instantly for saying it. It sounded so cliché, and so priggish. It must have played into every preconception he had formed about me. And it wasn't necessarily true. I knew quite well in that moment that I could probably be exactly that kind of girl, given the right kind of lead-up. But I thought William Upham had a lot of work to do on his seduction patter.

"Ah," he said, "Still a watcher then. Not quite ready to just *be*." He poured me another drink without asking if I wanted more. I hoped it meant I didn't have to run away like the little prude he probably thought me, that he thought we could just enjoy the rye now without the spectre of sex.

He barely spoke, though, after we clinked glasses, and as soon as I reasonably could, I muttered my thanks, unsure of whether a handshake or a peck on the cheek was in order, and so managing neither. He saw me to the door of the flat but did not linger there. I clattered noisily up the stairs, opened my apartment door, and slammed it again as though I had never made any secret of our living in the same building.

I lay awake for hours that night, wondering what he had meant by "not quite ready."

FOUR

EARLY SPRING 1939

I HAD NEVER SEEN HENRY'S APARTMENT IN DAYLIGHT UNTIL THE day he sent along a note to ask for my help. The request struck me as odd. Of all the guests at Henry's soirées, I was, I thought, the least likely to have the skills he might need. Unless he wanted to write a sonnet, which I doubted. When he greeted me at the door I said as much, and then I commented on how large the place looked.

"I do rattle around when I am on my own," he said, smiling. "But then, I am seldom on my own."

He must have meant his nightly salons, but I wondered about the bed that lay, barely concealed, behind the Japanese screen. Henry was an enigma in that area. There might well have been a line of women, or men, snaking its way across his crisp sheets, but his absolute discretion made it impossible to guess at whom or when. I had become quite comfortable in his company. I never felt the slightest sizzle of sexual interest from him.

As if reading my mind, he volunteered, "I hope you don't mind that I've asked you here on your own. Bea says you're interested in the marionettes. I thought you might like to help me to restring one. It's the ideal way to develop a proper sympathetic understanding of them."

I was not sure whether Bea had mischievously amplified my very slight interest or whether Henry had hopefully read more into some passing remark than she had intended. In any case, since I was there, I decided I might as well play along.

"Sometimes it helps to understand the principles if we look at a ball and a string." He produced a very scuffed tennis ball to which he had attached a strand of purple yarn. On the ball he had painted a sad Grimaldi clown face. "I can make him go up and down, with only one string. I can make him spin a little. But look what happens when I move to two strings and attach them along the equator." He had a second tennis ball with the same sad clown face to demonstrate this; I supposed he used them to teach his students. "Now I can make him tilt and shake, look at you quizzically, mourn a loss. He can communicate. Two strings, and already he is an expressive creature."

"In the right hands." I was quite sure I could not make a tennis ball run this range of gestures.

"It's quite simple, the manipulation." He set the ball aside. "All right then. Let's have a look at our candidate for restringing. This poor fellow has been through the wars." Henry sighed as he lifted our patient onto the worktable. With his right hand he cupped the marionette's head while his left cradled the body, allowing the legs to dangle over his fingers: a *commedia dell'arte* Pietà.

"We shall have to get his face paint touched up too, but that is just cosmetics." He paused and I laughed dutifully at the pun on make-up. Then, with a tiny pair of nail scissors, he severed the strings from the series of eye hooks embedded in its wooden flesh, and then from similar hooks in two bars of wood. "He is quite a simple chap," Henry pronounced. "Two control bars only."

I did my best to appear interested. "Yes, I see."

"I hear you had a drink the other day with William."

It took me a second to process the sudden shift of topic. "How did you—?"

"Not much happens that I don't hear about. I know a lot of people. People like to tell me things. You are relatively new. There are things you need to be told."

"We bumped into one another near Long Wharf."

"He was studying the longshoremen again?" There was a note of jealousy in Henry's voice. Was it William's attentions or William's commitment to his art that he wished for himself?

"Something like that. He invited me for a drink."

"At his flat."

"Which happens to be in the same building as mine." I tried to minimize the encounter. "But maybe someone has told you that already too."

"William is an excellent demonstration of the principle that the greater the artist, the more wanting the man. I'm talking morally," he added, perhaps misinterpreting the dumbfounded look on my face.

"So I gathered," I said, hoping it sounded as tart to him as it did to me. I was not looking for another parent.

"I am only saying to be careful." Then he gave himself a shake and changed tack once more. "We will start with the head strings. One attaches to either side, like this." He had cut off two lengths of string, and now slipped an end of each through an eye hook and deftly knotted them off. He carefully stretched them to full length along the table. "Those we will attach to the main bar in a few minutes."

I didn't know how to change the subject back, so I simply nodded and made a humming noise that I hoped would give the impression that I was absorbing the lesson carefully.

"Now the shoulder strings. They will need to be a bit longer as they also go to the middle of the main bar. We wouldn't want our fellow to be perpetually shrugging while at rest, would we?"

I struggled to keep myself from shrugging in response. After he had cut the shoulder strings to length and tied them off on the marionette, he nodded at me and I laid the strings out along the table, parallel to the head strings.

"You see? Nice and simple and orderly. Everything lined up and uncomplicated."

I was unsure whether he had again changed the subject.

"Did you warn Suzanne about William? If getting involved with him is so dangerous, did you tell her?"

"Suzanne has always been able to handle herself."

"I can handle myself."

"My dear, you can do many things, no doubt. But handling yourself with a man like William is not one of them. He is manipulative. He would devour you, consume you. I don't mean sexually, though perhaps that too."

I was about to blurt that I was not a virgin, whatever they might all think of me, but I bit my tongue in time. He really wasn't talking about sex.

"William's genius is destructive. It has to feed."

"You make him sound like something from a Bram Stoker novel."

"It is how addicts are."

"I think we all have our addictions, don't you? Artists, I mean. Painters and writers. Even teachers."

Henry winced at the way I added the reference to teachers as an afterthought. He was sensitive about any references to his decision to put the teaching of art before the doing of it. It was something I had heard both William and Frank use to win arguments with him when they had all had too much to drink.

"We'll do the back string next. There is just the one, in the centre of the back, very useful for making the marionette bow." He laid the tied-off string carefully up the marionette's spine, over the centre of the head, and along the table, between all the other strings. "This will go to the back of the main bar. And finally, the hand strings, which will go to the front to finish the main bar." When he had run these last two strings along the table to the outside of all the others, he picked up one of the bars and asked me to hold it. "You'll notice how long the bar is. That's what gives the mechanical advantage. The strings are close together at the marionette, but quite far apart at the bar. Leverage. Do you sail, Libby?"

I wondered whether he was about to warn me about going out in a boat with William.

"Pitch and yaw. Are those terms familiar to you?"

They were. My father had briefly sailed a twenty-eight-foot sloop on the Kennebecasis, before he had to sell it. "Vaguely."

"It's the same principle with marionettes." As he talked, he nimbly tied off each of the strings. "That's what the strings and the bars control: pitch and yaw." He held up the bar and marionette and demonstrated with elegant twists of his elegant wrists. "I can make him do anything. Anything I want. See?"

"Except walk, at the moment."

"Quite right." He set the marionette down once again, careful to keep the strings all running parallel. "That's what the other bar is for. The legs. I find that quite fascinating about this fellow. All the important bits of his upper half, his head, shoulders, back, and hands, are consigned to one bar, while the baser parts, the legs, enjoy a whole bar all to themselves."

If there was a moral to be drawn from this, he did not press it, and I was grateful. When he had finished securing the leg strings at either end, he again raised the patient from the table and made him do a charming little dance.

"Amazing." I found I actually meant it. "The effects you can get."

"And this is a fairly simple fellow. A mere nine strings. Imagine the nuance that is possible with more strings."

"And the risk of tangling."

"Exactly."

"How many strings for a human being?" I asked.

"You are very quick to understand." He bowed to me in a way that clearly signalled the lesson was at an end. Then he poured us both a very large drink.

The atmosphere in William's studio seemed to thicken; its free and easy energy changed after my visit to his apartment. Perhaps it was guilt, or the sense of a secret. I should have mentioned the drink to Suzanne. I suppose I thought she would have raised it if William had said anything to her about it. So either he hadn't or she didn't care, and I ended up leaving it alone even after Henry had issued his dire warnings. I had not let William kiss me, after all.

I did, however, begin what I came to think of as a small campaign of secret amends to Suzanne. It began with my agreeing, finally, to attend a rehearsal of the Little Theatre company. This was not an enormous sacrifice. I had become fascinated with Noel Coward over the winter, his sharp observations, his wit (obviously), and the fact that he had no compunctions about drawing characters considerably larger than life. If William was right and I too was a watcher, an observer, then I could learn from worse writers, I thought.

The rehearsal room for *Private Lives* was freezing. The actors kept their overcoats on, which certainly spoiled any illusion that the play's action was taking place in the south of France. There was a tiny kerosene heater by the director's table, but even he and the stage manager were shivering. If there had been a kettle, we could have made coffee that might have warmed us all up, but apparently the churchwardens had said no kettles outside the church kitchen, and the Little Theatre people were not allowed to use the church kitchen. The wardens had also said no alcohol, and no profanity. I loved and admired Noel Coward, but I adored the irony that his sophisticated plays were being rehearsed under similarly unsympathetic circumstances by Little Theatre groups in church halls across the country.

Everything went to hell when Suzanne couldn't get past the line "Nothing too peculiar, I hope?" without dissolving in giggles. The play is only a minute old at that point in the script. Victor tells Amanda that she looks beautiful enough to be an advertisement for something and she comes back with that quip. When we had run the lines the previous night, Suzanne and I had dreamt up a list of things she could be an advertisement for. Peculiar things, risqué things.

The objective of playing Coward, the frustrated director repeated, was to make the audience, not the actors, laugh. Suzanne had never liked the director, whose first or last name was Marlborough though everybody called him Marley. She said he was a wizened-up old duchess without a funny bone in his body. I began to think, however, that he did have a point, and I wished Suzanne would stop giggling, if only so they could get through the scene and we could go somewhere warmer.

They took a break for cigarettes (which were apparently allowed) and some calisthenics arranged by Janice, the stage manager, to help everyone warm up. Suzanne opted out and plunked herself down beside me.

"I think they're all getting a little annoyed." She sighed. "I wish I could help it. Maybe Coward wasn't a good idea. Just too damned funny. Maybe we should be trying something with more social *conscience* and less social *register.*"

Having heard her a lot recently on the difference between *society* theatre (as in high society, as in Coward) and *social* theatre (as in theatre that addresses what's wrong with society), I was afraid she was going to launch again into her description of the agitprop pieces she and some of the others had been reading about. The name stood for *agitation/propaganda*, she was fond of reminding me, as if that was a huge revelation or hard to work out for myself. The plays themselves sounded quite primitive. They almost always involved actors, dressed in top hats and bandoliers with the words WORLD CAPITAL emblazoned across them, shouting their plans to crush the workers. Suzanne assured me that the primitive nature of the plots and characters was the point: the plays struck directly at people's hearts. I suspected that the real appeal for her was the prospect of being able to drive around the countryside with her whole theatre in a suitcase. Mercifully, any plans she might have had for another lecture on the virtues of agitprop were stymied by the entrance of Movina Sudorfsky.

Movina also used the hall for classes and rehearsals, but it was clear that she was not there to dance. Not classical Russian ballet at any rate.

"Where is she? Where is the little she-wolf?" she snarled.

Gregory, who was playing Elyot in the show and remained in character, quipped: "You are going to have to be more specific, darling. This is a veritable *den* of she-wolves."

Suzanne was leaning back in her chair so that I was blocking Movina's sightline to her. I wished I had brought along my notebook; it was a shame not to record such wonderful material.

"You!" Movina swept her right arm in a large arc, stopping abruptly when her finger pointed exactly between my eyes. "You are her friend! Where—"

Suzanne stood up as if to stretch, as if she wasn't ten seconds ago trying to hide behind me. She towered over the tiny Russian by about six inches. "Movina, darling, what can I do for you? Mind, it can't be much. We are rehearsing, darling. You of all people know how important it is to practice." Her performance was calculated to send a message of indifference, insouciance.

Movina ignored her and addressed me: "You are a woman." She sent a small shower of spittle with the *v* in 'woman.' "Is this how women behave to one another in this country?" She did not wait for an answer. "How would she like it, your Miss-Martha-Graham-friend there, if I did the same thing with her William?" It took me a moment to figure out who Villiam was.

By then, the other members of the Little Theatre had formed a tight knot around us, which only fed Movina's natural instinct for performance. She reached for one of the gunmetal chairs and did the dying swan into it, finally burying her face in her hands while her shoulders heaved up and down in the universal language of grief.

I knew I should tell Suzanne to walk away. But her love of a scene was not much less than Movina's.

"You knew I was sitting for him. You knew you weren't the only one. What was I to do? I am only a woman."

I wanted to strangle her for that comment, even if I knew she did not mean it. And was there a hint of a *v* in the last word? "Frank is only a man. These things happen."

"Not to me," Movina sobbed. "Not to me."

"You should talk to Frank about it. It was his idea." Suzanne grinned from ear to ear then.

"Lies!" Movina was back on her feet again. "He would never think about you in that way. No man would when he has Movina!"

The giggles this provoked would either feed the fire or quench it, I thought.

Movina swept wordlessly from the room, her body language a remarkable mixture of contempt and defeat that I was afraid I would never be able to do justice to in words.

Only when the little audience began to break up did one of them notice the thin portfolio.

"Whose is that?" asked the young woman who was playing Sybil. (Nobody could ever remember her real name, which was why she was so well cast.) "Oh dear. She left this behind. Should I go after her?"

"The line is not 'Whose is that?' it's 'Whose *yacht* is that?'" cried Suzanne. "Let's get back to rehearsal. There's work to do."

As if the scene with Movina hadn't happened, the cast returned to act one of the play, navigating easily now beyond the line that had made Suzanne giggle. The portfolio was no more than a folded scrap of cardboard, but I couldn't resist looking inside. In it was a single piece of art paper, grey, on which was drawn a remarkably delicate full-length pastel portrait of Suzanne. She was wearing a leotard, her hair was in a bun, and Frank (it was clearly Frank's work) had represented her *en pointe*. The betrayal wasn't sexual at all. Frank had simply drawn her as a ballet dancer. I thought it was a bit cruel of Suzanne to allow her theatre friends to believe that it was something more, and I felt sorry for Movina. For her, Suzanne was the woman she hoped to ridicule and shame by calling her "Miss-Martha-Graham-friend." It must have been heartbreaking to have Frank portray such a woman dancing Movina's beloved classical ballet.

While *Private Lives* continued in rehearsals, the Phaethon project for the marionette theatre was abandoned in April. As far as I was able to reconstruct, Reuben mentioned to Henry, that first night in Henry's studio, that he had an idea for a play; a kind of contemporary parable. Henry had asked to see a script, said it might be something for the marionettes. Reuben had demurred, likely reluctant to have his work performed by a troupe of jointed wooden figures on strings. But then, months later, he had slid a typescript under Henry's door. Henry showed it around and, within another week, the Phaethon project was thrown over in favour of this new, more timely drama. Bea surprised me by being very gracious about it and refusing to point a finger. And if the Bojilovs were unhappy about all the now wasted work they had put into the clay figures, they didn't show it. Everyone was smitten with Reuben Weiss by then, and nobody wanted to say a word against him.

Early rehearsals of the new piece were managed with stock marionettes from Henry's collection, including the one he and I had restrung. Bea reported that the work was going very well. Not only had she accepted that her Phaethon script wouldn't be produced but she had agreed to operate one of the marionettes for the new project. That's how much she believed in what Henry was doing. That was what she said.

I was invited to the first run-through, at which they were going to use the actual figures that would appear in the play. These had been carved, to Reuben's and Henry's exacting specifications, by a man down the Fundy coast in Dipper Harbour. Frank had agreed to paint them following some arm-twisting by Henry. (William had turned him down flat.)

The night of the run-through Bea and I walked to Henry's studio together. She was as nervous as if it were opening night, and she were going on stage herself. She chattered non-stop about the play and the finer problems of choreography, which mainly seemed to mean avoiding getting the strings tangled up. Mostly, though, she talked about Reuben.

"Have you noticed his eyes?" she asked, not for the first time. "So wise and sad. Old eyes for a young man. He is quite young, don't you think?"

"Quite young," I agreed.

"How old, would you say?"

"Roughly your age?" I really had no idea, but I suspected this was the answer she wanted.

"He is a beautiful writer. His poetry, I mean. The play is good, of course, but his poetry is really strong. He could really do something with it. Make a name for himself." She made it sound like he was in a whole different league from us.

"*You* are doing something with *your* poetry. *I* am doing something with mine."

In fact, I had not written a line of poetry for months and our Tuesday meetings had tapered off since Bea had got to know Reuben. She told me one day she thought Reuben could be the next Ezra Pound. I told her not to tell him that. Not to tell anyone that just then, given Pound's Fascist affiliations.

"You should read his stuff. I'll ask him, if you like."

"Here we are." A small group of marionettists and well-wishers had already assembled by the time we mounted the stairs to Henry's studio. The air was humming. Frank Gray motioned to the empty chair beside him; Bea had already flitted towards the flame that was Reuben Weiss, so I accepted his invitation.

"I know why *I* am here. What are *you* doing for this project?" he asked.

"Watching."

"The usual then."

It was essentially the same observation William had made about me that day in his apartment. From Frank it sounded more offhand, less dismissive. I appreciated that. "They've asked me to give them notes," I told him. "As a kind of ideal audience member. Seeing it for the first time, with fresh eyes."

"And would you tell them if you thought it didn't work?"

"It's going to be wonderful."

Henry was giving last-minute instructions, helping Bea check her strings. It was all remarkably like what I had seen at the Little Theatre rehearsals, although the actual performers, the marionettes, sat through the preparations with far less fuss. What unfolded on the marionette stage, though, was as unlike Noel Coward as I imagined it was possible to get.

A narrator began the story, which I supposed I had to accept as part of a style, although I have never liked narrators in a drama. In a play, I want the story told in the action; otherwise, why is it a play? It might as well be a novel.

"Once upon a time," Bea's voice boomed from behind the screen, "there was a kingdom that had fallen on hard times. Recent wars had left its population decimated. The price of bread had risen and risen. The people were starving and unhappy." To demonstrate this, one figure rubbed its tummy and one its eyes. I tried to focus on the technique, remembering Henry's lesson in how pitch and yaw conspire to create expressivity. I snuck a peek at Reuben and Henry, who had sat down on the other side of Frank from me. Both of them appeared transfixed.

A scene followed in which the people agreed they needed a saviour. It built quite nicely to a peak and ended with a kind of dirge that was actually very moving. Bea was perhaps right about Reuben's talents as a poet. Then a misfit young man arrives in the kingdom and announces he can fix things, if only they will make him a prince. With nothing to lose, the people eagerly agree. The new prince gathers his ministers about him and diagnoses the cause of the kingdom's sufferings. He asks the ministers whether they have not noticed that some seem to be thriving while others starve. There are vigorous nods, conjuring in my mind's eye the busy fingers behind the screen. He asks the ministers whether they have not noticed that there are some who engage in practices that veer from the old teachings. Again, the marionette heads bob furiously. These groups are responsible, the new prince shrieks, for the sickness of the kingdom. To return to our former greatness, he argues, we must root out these evil influences. The ministers hesitate a moment (which was to Reuben's credit, I thought), but ultimately they agree. And the new prince sends his knights around the kingdom, rounding up all of those who are different. I could see Frank desperately making notes, trying, I supposed, to sort out how he would paint the important differences onto the carved pine faces.

One of the knights became too rambunctious and an entanglement that had to be managed ensued, so the play ground to a halt. Henry and Reuben rushed the tiny theatre, leaving Frank and me alone in our seats.

Frank turned to me. "How is the 'ideal audience' faring?"

"The message is very clear."

"He hasn't left much room for ambiguity."

"It is a fairy tale."

"Fairy tales leave *some* room. It's agitprop. Our friend Suzanne would be fascinated. And a little jealous."

"It's better than agitprop. More sophisticated. Because of the marionettes. They're already abstractions, types. They have no personality."

Frank sighed. "I have to give them little faces all the same."

"But the faces you will give them won't be capable of changing expression. I know that a change in the angle of the head can make it *seem* that the expression has changed, but they are still, essentially, masks. That is what I can't accept with agitprop: that a man with a million different expressions, a body that is constantly changing, is supposed to represent an abstraction. Like World Capital."

"But the prince, the prince *marionette* I mean, can represent fascism?"

"I think so. Yes."

"Maybe you should try your hand at writing one of these, Libby."

I didn't like that he was reading my mind.

"We all wear masks, you know," he continued.

"What?"

"You mentioned masks a moment ago as if they were different from faces."

"I meant—"

"I know. You meant the human face has the *potential* to change. But wouldn't you agree that most of us put on masks every day?"

From someone else, the question might have been an invitation to a serious conversation on social behaviours, but Frank uttered it lightly, as a simple statement of how things are. The play resumed, as though it had started itself, as though the marionettes had become impatient with the impotent fussing of the humans over their strings, and Henry and Reuben had to lunge for their seats. The narrator intervened to intone, "Meanwhile, in a neighbouring kingdom...."

The scene was a cocktail bar. I worried about how the marionettes would negotiate the tiny tables and chairs but then realized that failure would only add to the general impression of drunkenness that was apparently being sought. The denizens of the neighbouring kingdom played their music very loud to drown out the noises issuing from the new prince's domain. They drank and caroused and stopped their ears. When one of them tried to draw attention to the atrocities that were going on next door, they drowned him out, dismissed him as deluded.

Bea had reported that there had been a lot of discussion among the company over how the play should end. Reuben's original script called for a party to be thrown by the new prince, a party to which all of the princes from neighbouring lands would be invited. He would then invite each of them to have a private drink with him and poison them, one by one, adding each to a stew he was preparing. The last surviving prince would be invited to sit down to dinner.

A couple of the marionettists had thought this was too dark, even though they fully acknowledged the menace of the Nazi rise that the rest of the play endeavoured to represent; one had thought the Atreus–Thyestes touch of the stew destroyed the piece's otherwise happy independence of Greek mythology (he was one of the ones who had never really liked the Phaethon project). Reuben was asked to write an alternative ending. Whether by way of protest or in despair, he had produced a much less gory but more chilling conclusion. The party scene stayed in the script, but, rather than sharing a drink with the evil prince and then being added to a stew, each of the neighbouring princes was invited to his bedroom where they were ravished in a different way. Each prince then returned, besotted, to his own kingdom and instituted there the program of exterminations championed by the evil prince.

At Bea's latest report, the group was still divided on the two alternatives. Half thought the cannibalism was preferable to the unnatural acts that occurred in the prince's bedroom, if only because there were fewer dangers of getting strings crossed. Bea herself favoured the new ending. She thought the fascist-as-lover metaphor was far more effective than the fascist-as-cannibal. The revulsion that people would feel at this little wooden Hitler cooking the other princes up in a stew would eclipse the central message, she thought. It's easier to dismiss a monster than a seducer, was how she had put it.

It dawned on me suddenly that part of my role as ideal audience member might be to serve as arbiter in the ongoing dispute.

They would show me both endings, I suddenly suspected, and ask me to choose. "Watch the ending particularly closely," I whispered to Frank. "I may need your opinion."

"Which ending?" he smirked. *Of course* he would have known. "Don't worry. You'll be fine. Just go with your gut. Or, preferably, your head."

We were both surprised then when a third ending, about which neither of us had heard, began to unfold. Instead of being invited to a party, the neighbouring princes were challenged to compete in a series of sporting events. Mostly, the host country's athletes won. When others managed to win, the evil prince decided whether to acknowledge them or not. While it had the obvious benefit of being easy to associate with the recent Olympic Games in Berlin, this ending seemed to me a little too on the nose. Art needed to leave some room for the receiver, I wanted to say. My opinion wasn't needed. Frank leaned over to Henry and Reuben and hissed simply: "Stick with the stew. The Greeks knew a thing or two." They nodded, and the decision appeared to be made.

The nursery school where Bea worked had interested me ever since William had talked about the measures some of our artist friends had to take to make ends meet. I wondered whether there might be a story there somewhere that I could work on: something about the sacrifices people make for art. Or how their art affects their other work. I had been reluctant to write about Bea, though. Recording things about the others didn't worry me much any longer, and I was amassing fat stacks of notes on them. But writing about a writer felt different. Maybe it was too close to home. And I knew Bea could be very critical.

As early April failed to bring any sign of spring, and everyone's spirits visibly sank, I suggested I might visit Bea at work some day to cheer her up. She put me off at first. I supposed she was embarrassed of the place, but finally she agreed, after I fibbed a little about my need to see some children. She gave me directions that at the time I thought perfectly adequate: the school was in a brick building on the north side of Queen Square, about halfway along. I don't know why I didn't ask for a number. I suppose I assumed the building would identify itself, but everything in this area had burned to the ground in the Great Fire. All of the houses that stood now had been built on the ashes, following a uniform design in the same shade of red brick. The few variations in ornament around windows and doors meant nothing to me, and there was no shingle advertising the nursery school.

I counted off doors and climbed a set of crumbling steps exactly halfway down the block. It seemed as good a place as any to start. When I put my ear to the door, I realized that I did not even know which floor the nursery school occupied; or was it all of them? Just as I was turning away, the door opened to reveal a young woman in a bedraggled mobcap and threadbare apron, looking straight out of Dickens. Saint John could be like that, plunging a person into fleeting moments of uncertainty about which century it was.

"May I help you, ma'am?"

"I am sorry. I clearly have the wrong address. Sorry to have bothered you."

"Who was you looking for?"

"Less of a who and more of a what."

"What? I mean, I begs your pardon."

"A nursery school." When she looked blank, I said: "A place where they look after children."

"I knows what it is, ma'am. I'm just trying to work out why *you* might be asking about it." She looked behind me, obviously indicating the absence of a child.

"My friend works there. Bea Johnstone," I added when she looked doubtful, as if my being able to name a friend could render the facts of Bea's existence and occupation more believable.

"That would be the lot next door and under them steps." Her left thumb pointed the way. "And ask them, if you can, to try to keep the noise down. The missus's head doesn't ache half terrible." With that, she pushed the large wooden door shut, disappearing back into whatever Victorian fantasy she had come from, and returning me to the twentieth century.

The low door under the arched stone steps must have been designed for kitchen deliveries in more prosperous times, but it seemed to me, after the difficulty I had had locating it, like a portal into a secret club, or something Alice might find in her adventures. I had to turn the ringer three times before getting a response. It was Bea herself who finally came.

"We were singing," she panted. "'The Grand Old Duke of York'. We had to be sure they were neither up nor down before we stopped. Come in. It's down this way."

Before my eyes could adjust to the light, she had vanished before me down a narrow corridor, calling out to watch for toys as there might be some she had failed to tidy up.

The schoolroom itself must have been the old kitchen. It was roughly the size of Henry's studio, and its walls were just as full of art, though of a different kind. There were other similarities that I would note as the morning unfolded.

"Children, this is my friend Miss MacKinnon."

It took me a second to realize she meant me. I was about to say, reflexively, "Please call me Libby." Instead, I simply smiled and waved my fingers the way I had seen Suzanne do sometimes.

The chorus of "Good morning, Miss MacKinnon" nearly knocked me over. I suppose I made a face and that was why they all laughed. Then there was an awkward silence. I was apparently expected to continue entertaining them, but I had no idea how. Small children were not an audience I understood much about.

"We were about to do some painting, weren't we, children?"

I noticed then another young woman, in the corner assembling brushes and paints. Her shoulders were rounded and her hair needed washing. She threw me a tired smile and went on with her work. Bea joined her to fetch paper, which she then began distributing to the tiny tables that dotted the room. I would have offered to help, but it seemed that they were a very well-oiled machine.

I was amazed at how quickly the children settled down to painting. It was not that they were completely quiet or that they kept entirely still, but they were clearly engaged, and I envied that. I watched as one little girl (her name was Myra, Bea whispered to me) gradually managed to shift everyone's attention from their own work to hers. It was something in the way she held herself, something in how she flourished her brush and sighed from time to time as she made her painting. I thought, perhaps unfairly, of Movina. The girl's painting itself was nothing out of the ordinary for children's art: a square house, some gaunt trees, three improbably fluffy clouds. There were several pictures that I would have judged to be far more interesting. Myra's genius was for getting the attention. And that, I was beginning to understand, was more than half of what went into being a successful artist.

I did my best to help with snack time, pouring milk into fifteen tiny tumblers. I couldn't help thinking about pouring wine at Henry's. Reuben's play had got me looking for parallels everywhere. I thought there might be material for a parable in Bea's nursery school, something about a needy nurturing community that shared and created. When I asked how they afforded the milk, Bea just shrugged, leading me to suspect she took it out of the meagre salary that she drew. From the look of some of the children, I realized this might be the only time they tasted milk. Annie, the woman with the tired smile, put an arrowroot biscuit in each child's hand. There were three left over and I had bitten into mine before I noticed that Bea and Annie were putting theirs back in the tin. Bea laughed and said not to worry, I was their guest. But the circles under Annie's eyes seemed to grow darker.

We left Annie to supervise the snack, which, Bea told me, was harder than it sounded, since the children worked out all kinds of deals among them, with milk and cookies as currency. I would be amazed, she told me, at the politics of the place. I muttered something about its being a training ground.

The backyard was enclosed by a high, greying wooden fence on three sides, with the back wall of the house closing off the fourth. Looking up, I could see the wooden stairs and clotheslines of the adjoining buildings, but, focusing on ground level, it was easy to see how it could be a children's paradise in the warmer months. There was a sandbox (presently dotted with frozen cat turds, though it was early April) and a seesaw that looked like it could be fun once its handles were repaired. The scarred wood of the fence disappeared at intervals beneath bright portraits of ladybugs and frogs, flaking in only a few places.

Bea lit a cigarette and exhaled her first puff so slowly that it seemed she might have been storing smoke all morning.

"So now you know how I spend my days. It's not exactly what I had in mind for myself in my senior year at Mount A."

"The Depression changed everyone's plans." I was about to tell her about my conversation with William and then thought better of it. Unlike most of the rest of our circle, Bea didn't like to think she was being talked about.

"At first I thought of myself as a poet who was also a kind of glorified nanny. Now I'm not so sure it's not the other way around, and the nanny comes first."

I started to tell her how much I admired her latest poem. It was a love poem set on a beach. It was more direct, less intellectualized than most of her work that I had read.

"No. I'm not looking for that, for flattery. It turns out that I don't really mind. I love the children. I think working with them is really important. Not more important than poetry," she added quickly. "Differently important. For now, I can live with letting my writing fill in around the edges. It doesn't have to be central to my life for me to feel okay."

It was hard to know how to respond to this. If I told her how different things were for me, she might take it as a rebuke, might think I was patronizing her. So I didn't tell her about the guilt I felt every hour that I was not writing or at least *thinking* about writing, and I didn't mention the contradictory, gut-sucking suspicion that I was wasting my time, that I would never be published properly. Instead, I put my hand on her shoulder in a way that I hoped said I understood, and I asked to take a drag on her cigarette.

"And you have the marionettes to satisfy your creative urges right now, don't you?" Reuben was what I meant.

"Henry's acquired an Asian one, did I tell you?"

It took me a minute to understand that she meant a marionette.

"Working the thing is like playing a musical instrument, Reuben says. All of its strings are attached to a solid paddle. You pluck them—play them, really—to create the movements of legs and arms and head. Like a guitar. A pipa, Reuben tells me. That's what the Chinese equivalent of a guitar is. Henry's trying to find one of those now. He has an idea about transcribing the string-plucking sequences for the marionette to see what they sound like on the pipa. If his hunch is right, there should be quintessential walking music, and waving music and so on."

"And nose-blowing music."

Bea's expression remained utterly serious. "I guess so, yes. It's a pretty interesting way of exploring the overlaps between the arts, don't you think?"

"What's happened to Reuben's play about Hitler?"

"We're still working on it. Rehearsals are on hold while Reuben and I make some changes to the script."

Whether she was blushing because of the work or because of the collaborator I couldn't be certain, but my money was on the man. When she asked me again whether I had seen Reuben's eyes, I knew I was right, and that it was time to go back inside before she poured her heart out about our refugee poet and demanded details about my (non-existent) love life in return.

Annie was reading to the children. She was able to do it upside down: balancing the book on her lap, facing the pictures out. I admired that kind of care for her audience. The children were silent, still, hostages to the narrative. I didn't stay around to hear how things ended for the Little Match Girl. I wanted to get back to my apartment to write up my observations of the outing.

FIVE

LATE SPRING 1939

SUZANNE HAD A COLD, FRANK MUTTERED AS HE ANSWERED MY knock on his studio door. She had cancelled her sitting by way of a note delivered by one of the Prince William Street urchins. Nobody we knew had a phone. I was annoyed that she hadn't bothered to send me a note, too. We were to have met up at Frank's after she was finished modelling and walk together to the Capitol for a late matinée, and then go on to Henry's. So there I was, disturbing Frank and in need of another way to spend the late afternoon. Worse, I would have to arrive by myself at Henry's, which I still did not like to do. I muttered something to Frank about how I was sorry he had lost an afternoon's work.

I was halfway down the hall when he called out, "What about you?"

"I'm sorry?"

"Would you sit for me?" When I didn't say anything, he continued. "Since your plans for the rest of the afternoon are shot. Or we could just have a drink."

"Perhaps we could do the one while I think about the other." I couldn't believe they were my words. They were more like a line

I might give a character. I felt prickles all over, as though I had already shed my clothes, which I then determined absolutely not to do.

Frank was a rum drinker, which, given the refinement of his other tastes, was a surprise. His glasses were new and clean, which was not. They rang musically when we touched them together, which made me think they were quite good, even crystal.

"Here's looking at you," he said, and then, likely noticing the colour in my cheeks, he immediately apologized for the silly joke. Everyone always said of Frank that he was a gentleman.

There was a long silence. We barely knew each other, after all. He showed me the marionettes he had been painting. They were without their strings, but he had fashioned a kind of gibbet on which he had suspended them, with cords looped around their necks. Like tiny condemned criminals. I couldn't tell whether he knew that the project appeared to be on hold. It was not my place to tell him, so I simply made approving noises as he pointed out various features and effects he had tried.

"Is it odd applying paint directly to a three-dimensional face?" I asked. "I mean, as distinct from looking at a three-dimensional face and then applying paint to a flat canvas like you usually do?"

"Do you wear make-up?"

"Everyone does these days."

"Then you tell me what it's like to apply paint."

"It's my own face."

"Fair enough."

I wondered for a second whether he meant my point or my face was fair.

"The real problem is the wood. It absorbs the paint. A little like pores, I suppose. The old fellow they got to carve the figures used a fairly thirsty pine." He freed a marionette from its halter.

"I should have applied several coats of white just to seal it. And then there are the knots."

"Like blemishes," I said, trying to move beyond wondering what he thought about my face. "What about linen? I seem to remember reading something about sized linen on wooden figures."

"On polychromed angels. My, you are good. Clearly no expense was spared in educating you." I waited for him to add that I was not just another pretty face, but he reverted immediately to his technical challenges. "If I'd thought of linen that would have been great, though a bit tricky with the small detail here and here." He had taken my right hand and was guiding my fingers over the face of the little dictator marionette. His own face was only a foot from mine. The rum smelled sweet on his breath. I thought there must be rosemary in his shaving soap. And mint. "And linen mattes the surface. Surfaces are so important. I think these figures need to be shiny, don't you? Hard and shiny. Brutal. That's what Reuben's script calls for. I just wish the wood wouldn't keep sucking in the bloody paint." He looped the string around the marionette's tiny neck once more and left him to dangle.

"Bea thinks Reuben is a genius." I was curious to hear what Frank thought. Suzanne had told me once that he never truly admired anyone else's art. I knew about his low opinion of William's methods—everyone did—but I was curious to hear what he might think about someone working in a different medium altogether.

"Reuben has suffered. And he has fire in his belly. Understandably. Does that make him a genius? I don't know."

I suspected his reference to fire in the belly was as much about William Upham as it was about Reuben Weiss. I was drinking Frank's rum, so I said what I thought he wanted to hear about them both. "Reuben lacks technique, discipline. Those are surely important to genius too."

"The difference between the way he works and the way I work is like the difference between puppets and marionettes."

"Henry's crowd doesn't think much of puppets."

"Exactly. Because puppets are controlled from below, through their baser bits. There's always a hand, or at least a finger, up in their guts, telling them what to do."

"While with a marionette the control all comes from above. I see what you mean. Puppets are Dionysian and marionettes are Apollonian." I was getting more accustomed to the unabashed showing off that typically happened in these conversations, and I had just struggled through *The Birth of Tragedy*.

"A woman who has read her Nietzsche. Even more impressive."

This sounded more patronizing than impressed, but I decided to ignore that. "The lay figure should represent the happy medium, then," I said.

"Meaning?"

I was glad to have left him a little behind. "You control it on the level. You manipulate its parts directly, straight on. Neither from above or below." I remembered William telling me how he had to make do with a single lay figure. Frank had four of them that I could see, on the shelf next to where he was drying the marionettes. I picked up the nearest one and was demonstrating my point when the arm came loose, just pulled away with a pop. I began to fumble with it, holding it up very close to my eyes, thinking I might be able to see how to reattach it to the torso. Frank lifted the little figure and the severed limb out of my hands, brushing a little hard against my cheek as he did.

"It's all right." But I could tell it wasn't. "It happens all the time." I knew it didn't.

Frank liked things just so, Suzanne had told me. Everything in its place. And I had managed to displace an arm. It was as though I had ceased to be in the room with him, so intent did he become on repairing the little stick figure. I wondered whether I should go, and drained my glass.

"We've had our drink," he said. "Shall we discuss the other?" He had managed to restore the lay figure's arm and placed it carefully up on a high shelf.

If it had been William asking me, I would have said no. I was not ready to be looked right through, to have what William might see in me translated into paint on canvas for others to look at. I didn't know Frank as well. And he operated completely differently from William. I had not had the chance to watch him work as I had William, but I could tell just the same, from his finished pieces and the perfect order of his studio. He would never try, never even think to look through me, I thought. He would produce an exquisitely wrought version of my surfaces, perhaps a little touched up, idealized. And if I was ever going to write authentically about artists and their models I supposed I needed to find out what it felt like to be looked at in a studio.

"Why not?" I laughed, hoping he would not hear the fear.

"I'll get set up." Was there a catch of anticipation in his voice?

Once again, I might as well have been absent as he focused on easel and palette and paints. I watched him as he worked. The easel was adjusted four times before the paints were set on the small side table. The tubes of colour were lined up, label up and with their caps all at the same end. He used a square piece of Masonite for a palette and he carefully set it down so that its corner was congruent with the corner of the table. I hesitated to interrupt the ritual, but I also didn't want to appear to be a fool. Or to lose my nerve.

"Shall I just go behind the screen?"

"Hmmm?"

"The screen. Shall I go? Would you like me to undress?" I was wishing then I could run out the door, but I took a deep breath and started to unbutton as I moved toward the screen for cover.

"What are you doing?"

"Um. Changing. I thought you'd want me, well, you know."

"I thought we would start with a quick portrait. Your face."

"Oh. Oh god. Sorry. I thought you wanted a life study."

"Don't worry about it. It's an easy mistake to make, unless you know."

"Know?"

"I never paint a woman naked if she is someone I might like to go to bed with later. It gets a bit confusing otherwise, don't you think?"

He couldn't possibly begin to fathom the depths of my confusion at that point. "Oh," I stammered, "Oh, yes, I do see. I suppose I do."

He painted in absolute silence for over an hour. Sitting was amazingly hard work. I developed a greater respect for Suzanne. Just when I began to think that if I didn't change position soon I would be frozen forever, he flipped his canvas around so I could see it.

"What do you think?" When I didn't say anything, he added: "It's just a start. We can work some more on it tomorrow."

"It's perfect." I was afraid that might sound conceited, as though I was suggesting that I was perfect. "What I mean is, it's beautiful."

"I know."

I cannot use the euphemism 'went to bed' for what happened next; we made love (another euphemism, I know) on the studio floor. I supposed he was good at it, well practiced. I had only a little basis for comparison, mostly inexperienced boys at university. The studio floor was very hard. The act itself gave me less pleasure than sitting for him had. I thought that might be true for him too. Afterward, I lay there for a few minutes, looking up at my still-wet portrait staring down at me, and all I could think about was William.

~~~

The idea to work on my handwriting came from watching Frank paint. After our first session, he let me sit with him and watch, just the two of us in the studio, while he worked from studies or developed details on a work in progress. I had to sit off to the side, looking at him in profile, and was never allowed to look over his shoulder to see the canvas. He hated anyone seeing anything but the polished product. But I became fascinated by the movements of his brush as they played out in his arm. There was, I could see, a pleasure to be had in the making itself, independent of the content of the painting. Some days, Frank would spend hours building up paint on a prepared board, chosen from a pile of scraps he kept in the studio, perfecting a technique for getting an effect he had in mind for a painting he was working on. I wanted to see whether something similar might work for me, whether paying more attention to *how* I produced words on the page might teach me something. My society sketches, if that's what the short pieces I had been working on more and more were, felt as though they were getting stale, and I had decided to try to work on some poetry again. I hoped that hours invested in refining the ways that I made my letters might pay off when I tried to arrange them into words.

I borrowed a book from the library that promised to teach me Copperplate. The Palmer cursive I was supposed to have learned in school never really took, and it had, over the years, deteriorated into an inconsistent backhand scrawl that made everything I wrote look as though it was produced in a storm at sea. Returning to the discipline of Roundhand, and the elegant flourishes of Copperplate in particular, would be a form of rehabilitation.

A shopping list becomes an object of beauty when produced in Copperplate. A note for the milkman begs to be framed. But I did force myself after a week to try to put my developing skills to work on some actual poetry. The disciplines of forming the script called out for parallel strictures of fixed forms. I began with several *hokku*, mimicking Pound and Amy Lowell, allowing the appearance of the Copperplate as much as the imagery to determine what went into the five and six and four syllables of the successive lines. As my wrist grew stronger, I moved to *terza rima*, letting the metre and the shapes of the letters take turns dictating the lengths of the chain-rhymed lines.

When I tackled the first of the sonnets, I finally felt the return of some of the joys that originally drew me to poetry in my university years. The pleasures of wrestling with the constraints of rhythm and rhyme scheme and conceptual architecture quickly outstripped the gratification of making well-formed individual letters. Might finding the ideal tension of a line break, I wondered, rival the fulfillment of sex?

I had adopted a cat, to be a second beating heart about the place. She was terrified of the typewriter, so I continued to write longhand. But the medium was by then largely only a medium, like Frank's oil paints.

Suzanne was the first reader of the new poems. Asking her was another part of my secret campaign of amends for having that drink with William. It didn't take more than a minute for me to regret the decision.

"So, it's supposed to be like Shakespeare?"

"Lots of poets have written sonnets."

"Dead ones."

"They weren't dead when they wrote them. Lots of living people are still writing sonnets."

"It looks beautiful. How did you learn to make your *b*'s like that?"

"What do you think of the poems?"

"It must be a lot of work. Do you have a special pen? A special nib?"

"The poems, Suzanne. What do you think of the poems?"

"I don't really know anything about poetry."

"Poetry is for everyone. You shouldn't have to know anything about it for it to move you."

"Honestly then?"

"I'd expect nothing less."

"They are kind of cold, aren't they? I mean, I can see they are carefully thought out, carefully made. And they *look* very beautiful on the page. I want to borrow that book you got, brush up my handwriting. But the poems? They leave me a little cold."

I decided it was a sign of my growing maturity as a writer that, rather than letting Suzanne's response crush me, I sought other (I hoped more informed) opinions.

Bea admired the handwriting, although she wondered how easy it would be to reproduce it on a press. I reminded her about where the name Copperplate comes from, and she reminded me that not much printing was done with copper anymore, and I said I know nobody uses bruins anymore but there must be blocks now of the type, all made up. We agreed to leave it there. I didn't dare ask her what she thought of the actual sonnets. If she had liked them, she would have said.

Henry's response was even more disturbing. He was, at the time, the only person I had told about Frank and me, although

I suppose some of the others might have begun to guess after the first few weeks. When I told him, I expected a scolding to do with hurting Movina, but he had simply nodded and said he wasn't surprised the two of us had found one another.

"I suppose it is inevitable," he said after he had read the sonnets. We were having tea at my pine-door desk and he drained his mug and stared into the leaves at the bottom to underline his pronouncement.

"What is inevitable?"

"That there should be so much influence. That he should change the way you write."

"You mean Frank?"

"Inseminate you with his style. That's good, isn't it? Rub off on you. His style, your stylus. Your pen, his—"

"You're just projecting. Because I told you about the two of us, you're now seeing something where there is nothing." I tried not to let this sound too desperate, too defensive. "What we are doing romantically has nothing to do with our art."

"Sexually, you mean. Romance is hardly the word, is it? Do you love him?"

I reached over and poured more tea in his cup.

"Right. What you are doing sexually. And I am not saying it has anything to do with *his* art. What made you give up those freeform pieces you were doing? The ones about artists and models? Why did you go on this goose chase learning Copperplate, for heaven's sake?"

He was right, of course. Bastard. "What do you think of them? As sonnets?"

"As sonnets, I am quite sure they are absolute perfection."

"But?"

"But, my dear, they leave me cold. Frankly cold, if you'll forgive the dreadful pun."

We turned to light gossip about our friends then, and finished our tea. After he left, I tucked the beautiful sonnets away in my desk drawer and began banging away at the prose sketches on the typewriter again. The cat would simply have to learn to live with it.

SIX

SUMMER 1939

DINNER WITH MY PARENTS WAS NOT PLANNED. THEY WERE supposed to be away when I invited Frank out to see the house in Rothesay. He was fascinated when I told him they owned one of his blue portraits and he wanted to know which one. When I couldn't describe it to his satisfaction, he said he'd like to see it sometime.

We were in his studio. I looked around at the canvases lined up along the walls. "Surely you must know where your paintings are, who has bought them."

"As long as I get the cheque from my dealer, I usually don't give them another thought."

"They aren't like your children?"

"Do you know everyone who's reading your poetry?" He didn't look up from the canvas he was working on.

"Pretty nearly at this point, actually. I think I do." I thought of the Copperplate sonnets imprisoned in my drawer.

"Once my paintings are launched, they're on their own. They have to make their own way in the world. But, in this case, I'd like a brief visitation. Even if only to confirm paternity." He put down his brush and came to stand behind me, his chin on my shoulder and his hands on my belly.

I realized he mostly wanted to see where I had come from, even though I had told him that Rothesay was not home. "My parents are going down to visit friends at New River Beach this weekend," I said. "We could go out then, I suppose."

"You don't want the parents to meet me?"

"I don't want you to meet them. Not yet." Afraid that the 'not yet' sounded like I might be expecting a long-term commitment, I quickly added: "We agreed to keep things simple. Isn't that what you said?" In fact, I had been the first to say it. "Besides, I try to keep my life with them and my life as a writer separate."

"And I am part of your life as a writer. I'll accept that. You'll introduce us when you're ready."

I didn't want to tell him I was not sure how I would ever be ready. My parents had difficulty grasping that I was no longer twelve years old. I was pretty sure they would smell the sex on us the moment we crossed the threshold. They were also likely to formulate ideas about Frank's intentions. I certainly wasn't ready for that.

"We'll borrow Suzanne's car and make the grand pilgrimage on the weekend then," he said. "She won't mind."

I wondered what she wouldn't mind: that we were borrowing her car, or that she was not included in the expedition.

We were too far into the driveway to turn back when I realized my plan was in trouble. By the time my parents' old Ford came into view, parked at the foot of the front steps, my father was just coming around the side of the house. He shielded his eyes, though it was not particularly sunny, and strained to see who had dared to trespass on his weekend's peace. Frank pulled the brake and killed the engine, leaving me no choice but to leap out and greet my father.

"Elizabeth! Were we expecting you? Your mother and I were supposed to be at New River, but the fog, and your mother's head..." he trailed off. Likely because he had suddenly noticed that I had gotten out of the passenger's side of the car and therefore there was someone behind the wheel, probably someone he had not met, someone whom he might not want to hear all about my mother's head. I could have told him that I had briefed Frank on mother's trials and tribulations, but I was afraid that would only suggest a relationship more advanced and deeper than ours actually was, so I simply beckoned to Frank to show himself.

"Daddy, this is my friend Frank Gray. My friend and colleague," I added, wanting to steer my father off any possible scent of a boyfriend.

"The painter? I'm delighted. We have one of your works."

"Your daughter mentioned. That's the reason we are here, actually. To see that portrait. " It was true up to a point, of course. On the slow drive up along the Kennebecasis, Frank told me that what he really wanted to do was to make love to me in my girlhood bedroom. I had to tell him again that I did not grow up in the house, at which point he had asked me where was my sense of fantasy. It was an odd question, I thought, coming from someone as buttoned-down as Frank.

"Well, you must come in."

"Not if Mother's not well," I exclaimed. "We can come back another time." I stressed the 'not well,' hoping my father would pick up the code and realize I didn't want my friend to see my mother in one of her states.

"She's feeling better," he said, meaning she was presentable, coherent. "You must stay for dinner."

"That's very kind," said Frank without a glance at me. And so it was decided.

I left the picnic that we had packed where it sat in the back seat of the car, hoping my father would not spy the basket and realize we had been expecting an empty house. I needn't have worried. He seemed to have eyes only for Frank.

"You must see the view from the back of the house first, Mr. Gray. I'd be interested in your opinion. As a connoisseur of landscapes."

"Frank paints the figure, not landscapes," I murmured, as my father ought to have known very well. But I followed them around the house to the rear patio. It was a marvellous view. Every time I saw it, it slowed my breathing, looking out as it did over the tiny yacht club and across the expanse of the Kennebecasis to the enormous cliffs that hold the river in at Long Island.

"That's Minister's Face," said my father. "See how it looks up to heaven? The water there is a hundred feet deep, at least. There's a definite Group-of-Seven feel to it, wouldn't you say? You'd be welcome to bring your paints out here any day, Mr. Gray."

Fortunately, my father was looking enrapt across the river and so he failed to see Frank's involuntary cringe at the mention of the Group. Perhaps the only thing that Frank and William had in common was their contempt for the Group of Seven and its continued stranglehold on how people defined Canadian painting.

"How did you say the two of you met, my dear?" My father was looking at me now, with an intensity even greater than that he had afforded the Minister's Face.

Frank came to the rescue. "The artistic community in Saint John is quite intimate—" he caught himself, too late—"quite *small*, I should say. We all get to know one another. We have to stick together, times being what they are. You may have heard of Henry Ward."

"The art teacher at the vocational school. He comes out here to the boys' school once a week, too."

"Among others, yes. His studio is a kind of clubhouse, I suppose you might say."

This seemed to satisfy my father; I imagined it was the

analogy of a club, something he could easily understand. He nodded appreciatively. "Her mother and I were a little worried when Elizabeth announced her plan to move into the city." If this was true, they had hidden it well. "I am glad to know she is getting to know some like-minded people."

He talked about me as though I wasn't there, and twelve years old…. He would become apoplectic, I thought, if he knew what was on the minds of some of those 'like-minded people.'

"I am happy to look out for her, sir."

I wished I could pinch Frank without my father seeing, or punch him. This was pure performance. He had never given any such indication to me. Nor did I want someone looking out for me.

"Who is looking out for whom?" my mother asked, articulating each word carefully as she came through the screen door.

"Mrs. MacKinnon?" Frank asked, knowing damn well she couldn't be anyone else. "Frank Gray. It is a pleasure."

"Don't we have a painting by Frank Gray?"

"Exactly."

"Is there something wrong? Have you come to take it away?" My mother was never convinced that my father had handled our financial affairs correctly. She lived in constant fear of a visit from the bailiff. The Depression had done its work on her.

"Mr. Gray—Frank—has only come to have a look at his painting, Mother," I said.

"Then you must come inside, Mr. Gray. And have a drink. I was just about to mix some."

We filed into the living room, an airy space with large windows that looked out at the river, gleaming white-painted wainscoting, and an enormous river stone fireplace. I couldn't help feeling a little flush of pride when Frank exclaimed at its beauty, even if my parents didn't own it and I had lived little more than a year in total in the house and couldn't wait to escape it for my garret in Saint John. Frank was careful to admire several paintings that I knew he couldn't possibly like before he allowed himself to stop in front of his own portrait in blue.

"You must have known the model very well," my father said. "To have captured her...her *soul* so completely."

"It's all about technique, isn't it? Creating an illusion. The right line here, a certain colour there, and you persuade us you know the subject down to her roots, that *we* know her. Even when she is actually a stranger to both of us." My mother could always be relied on to say the most surprising things. They were either so far from appropriate that nobody knew where to look, or they were bang on.

"What my wife means, Mr. Gray is—"

"You are quite right, Mrs. MacKinnon. The work, much of it, is simply surfaces pretending to be depths." I could tell that Frank was genuinely impressed by my mother's grasp of what he did. I decided that I would not bother to tell him, even later, that she might as easily have taken an opposite position, depending on what the vodka told her.

My father took up that opposite position instead. "You are too modest, Mr. Gray."

"It's not modesty, Daddy."

Frank shot me a withering look although he knew as well as I that modesty was not something he could usually be accused of. Understatement, perhaps.

I persevered. "It is an amazing feat to pull off, if you think about it, creating that illusion."

"Like a perfect poem," Frank chimed in and I wanted to hug him. "A few choice words, carefully ordered, and your daughter can create whole worlds of meaning."

The argument was wasted on my father, whose keen admiration of the visual arts was balanced by his hefty suspicion of anything literary.

"But you must have known this model very, very well. There is a whole series of paintings of her, if I am not mistaken. It's obvious you had a special insight into this woman, this girl."

"Now *there* is a question." My mother started to hand Frank a martini he had not asked for. She preferred gin when the drinking was public. "Is she a woman or a girl?" She looked at me as she held the glass out to him and the drink almost spilled.

Frank was clearly confused for a moment about which 'she' we were talking about, but he went for the easy option: the subject of the portrait. "She was a member of an AYPA group run by a friend."

"A girl, then," pronounced my mother, again fixing me with her martini eye. "And a good Anglican, not that that has any bearing. Unless you were doing a life study. The church might have something to say about your friend providing nude models from her young people's association."

"I will go and see what's in the kitchen. Daddy has invited Frank and me for supper, Mother." I knew she would not have begun to think about what they were going to eat, but I was sure I could find something. And it would spare me a few minutes of the conversation.

There was a hunk of ham and some cold boiled potatoes I could cube and fry, and a few carrots I thought I could get the fur off. It would be good for Frank to see for himself how frugally my parents had to live. Perhaps he could report to some of the others who had it in their heads that I was a rich girl from the suburbs. The frying pan was coated in bacon grease, but it would give the mealy potatoes some flavour. I had to wash three plates. Cutlery, on the other hand, was no problem. The sterling was all shined up and ready to go. I thought about how this provided a perfect little portrait of my mother's priorities as I overheard her regaling Frank with stories of my father's various postings around the world and her attendant social triumphs.

When I rejoined them, my father had pulled Frank away from my still chattering mother to admire the view from the windows. I wanted to tell him it was the same view he had shown him from the patio. I wanted to tell him again that Frank painted people. As far as I knew, he had never even tried to paint a landscape. But I understood the urge to rescue visitors from my mother sometimes, no matter how redundant the distraction.

"We could have had the Limoges," my mother scolded when we went into the dining room. She must have forgotten that what hadn't been smashed in one of her outbursts had been sold.

"I am sure Mr. Gray doesn't mind, my dear."

Frank pretended to admire the plain plates. I could tell he was checking the heft of the silverware, though. He knew good things.

Nobody commented on the food, which was a relief. The conversation turned back to painting, which was not.

"You must have canvases hanging in all kinds of interesting places, Mr. Gray." My father's implication that his living room was one of these interesting places filled me suddenly with pity.

"Frank doesn't keep track," I snapped, instantly regretting it.

"Of course not. The art has to have a life independent of the creator. His paintings are not his children." Once again my mother's insight into Frank's practice and outlook was surprising. I was not sure whether this was meant for me or not. It was always hard to gauge the extent of my mother's intuition.

"I am only saying it must be satisfying to know your art is enjoyed by people all over the city."

"The country," I quickly corrected my father.

Frank and William had been competing for years over who would gain the widest reputation, although their strategies for getting there couldn't be more different.

"Now the model, well, the model is another matter," my mother began, drawing out each *m* a fraction too long. I could tell she had changed tack, come about completely. "Poor little blue girl. Imagine being she, not knowing where your image is being seen, in whose living room you might be hanging…subject without recourse to the gaze of strangers."

"I can see where Libby gets her gift with words from," said Frank. I wanted to shove a sterling silver fork in his sycophantic jugular.

"Oh words, words are cheap." The effort it took my mother to get these ones out undermined her argument. "We all have words. Which of us can paint a moving portrait?"

My father must have seen the look on my face. "How is the writing going, Elizabeth? The poems?" He said the word poems as if it were soaked in lemon juice, but at least he was making an effort.

I should have taken the opportunity to dazzle them with declarations of the importance of what I was working on, the ingenuity of it. Instead, I merely said: "Oh, you know, some days are slower than others." And the conversation moved on to politics, the beleaguered state of the world, and the evident failure of the Paris Conference to fix Europe two decades previous. I was astonished at how much my father and Frank found upon which to agree.

On the way back into town, Frank stopped the car at the Renforth Wharf under the glow of the single streetlight. When we rolled down the windows we could hear the river lapping at the pilings.

"That must have been ghastly for you," I began.

"Not a bit."

This was exactly what I was afraid of. "My parents and I are nothing alike. You can't tell anything real about a person from their parents."

"We don't choose our parents, no." He was silent for a long time, which made me doubt the sincerity of his pronouncement.

"I'm sorry you didn't get the full tour."

"Ah yes, your girlhood boudoir and so on. Another time."

We crawled into the back seat of the Packard then. The fog had rolled up the Kennebecasis and the temperature had dropped ten degrees. I was glad that the cramped quarters meant we ended up leaving most of our clothes on. Just as we were finishing, I was able to catch a glimpse of my face in the rear-view mirror. Looking straight back at me was one of Frank's endless series of portraits in blue. The painter, I noticed, was stealing a look out the car's side window, at the river and the hills beyond.

～⌒～

I almost turned down the invitation for a picnic in St. Andrews the following week, having heard from my father about the fog at New River Beach. Henry had also invited Emil and Marijke, whom I didn't really know. I suspected he was still trying to make it up to them for cancelling the Phaethon project. But I had never been to that part of Charlotte County before, and I thought the change of scene might do me good. There were only so many hours that I could spend in Frank's studio trying to be quiet. So I said yes. The least I could do, I added, was make the lunch. Henry didn't argue.

We left Saint John in a thick fog and all the way to St. George I regretted my decision to go along. There was nothing to see. At every turn in the road I was sure that Henry was about to roll his car into a ditch. Or into a moose. None of us spoke, which made the thickening atmosphere of dread even worse. Then, the moment we reached some river with an unpronounceable name, the curtain of fog lifted and we were treated to a view that took my breath away. The evergreen forest ran right up to the cliffs, the height of which was exaggerated by the very low tide. Dotting the estuary and the bay beyond, a series of small wooded islands gave the illusion that they had been torn off from the mainland and tossed carelessly into the ocean. The silence in the car changed from anxious to awed in an instant. Henry looked over at me with an I-told-you-so expression, and I smiled back. In the back seat, the Bojilovs were holding hands.

The town was a painter's paradise. I could tell that as soon as we drove down Water Street. There were three or four little shops that Henry said were must-sees. The last of these was part gallery, part cooperative, and part shop, an interesting economic experiment for a county hit especially hard by the Depression. In their homes people spun, dyed, knitted, wove, and hooked; and then, in this hole-in-the-wall, they sold. If they could.

"Am I supposed to admire the technique? Or the fact that it looks a little, a very little, like a scene at New River Beach?" I whispered to Henry as we stared at a large hooked rug. I didn't think the shopkeeper could hear me.

"Both," said Henry, "Although I usually stick with the technique."

"Beautiful," I exclaimed quite loudly to the woman. "The knots are so tight." I had no idea whether rug hookers referred to them as knots, but it was the best I could do. I squinted at the piece, imagining oil paint in place of the wool, trying to assess it on a standard I was beginning to feel confident I knew quite a lot about. I was still a relative innocent regarding landscape, though.

Henry asked the shopkeeper about a few actual painters he knew in the tiny town, and the two of them traded stories for fifteen minutes while I studied Fair Isle sweaters and woven handbags and bolts of mulberry-dyed wool as rough as Harris tweed and skeins of yarn the colour of the spruce forest we drove through to get there. I began to suspect why Henry had brought me. He wanted to expand my definition of art.

Just as I was mulling how I might formulate a list of some shared principles between art and craft, the Bojilovs appeared as if on cue at the shop window. They wouldn't come in, I knew. Henry had explained that they did not get along with the proprietor. It was a long story, he said, that in the end only served to demonstrate that bitter rivalries could exist as easily in the world of handcrafts as in fine art circles.

Emil and Marijke had scouted a picnic spot and told us excitedly about the old fortifications as they ushered us along Water Street. Their interest leaned more to its picturesque qualities than to the historical significance, but Henry filled the latter in for me. "See the shoreline over there? Not the nearest part. That's an island. But the shoreline over there? That's Maine. Right there. The threat of invasion must have been quite present always."

I looked at the dilapidated blockhouse and thought about my friends in London. I wondered how long it would be before they had to listen nightly for the drone of German aircraft. I had grown up on my mother's tales of the Kaiser's bombardments in the years just before I was born, and it all appeared ready to happen again.

My picnic was quite simple: slices of ham and cheese, pickled onions, and a loaf of bread that I had forgotten to slice. For dessert there was a blueberry cake that had taken me hours to make. Henry had put himself in charge of wine and he produced the obligatory straw-bottomed bottle with a proud flourish that suggested none of us had ever seen such a thing before. It did, in fact, seem a little exotic in this setting. When Henry had reported that the Bojilovs would bring the rest of what we needed, I wondered what that might be. They had been lugging a large knapsack all morning. As Henry and I were producing food and drink, Emil pulled a large blue-checked tablecloth from the top of the sack and spread it on the grass. Once we are all seated, he retrieved eight bundles of newspaper and handed them to Marijke, who began undoing them. Four dinner plates in a deep blue emerged first, followed by four matching pottery goblets.

"Marijke, they are beautiful," I gasped.

"Emil made them. Emil makes the useful things. I am for the whimsy."

"But they are so much more than useful!" I thought about the chipped enamelled metal I would have brought along, if I had even thought of dishes.

"They are modelled on a Greek shape. The plates. The colour, obviously, is not Greek." Emil made it sound like a huge compromise.

"Emil loves symmetry. Order." Marijke said this with undisguised admiration. In someone else's mouth it might have been a criticism, or at least expressed regret. I was thinking about William and the scathing things he sometimes said about Frank. "Me, I am rather more...chaotic."

"Apollo and Dionysus," said Henry, pouring wine into the four goblets. "To order and chaos, and the indispensible tension between them." He mouthed something at me that might have been *Frank and William.*

"Emil's work is timeless. It will last forever," Marijke said as she raised her cup.

"Unless it is smashed," her husband reminded her.

"Mine is of the moment. I make what I feel. Small comments on the humanity I find around me." She made it sound like the act of a naughty child. I wondered what she would have thought of the social sketches I had started back in on.

"'Nothing human is alien to me,'" intoned Henry, sparing us the Latin. "Including appetite. Shall we eat?"

"We will have to pull at the bread, I am afraid. I should have sliced it at home."

"Like *maenads*," Henry laughed, taking the loaf, pulling off a large hunk, and setting it on his plate. "What a marvellous way to start our lunchtime bacchanal. Take that, Pentheus."

"I remembered to cut the ham, and the cheese," I said, passing around the greased paper parcels in which I had wrapped them. Henry fished out pickled onions for everyone. We ate in silence for a while, pensive nymphs and satyrs watching as the receding tide miraculously began to reveal the red rocks of the reef below us. It was a scene begging to be painted, but it changed too fast. Emil reached over and took Marijke's hand. I tried to remember then what Henry had told me about how many years they had been married. More than twenty, I recalled. Their earlier conversation about order and chaos, ideal form and human idiosyncrasy, made perfect sense as I watched them holding hands and looking at the seascape. Henry had said he believed that that balance, the tension, was the secret of their marriage. I began to suspect why he had really asked me along for this picnic with them. It had very little to do with the scenery, or with the relation between art and craft, and quite a lot to do with developing an understanding of the very different ways in which our other friends made their art, and who they were. And (but this understanding came later) with choices I would have to make.

To show Henry I had understood his intentions, I shifted my position so that my gaze was clearly focused on the two potters. I watched them even more intently. They ate very quickly, like people who do not always have enough to eat. Marijke tore off chunks of bread and Emil deftly split them into perfect halves and slipped in slices of ham and cheese, carefully lining up the edges.

I was glad I had brought plenty. At the same time I felt my usual pangs of guilt over having been able to afford to bring so much. I worried they would think of me as a wealthy amateur, a dilettante generously admitted to the ranks of the starving artist, never truly to belong. I had heard that they grew their own vegetables and that Emil was forced to set traps for small animals they could eat. If any of this bothered them, they were very successful at hiding it. The cake, half of which I expected to return with me to Saint John, vanished in ten minutes.

"Time for a walk," murmured Henry, obviously sleepy from the sun and the wine and the cake.

"I know a very good route," offered Emil, and he began packing things away into his knapsack. When I tried to hand him my plate and goblet he looked as though I had proffered a dead mackerel.

"He would like you to keep them," Marijke interpreted. "They are for you. As a thank you. A gift."

I knew how their pottery was priced and how little the food had cost me. "I couldn't. It's not right." I was on the verge of offering to pay when Henry sharply shook his head. "Thank you," I said. "They will be a wonderful reminder of the day." Marijke handed me some newspaper to wrap them in.

We walked back into town to deposit our things in the car, from which Emil produced two buckets he had stored in the trunk. As we retraced our steps once again past the picnic spot, Emil explained. "There is a very good place for clay along here."

"Also a good golf course," said Henry.

"The clay is before you get to that. In a creek," Emil replied.

We smelled it before we saw it. The tang of wrack weed exposed by the tide was mixed with a much deeper note of sulphur. It was one of those creeks that rushes down out of the hills, only to be slowed to a crawl by tidal flats through which it has nevertheless carved its way for thousands of years. The range of colours, of mud and sandstone and water, and the contrasts in light were a feast for the eyes. I could see Henry planning how he might paint the scene, if only he could plug his nose.

Marijke was unbothered by the smell. She had removed her shoes and stockings and hitched her skirt up somehow into its own waistband, exposing her strong smooth thighs. I wondered that neither Frank nor William had ever painted her. Emil handed her the buckets and she made her way down onto the mud flats, her head cocked to one side, a retriever looking for a covey.

"A little to the right," Emil called, and she splashed through a rivulet and over an outcrop of red stone, nodding and looking. "We have our own clay at home up the river," Emil assured me. "But Marijke likes to work with this. We do not often get here. I hope you do not mind."

I was about to say something about what a golden opportunity it was to see an artist so in touch with her medium, reaching down into the mud from which we all came, but instead I just muttered something about how pretty the place was. Conversations that fit neatly in studios seemed entirely out of place in all that natural beauty.

"I suppose you are right. We have only eyes for the clay. Look, she has found a deposit."

The three of us watched while Marijke, her glorious legs now spattered, filled the two buckets.

"Should I help her?" I asked half-heartedly.

"She will be fine."

As she struggled to carry the two buckets back across the mud and up the bank, I was for an instant less convinced about the excellence of their partnership, but Marijke was beaming when she reached us. And Emil did carry one bucket back to Henry's car.

I found William alone in his studio one afternoon late in August. Suzanne, he said, had been called to an emergency rehearsal, though he couldn't imagine how Noel Coward demanded that kind of urgent attention. Without a model he was having to make alternative arrangements. He hated to waste a whole afternoon. He hoped I would stay even if Suzanne was not there.

It had been months since our drink in his apartment, but we had not had a minute alone since to talk about what had and what hadn't happened. I hoped that was not about to change. He must have sensed my hesitation.

"Suzanne wouldn't mind," he said. "It's just two artists working together in the same space. Like always. Right?"

I wasn't sure that was an exhaustive description of the situation from either of our points of view, and now there was Frank to consider too, but I smiled and murmured, "Of course. Just two artists."

"I've been meaning to try another self-portrait for a while now," he said after I had settled into my usual chair with my notebook. "We did them all the time at art school. It was equal parts about learning to see yourself clearly and working with what was cheap and available. And there was never any of the usual awkwardness about whether you had misrepresented your subject, or who owned the image."

"Narcissus looking into the pool."

"And trying not to fall in. Exactly." He had suspended a hand mirror on a string from an eye hook stuck in the upper right corner of the canvas on his easel. "I've tried working from memory, but it's not the same. It ends up softening everything, glossing over the troubling parts. This isn't ideal either, though. I find I become obsessed with the fact the mirror has reversed my features."

"Does it matter? Your face is," I paused for a second, searching for the right neutral word. "You face is symmetrical."

"Nobody's face is symmetrical. Bodies aren't either. You must have noticed."

Before he could turn the conversation to breasts and buttocks, I asked him what he planned to do with his self-portrait.

"I'll probably paint over it. Canvases are expensive."

I looked around the room at the dozens of unfinished paintings that suggested otherwise.

"Sometimes it's fun to know I am at the bottom of a painting. Literally."

"Even if nobody ever knows? Isn't it enough to sign them?"

"That's just words."

"You are talking to a writer. I'm rather fond of words."

"Describe me then. Put me into words." He put his brush down and turned to face me full on. I noticed for the first time that his left eye was slightly smaller than his right. "I'll sketch what you say." He picked up his sketchpad from the floor beside the easel.

"I don't think that's a good idea."

"What kind of writer are you? Are you worried about my feelings, that you'll say something truthful about my nose and I'll be crushed? Artists need to be tough, uncompromising. You be my mirror. It's only a face."

"Only?"

"A convenient covering for the front of the head, a necessary evil if you want to paint people. I always finish the face last. I'll describe you first, if you want." He fixed his gaze on me, an eagle sizing up a mouse. "Oval-shaped. Could even be almond, with the ginger hair effectively covering up the point on the top. Pale forehead like some Irish queen."

"William, you can stop."

"Eyes the colour of cow shit. Fresh, not dried. A little upturned at the outer corners."

"Hazel. The colour is hazel."

"Whatever *that* means. Nose like a hawk. Noble. Mouth wider than you'd expect in such a long face. One slightly crooked tooth that makes the smile more real—endearing, actually. Narrow shoulders, but enough to support the breasts."

"We were talking about faces." Mine was burning.

"But the face can't be understood in isolation. You need the whole figure, the entire attitude, to capture the essence, even if it doesn't find its way onto the canvas with the face."

"Your face is the shape of a shield, I think," I began.

He picked up his pencil and began to sketch as I moved on to describe his forehead. When I reached his shoulders, I stopped. He looked up from the paper, frowning.

"You didn't really think I was going to do the rest, did you?"

"I was a little curious. Not so much about what you would say, but how you would say it."

"*If* I would say it, you mean."

"Here." He handed me his sketchpad. "What do you think?"

I could see that he had followed every phrase I had used to describe him, every word and image. But the sketch didn't look a bit like him. I held it out. "Oh dear."

"No. Keep it. A memento." He tore the sheet from the top of the sketchpad and handed it over.

"A warning about what gets lost in translation."

"We all see things differently. Telling the truth about what you see doesn't necessarily mean telling the Truth."

When I left him that day, he was lining his easel up next to the windows, trying to get the angle right so he could see his reflection and the canvas with the least possible movement of his beautiful head.

SEVEN

FALL 1939

WHEN THE WAR BEGAN, BEA AND I WERE HAVING TEA. IT SOUNDS dreadful, as if we were deaf to the shrieks of world affairs, but it would not be far wrong. We were having a lot of tea together in those days. She had found more time for me through the summer. The nursery school was in recess and even the marionette theatre was on a break while everyone tried to make the most of the small window of summer that Saint John afforded. We were even talking more about poetry again, and less about Reuben Weiss. By the end of the summer we didn't talk about Reuben at all. Of course there was a story there, but Bea was not eager to tell me, apparently, and I knew not to ask. She would talk when she was ready.

We had graduated from our customary Red Rose to something more exotic that Bea was having brought in specially to a little shop in the city. At first, with every sip, I felt guilty for betraying the local brand, but with time I was able to persuade myself that the heavy smoke in a cup of lapsang souchong was as little like Estabrooks' special blend as a lion is like a housecat.

The day Hitler invaded Poland, Bea was in her kitchen shaking out the bamboo strainer she used, and I was leafing through a new volume by T. S. Eliot. There was a knock at the door.

"See who that is, won't you, Libby? Maybe it's *The New Yorker* coming to scout talent."

It was Suzanne. As soon as the door was open a crack, she burst in. I barely avoided getting knocked over. "I *thought* you'd both be here. What's that stink?"

"It's tea. Very nice tea. I'd offer you some but clearly it would be wasted. Have you come to talk trochees and spondees?"

"If that's poetry, no. If it has something to do with international politics, then yes. It sounds very prickly in any case."

"Is that line Coward or Oscar Wilde?" Bea, I knew, admired neither.

"Pure me, darling."

"And since when are you interested in international politics?" Bea's view of Suzanne was that she was a pretty ornament. She refused to believe her capable of anything but the shallowest of thoughts. We argued about it quite often. Bea would not accept that acting, nor what was coming to be called modern dance, required a great deal of intellectual capacity. Her contempt for the performing arts that involved living bodies intrigued me in light of her reverence for the marionette theatre. We had not argued about that.

Suzanne made a moue. I wanted to tell her that would do nothing to improve Bea's assessment of her. "It's true that not all of us are mooning about over a certain handsome European refugee, but that doesn't mean we are not interested in the state of the world."

I waited for Bea to throw something, to spit at her, to tell her she must leave immediately. Instead, she did something I had never seen her do. She cried. It was not the theatrical sobbing of Movina's repertoire. Rather, she produced a single tear that grew impossibly large in the corner of her left eye before finally trickling down her cheek.

"That's not fair, Suzanne," I said. "Bea is not interested in Reuben Weiss." It was a risk. I had no idea whether she still was or not, but that single tear had made me want to defend her, and this was the only way that sprang to mind.

"Reuben Weiss is not interested in me!" It came out in a rush, at once a confession that had been long bottled up and a bitter self-indictment.

"Then Reuben Weiss is a fool."

With those six words, Suzanne was suddenly lined up to be Bea's best friend and support. I tried to tell myself this could be a good thing, but I couldn't suppress the jealousy completely. They sat on the couch and railed against the fickleness of men. I was surprised by how many stories they had, and how many were in common, but then they had known one another for years.

To hear Bea tell it, Suzanne and I appeared to be the last people on earth to know about Reuben's involvement with Movina. She didn't once imply that either of us had any part to play in events. I knew, though, that Suzanne must be thinking about how she had provoked Movina's jealousy of Frank by sitting for that ballerina portrait. Movina's furious reaction to that purely aesthetic infidelity had (I happened to know) killed what little interest Frank still had left in their affair by then. When I replaced her in Frank's bed, Movina had no choice but to look elsewhere. Women like Movina do not feel complete unless they have a lover. Reuben was available.

"Apparently, Reuben has a passion for the ballet. He needed an *artiste*," said Bea.

"You're an artist."

"A poet. So is he. That's maybe part of the problem. Too much alike. Endogamy is not always appealing. I mean that in the botanical sense, of course: the pollination of two flowers on the same plant." This was Bea showing off. She did it when she was uncomfortable. I was sure she was also doing it to make Suzanne feel stupid. Perhaps they wouldn't be the very best of friends after all.

"Ah," said Suzanne, sounding puzzled. Then, "I've only ever thought of endogamy in the anthropological sense, but of course the etymology makes sense. From gametes."

If she was impressed, Bea didn't show it. "So what *is* going on in the world, Suzanne?"

"Germany has invaded Poland."

"Europe is a long way away."

I thought Bea might as well have said she wished Reuben Weiss and Movina Sudorfsky were a long way away.

"Britain will declare war. They must. And we won't be far behind."

I knew she was right. On my latest weekly visit out to Rothesay, my father could talk of little else. My uncle, who was visiting from Montreal, was elated at the prospect. Wars lift depressions was what he had said. The economy would boom again. I supposed he might be right, and I hated that.

Suzanne's interest in the impending declaration of war was not economic, or military, or humanitarian. It was William she worried about. "You remember what happened in April with the end of the Spanish Civil War?"

Bea and I both knew the story. William had finally mustered the resolve and the funds to go and join what some were already calling the Last Great Cause. He had by then sorted out who was on which side (we never reminded him of his drunken speech at what he persisted in calling 'that country club party') and he was determined to take a stand. I thought it was a terrible idea, but Suzanne had been entirely supportive despite her worries for his safety.

The way he responded to the news of Franco's victory was, then, utterly unfair.

He was in his studio. Suzanne had brought him the newspaper and he flung it back in her face.

"There! Are you happy?" he shrieked.

When she said she was sorry that he would not be able to go he called her a liar, accused her of secretly rejoicing at the defeat of the Loyalists so she could keep him in Saint John. Then he stormed out of the studio and got so drunk that nobody saw him for a week. Henry found him finally in the upstairs hallway of a paint-peeling, sagging-silled dump on Britain Street. When he regained consciousness, he had no recollection of how he had ended up there. Henry developed a convincing theory that involved the heavily rouged death's-head of a woman who lived in one of the building's four apartments, but he never shared his speculations with Suzanne.

"Who knows what he'll do now?" Suzanne asked. "Something desperate. He won't want another war to pass him by."

"Will they *want* war artists, I wonder?" Bea may have been trying to offer comfort with this, but Suzanne and I knew that William would have different plans. He had completely given up painting the longshoremen and the shop girls, paralyzed by his doubts about the morality of furthering his career by representing their pathetic situations. He would certainly not want to paint the horrors of war.

"He would want to be right in the thick of it," I said.

"How will that be different from his wanting to join the battle in Spain?"

"This war will be different. That's all I know. Bigger. More impersonal. Less human. Does that sound stupid?" Suzanne's voice, usually so perfectly produced, sounded like all the wind had gone out of it.

"Not a bit," Bea said. And she poured Suzanne some lapsang souchong.

Throughout the long week between Britain's declaration of war and Canada's following suit, none of us could talk about much of anything else. But then, once the decision to go to war was made, we settled back into our daily lives. Perhaps it was the distance from Europe, or perhaps it was our proximity to the United States, which had decided simply to ignore Hitler for the time being. In any case, we just stopped talking about it. Suzanne's fears about William's joining up appeared more and more unfounded. He even started talking about looking for work, although he didn't act on that for several months.

The three of us were in his studio when he first raised the subject of giving up painting for what he called 'a real job.' Suzanne was fidgeting on the throne. I was writing in my notebook, much as I had been doing since that very first day. I was still getting my best work done in William's studio, although by then I was no longer writing as much about what I saw there in front of me. The smell of linseed oil seemed to have become necessary for any smooth flow of words onto paper. In the evenings, typing up what I had written, I found I had very few additions or other changes to make. When I told Bea about how well I was able to write in the studio, she put it down to what she called the sexual tension in the room. I was afraid to ask her whether she meant between William and Suzanne or whether she was talking about something to do with me and William. I didn't mention to her that I never felt the same way working in Frank's studio.

"Do you ever think about just packing it in? Getting a real job?" William's face was about three inches from the painting he was working on. I couldn't tell right away whether he was addressing Suzanne or me. He had a tendency to toss off remarks without looking up from his canvas. And by then he used the same tone of voice for both of us.

"Has custom staled my infinite variety?" asked Suzanne with an exaggerated yawn and stretch that completely transformed the shape of her right breast and seemed to answer her own question in the negative.

"I was asking Libby."

"What should Libby be thinking about packing in?"

"Poetry?"

"I'm working on something else right now," I said.

"What's wrong with poetry suddenly?"

I was about to answer it was not sudden when I realized that Suzanne was asking William.

"What does it achieve? How does it change the world?"

"Improve it, you mean?" Suzanne laughed dismissively.

"Change it in any way at all. For better or worse? I mean, she labours away, composing, changing, polishing, trying to capture an essence, but what good does it do? Whose life is changed?"

"I'm working on something else right now," I repeated.

"Ah, I see. This isn't really about poetry at all, is it?" Suzanne had thrown on her robe and was guiding William to a chair where she lowered herself to sit astride him. They used to make me uncomfortable, these sudden displays of affection, but I had by then become inured. I even watched them with interest, perhaps tinged with a little jealousy. For all their erotic potential, though, the displays never led to actual sex, not while I was in the room anyway; and Suzanne and I usually left together. Sex was something she told me they did in William's apartment. The studio was for work. And work sometimes included the model nurturing the artist, stroking his face as well as his ego. "Those idiots in Toronto don't know a masterpiece from a mastur-bates. You can't pay any attention to them. People love your work, William. Real people. They are moved by it."

"That and fifteen cents will get you a bowl of soup."

"You'll sell some more paintings soon, you'll see. Won't he, Libby?"

I nodded. It felt like the best way to preserve both my integrity, and peace in the room. As long as I didn't utter actual words, I wasn't actually lying. In fact, I was not convinced that William's latest work would sell. He was experimenting with Fauvism and I was not sure there was a market for impossibly coloured Suzannes.

"And it's not about sales, anyway, is it?" I added.

"What's that?" William snarled. "I couldn't understand you with that silver spoon in your mouth."

"Don't be a beast," said Suzanne, laying her hand gently on his lips.

"I said her mouth, not her ass."

Suzanne sprang off him. "Apologize, William. Filthy beast."

"It doesn't matter," I muttered, although it did. I hated that he thought of me as a dilettante, a spoiled rich girl who could afford to flirt with the arts without any consequences. In fact, as I had told him many times before, my family was probably no better off than his, which made his accusations absurd but no less hurtful.

"Libby is an excellent poet who works hard to try to sell her work. She toils away here day after day, sweating every detail just like you do."

"I'm working on something else right now," I told them for the third time.

Whether they were actually interested or whether it was to diffuse the tension in the studio, they both asked me what. And that was when I showed them, and when I began providing William with the carbon copies of the typed-up manuscript that I never finished: my thumbnail portraits of us all, of the way we were.

Bea had been suggesting the experiment with automatic writing for months before we finally got down to it. The delay owed, in part, to our failure to agree on the purpose. Bea insisted that the exercise would be like a séance, tapping into unseen forces and spirits, while I maintained it should be our own deeper selves we would be trying to tap. She claimed to be worried that she didn't have a deeper self, and then we would leave the idea alone.

Suzanne's and William's reactions to the first of the sketches I shared with them convinced me that Bea and I should go ahead with the experiment on whatever terms. "Brilliantly executed," Suzanne had said. I put that down to supportive flattery, until I realized it was also a way of avoiding addressing anything but technique. "Closely observed," was William's phrase. He at least had had the nerve to go on. "But not much inner light there, is there?" That got me worrying that what Henry had said about Frank's influence on my writing might be accurate. I was paying too much attention to surfaces and technique. Perhaps automatic writing, if it could tap my deeper self, would be the antidote.

We settled on Bea's apartment, which occupied the bottom floor of a brick house on King Street East. The building had been in Bea's family since it was built, but it had, within the last decade, been divided into flats that were mostly rented to strangers. Bea had hers at a preferred rate. She had set the scene before I arrived. I hated to think what she had spent on candles or how long it took to get them all lit. They were in every conceivable form of container, from empty Chianti bottles to chipped saucers. I counted twenty-eight flames in all. She had read somewhere, probably in a biography of Yeats's wife, that multiples of seven were conducive. When I asked conducive to what, she Cheshire-catted the single word, 'receptivity.'

The mahogany shutters that had graced the windows for the sixty years since the house was built were still in place. They matched the wainscoting perfectly. When they were closed it was as though the room had never had any windows. For the session, though, Bea argued we should leave the shutters open, to avoid closing out any spirits that might want to reach us. She had instead draped the windows with swaths of white tulle that were at once meant to soften the room's edges, she said, and to suggest that we were brides awaiting our spirit lovers. I told her that the bridal image made me uncomfortable, but she was very persistent and accused me of being a prude. It wasn't the sexual connotation that bothered me, actually, but the open invitation to spirits from outside to guide my writing.

She suggested we start with a glass of wine. To open ourselves up, she said. Since the opening up could equally be to either internal or external forces, I agreed. My head was pounding in any case and I hoped the wine might calm me. I had not eaten all day, but I didn't think of that until I had swilled three quarters of the glass. The effect was almost immediate. I could feel my cheeks warming and a pleasant sense of imbalance between my ears.

"Should we have music?" Bea asked. "Schubert? Mahler?" She was very proud of her brand-new record player, its mahogany cabinet a nearly perfect match for the room's original woodwork. Above it she had hung a reproduction of a painting she said was by someone called Karl Hofer. In it, a gaunt woman lifts a record from a stack, ready to put it on a turntable. The woman's chemise has slipped to reveal a pale breast the size and shape of a tennis ball. The Nazis had declared the painting degenerate, but so, Bea told me, had her father. He put up with it though, when he visited, because of his fascination with the unusual record player. Bea had explained the Philco's novel technical features to me several times, how it was able to broadcast entirely without wires to any nearby radio set that was tuned to a certain frequency. That ethereal ability had never seemed particularly interesting to me until then.

"Of course," I said. "How perfect, one apparatus transmitting signals to another entirely through the air. What more appropriate way to set us up?"

She put on "Death and the Maiden," which would not have been my choice. We sat side by side on her chesterfield for a few minutes, holding hands like two frightened schoolchildren about to enter a haunted house, two virgins about to enter the *seraglio*.

The Victorian aura of the apartment was unmistakable, with a large round table in the centre of the room, no doubt exactly where it had stood since the house was built on the ashes of the Great Fire. It was easy to picture the family Bible that would have adorned it in years gone by. The needlepoint seats on the two lyre-back chairs that Bea had pushed up to the table were worn in the middle but still quite bright around the edges. There were two small stacks of paper, one in front of each chair, and a pen and pencil at each place. We had agreed that we might feel moved to use either implement, so both should be ready to hand. At one point, we had considered alternatives to paper, but in the end we couldn't imagine what they might feasibly be.

"Ready?" She drained the last of her wine and led me to the table, where we sat on the lyre-back chairs. "Should we shut our eyes, do you think?"

I was about to remind her we had agreed that, above all, the experiment was not to be about *thinking* but about *feeling*, but she quickly caught herself.

"Sorry. We'll just go with the flow, right? Feelings. "

I nodded, feeling a little dogmatic. She shut her eyes. I shut mine. Our hands touched. The Schubert played on.

We had talked about what to do if nothing happened. Would we try another glass of wine or look for some other means to nudge things along? That kind of thing. These conversations always dissolved into more general discussions of the nature of inspiration itself. We debated the distinctions between being 'inspired by' and being 'inspired to,' and chewed over whether it was important to have the subject of inspiration near at hand, if not in front of you, when you wrote, or whether the mind's eye and memory were enough. We talked about debts to one's muse, and whether the balance owing in the exchange between subject and writer was on the giver's side or the taker's. Sometimes, I found, I was thinking about writing when we talked, and sometimes about William.

Under normal conditions, Bea and I worked very differently from one another. She was more given than I was to sitting at a desk waiting patiently for inspiration. If I didn't start typing or scribbling nearly as soon as I sat down, I quickly found other things to do with my body while my mind prepared itself. My apartment, as a consequence, was much cleaner than Bea's and my laundry always done on time. I had never understood, I told her, those people who sit on the toilet for ages, reading, waiting for a bowel movement. Either I go or I get up, I said. Bea had had a field day with my likening my writing to my bowel movements. I was surprised, then, when she was the first to become impatient.

"Are you getting anything? I'm not getting anything. Maybe it's the candles. Too many. Or the music. I should turn the music off."

"It's only been a couple of minutes. Give it a few more." The truth was, I was finding the whole experience quite restful, even if it led nowhere in the end.

Bea had left a window open. The tulle fluttered.

"There. Did you see that, Libby? Hello? Is someone there?"

I wanted to tell her it was not a séance, but then I realized that it really was, for her. If she believed the spirits were to guide her writing, then expecting them to give the conventional signs of their presence was not unreasonable.

"Hello? Can you knock to let us know you are there?"

The Schubert had stopped and there was only the rhythmic scratch of the needle as it skated across the smooth black ring around the disc's orange cardboard centre. I was afraid that if I got up to take the record off Bea would accuse me of ruining the moment. At the same time, if I were a spirit I would have been driven right back where I came from by the nerve-grating sound.

"Bea? Can I...can I just stop the record?"

She was across the room at the precious record player before I had finished the question. All my friends knew I was bad with machinery. The room went silent. No knocks. Bea rejoined me at the table, her left hand poised, twitching above the pen, and her right above the pencil, an inexperienced diner uncertain about which fork to use.

"We could try breathing," I suggested.

"I haven't exactly been holding my breath."

"In concert. The way we talked about." The idea was to breathe in through your nose to the slow count of seven and then out through your mouth to a count of fourteen. It was basic relaxation and there was probably no merit in doing it in concert. That part was my concession to Bea's spirit thesis.

After twenty-one repetitions of the inhaling and exhaling, I was nearly asleep. Then I heard Bea's pencil scratching across her paper.

We had weighed the pros and cons of looking at the other person's writing. Bea had been against it. I accused her of inconsistency. If this was like a séance, as she insisted it was, then it was a shared event and everyone present should have equal access to what the spirits were communicating. She had responded that my position on this was equally inconsistent. I should not want the outpourings of my deeper self to be shared around like common property, should I?

I looked over at her paper anyway. She was rapidly covering it with hieroglyphs and doodles that bore no relationship to any written language I knew. Even though she was not looking down at the paper, the unfamiliar movements of her hand must have told her she was writing gibberish, but she persisted, mechanically replacing the first sheet with a second, which she covered in the same way.

It was not exactly jealousy that I felt, I told myself. I was not interested in producing automatic writing that couldn't be read. Bea was not doing anything I wanted to do. But she was doing something. She had opened herself up to something. Unless she was faking. I immediately dismissed the thought as unworthy, but as quickly replaced it with another. What if I were to rap gently on the underside of the table? Would Bea break off her writing to make contact with a new presence, or would she assume it was her current guide finally doing what was asked of her? Or would she be terrified by the prospect that the whole thing might actually be legitimate and that we had attracted forces from beyond? She must have known that was impossible.

Any knocking proved unnecessary as Bea herself suddenly broke from the spell. She dropped the pencil and stared at her shaking hand. "Jesus," she said. Then she looked down at the pages in front of her. "Damn. Did you look?"

There was no point in lying. "I did."

"You could have stopped me."

"Could I?"

"What about you? Anything?" I couldn't tell whether she was putting me on.

"Afraid not. How about another glass of wine?"

"I need the loo. Help yourself."

I poured for both of us and set the glasses on the table rather than beside the chesterfield. I was already writing when Bea returned from the bathroom.

"It's all right," I said. "You can talk. It's just me at the controls. Manual writing." It was a joke we made when trying to distinguish the day-to-day of what we usually did from the exotic automatic writing we wanted to try.

"What rubbish," Bea snorted as she sat to examine her pages. I had been afraid she might pretend to see some meaning. "What's the point of messages that nobody can decipher?"

"Art for art's sake?" I ventured, without looking up from my page.

"It is odd, though, isn't it? I mean, that I would do that, that that would happen to me, and not to you. There must be *something* in it, mustn't there?"

"If only we knew what. Do you mind if we snuff some of the candles? It's getting quite thick in here. I'd like to stay for a while, though, maybe finish my wine and try to write a little."

"Of course. It's not very late."

The next day was Monday and she would have to go to work at the nursery school in the morning. I knew she would prefer me to leave, but the wine was good, and if the experiment in automatism had worked out properly we might have been at it until the small hours. Besides, I suddenly felt that I could not leave the room without something to show for all the preparatory trouble we had gone to.

"I can't even tell which side is up," Bea moaned, turning her sheets this way and that. "That bit there could be a chimera or a phoenix or something, couldn't it?"

I looked up in spite of myself and got drawn into a protracted discussion of whether the communications (if that is what they truly were) were directly pictographic or whether they were sophisticated ideograms, possibly rebus puzzles. Ultimately, I thought, it didn't matter, because there was not a single instance where we could agree on what object or objects in the visible world any of the scribbles might resemble.

Bea yawned dramatically and I drained my glass and began to pack up my things.

"I'm sorry it didn't work out for you," she said. So she really had decided that she was being guided, even if we couldn't understand the message.

"I'm glad your spirits spoke to you," I said. It didn't cost me anything, and I knew how good it would make her feel.

"I'm sorry you didn't find your deeper self. But don't give up, Libby. You'll find your inspiration one day."

We hugged goodnight and I headed down Carmarthen towards home.

What I didn't tell Bea the next time we met, what I didn't tell anyone, was that I did eventually have a kind of success that night. It was late, well after midnight, and I was half asleep at my kitchen table, I think. My hand began moving of its own accord, or at least not through any conscious effort of mine. The pencil scratched out actual words, whole sentences, until a kind of love letter emerged. I read it through four or five times and then tore it up and tossed it in the trash. I could never send William Upham such a message.

~~~

I didn't, as a rule, drop in on Frank unannounced at the studio, even after we became involved. Unless we had a prearranged sitting or he had invited me to watch while he painted someone else, it was understood that he continued his practice in his regular working space and I in mine. From our conversations over dinner and in bed, I gathered that Suzanne was continuing to sit for him. Movina was apparently modelling again, too, though he said he still hadn't painted anything of her that he felt he could sell. So when I decided on a whim one day to stop in to ask whether he wanted to see a late matinée at the Capitol with me, I expected to find either Suzanne or Movina on the throne.

I paused a moment on the landing outside the studio, hoping to hear a snippet of dialogue I might be able to use, maybe to get a sense of how he was with his other models, but all was silence. When I stepped into the doorway, I could see that Frank was leaned in to his easel, utterly engrossed, but when I looked to see who commanded such attention, there was nobody else in the room. On a small table about six feet in front of him was a single lay figure, posed in exact mimicry of a painting he had made of Suzanne several months before.

"Libby." He had looked over to load up his brush. "Was I expecting you?"

"You must introduce me to your model." I thought it was a droll thing to say and might distract from the unexpected pang of jealousy I was suddenly feeling for this inanimate object.

Frank did not get the joke, and was unlikely to detect the jealousy. "Oh, I don't give them names. That would defeat the purpose, wouldn't it? That's what's so attractive about lay figures. They have no personhood of their own, but they can stand for anyone. Everyone."

"I thought Suzanne would be here. Or Movina." I remembered that first day I had visited Frank's studio, how jealous Movina had been of Suzanne's presence, and I hoped I was not sounding the same.

"How about a sitting? Now that you are here?"

I looked at the jointed figure on the table. "I'm not sure I could hold that pose."

"Oh no. I can leave that for later." He grabbed the little mannequin around its waist and balanced it back on the shelf with the others. I wondered whether the one I had injured was recuperating well, but I couldn't pick it out of the line.

"I was thinking about a movie." It felt awkward, like I was trying to ask him on a date. "Of course, I'd love to sit." I took off my hat and coat, preparing myself to be manipulated like the wooden figure he had just returned to the shelf, though I was less endlessly biddable, I hoped.

He guided me to a straight chair. It had a ladder back and rush seat, and I knew it would be hell after five minutes. When he adjusted my shoulders at a slight angle to my hips and then turned my head the other way, I wished I had just gone to the movies alone. Once he settled in with his paints, though, I immediately felt more at ease. I had already, after my first sitting for him, coined the phrase *looking with intent* for what was happening. Frank was staring at me in order to translate me. It made it all right. To be self-conscious would have been to be selfish, to deny him something that cost me nothing. The portrait was more important than any small discomfort I might feel as its model.

I was still trying to discover his rules about talking, but thought I would take a chance. "Did one of them cancel a sitting?"

"One of whom?"

"Movina. Suzanne."

"No."

"I just thought."

"Sometimes the mannequin is what I want to work with."

"Less talkative."

"More expressive."

"Than a human being?" I reached down to scratch my right knee. I had learned how to cater to such calls of nature without altering the angles he had carefully set. I knew he wasn't painting anything below the shoulder.

"More expressive because you get the pure gesture only, without all the distraction. You capture the essence. I suppose it's a little like those *übermarionettes* that Bea likes to chatter on about."

"But a little cold." I was suddenly reminded of what Henry had said about Frank's influence on me. "You can't get inspired by a handful of jointed wood."

"But you can use it to store the original feeling. I think the lay figure stores up the inspiration…its joints remember it. And, of course, it never gets tired."

"Sorry." I had shifted my position on the uncomfortable chair and couldn't recover the exact angles Frank had set. He put down his brush and came across to massage my shoulders. "That feels nice." It was true. But there was none of the electrical charge I felt when William touched Suzanne in the studio. "What stored up inspiration were you getting when I came in? It looked very much like a painting you did of Suzanne a while back."

"Did it? I don't remember."

"I suppose it's inevitable that you would repeat yourself sometimes." I watched his face closely. It did not change.

"Every model is only an instance of the ideal. The essential gesture finds many individual bodies."

"I think I am glad you paint only my face then."

"Faces have types, too."

"But no two are exactly alike."

"I'm sure you're right. Can I have just ten more minutes of yours, please?" He adjusted my hips and shoulders and chin and returned to his easel. I wondered then whether I really needed to be there at all. I tried not to disturb the pose as I shivered at the thought.

EIGHT

WINTER 1940

MY DECISION TO TRY WRITING IN THE SAINT JOHN FREE PUBLIC Library was supposed to provide an elegant simultaneous solution to three problems I was having with my work.

The first and most pressing problem was my growing impulse to focus entirely on recording the doings and sayings of the people with whom I had now surrounded myself. My afternoons in William's studio with William and Suzanne, and my sessions sitting for Frank, were still producing pages of notes on artists and their models. These ranged from abstract musings on the reproducibility (or not) of the original to more embodied observations of the physical chemistry between painter and painted. But the social sketches were taking more and more of my time. Evenings spent at Henry's were all being painstakingly transcribed in a veritable Hansard of prolonged aesthetic debates that never reached a conclusion. Rehearsals, walks, and visits added to the piles of notes—enough to fuel dozens of sketches and short stories, which threatened to devour me completely if I let them.

The second problem I was facing was a feeling of guilt about losing touch with the great literary tradition. Consorting with visual artists, which most of my new friends were, had seduced me away from the words of Shakespeare and Donne, and even from Eliot and Mrs. Woolf. The world of painters and potters provided a whole new way of seeing for me, and I was eager to master its codes and networks of allusion. But I had begun to fear it was cutting me off from my roots in literature. Observing artists' models and becoming one myself had taken the place of studying literary models.

My third problem had to do with venue. My apartment provided me with a refuge from the demands of visual art and artists, but it replaced them with the mundane responsibilities of everyday life. There seemed always to be dishes to be done and floors to be swept. The cat was eternally hungry. I felt no responsibility to clean the free public library. It was decidedly not a stronghold of visual arts, although, thanks to the Carnegie Foundation, the building itself was a rich architectural feast. Rather, it was the natural home of Donne and Shakespeare and even, thanks to some enlightened collecting, of T. S. Eliot and Virginia Woolf. And nobody I knew had ever reported going there.

The plan worked perfectly for a full week. I left the apartment religiously just before ten, allowing myself exactly the time needed to climb Chipman Hill, regain my breath, and appear at the grand entrance just as Trinity Church was chiming the hour and the massive oak doors were unlocked. I climbed straight to the second floor and staked claim to a small table in the reference section. The reading room on the main floor was, I decided, far too public, too social, a space. On my way by the stacks, I plucked from the poetry shelves a different volume each day at random. Once seated, I played a medieval kind of game, letting the volume, whatever it was, flop open where it would, and beginning my reading there. After half an hour I would make myself stop, close the book, and shut my eyes for a full two minutes.

Then I took up my pen. The trick was not to mimic what I had read, but to join a conversation with it, maintaining reverence while avoiding imitation. Usually, setting myself a particular formal challenge helped.

One morning while I was labouring away on the very early stages of a sestina, trying to identify a set of *répétons* that could sustain the piece, I was interrupted by a grizzled face that popped around the end of the shelving next to my table.

"Sorry to disturb you," the man said. "Do you have a minute?"

It would have been hard to argue that I didn't, since to a casual eye I was merely sitting chewing a pencil end and staring into space.

"Um. I do."

"How do you spell *succumb*?"

I began to spell it. When I got to the second *c* the man spluttered. Then the *umb* utterly floored him.

"Really? Who'd have thought? What's the point of the *b*? What about Nova Scotia?"

Listening to him, I thought I could guess what was challenging him. "*N-o-v-a*," I spelled; then, "new word, *S-c-o-t-i-a*."

"Oh my god. Two words. Of course. Thank you." And he disappeared.

I nearly had my first stanza hammered out when he materialized again. "Sorry. Last one." I knew this was unlikely. "Hurricane."

I rattled it off. Like the two *c*'s in succumb, the double *r* made him skeptical, but the *u* was hardest for him to swallow.

"Are you sure? So *h-u-r-r* as in jurry. Not *h-e-r* as in, well, you know."

"Right."

"How do you remember all this? How all the words are spelled?"

I hadn't ever thought of it like that before. I found I couldn't remember not being able to spell. "Plenty of practice," I said, which was part of an answer.

He interrupted me three more times before I left for the day. I began to see a pattern in the words he asked me to spell, words of weather and disaster, but I didn't ask him what he was trying to write. I was afraid that he might then ask me about my writing, which was a good deal less interesting.

At home that evening, I couldn't stop thinking about the encounter, about what it said about the nature of stories that I could be hooked so thoroughly by those few words, and what it said about me that I had never thought about where command of vocabulary and spelling comes from.

I changed my seat the next day, and that was how I came across Henry. He had staked out a table in a corner of the reading room, which turned out to be less populated than I had imagined. Piles of bound periodicals surrounded him and his head was bent. He was poring over something, so I couldn't see his face, but the shock of thinning blond hair was unmistakably Henry's. I hesitated for a moment. Perhaps he did not want to be seen. Then I considered the possible consequences of appearing to snub him.

"Good morning, Henry."

There was a rustling of paper behind his periodical fortification. "Libby, my dear. Hello. Are you borrowing a book?"

"I have been coming here to work lately. To write."

"Among the old masters. And mistresses, I suppose." As always, Henry understood immediately. "I heard about your little experiment with automatic writing. Bea seemed quite excited, all that getting in touch with deep-down things. Still, there's no substitute for the Greats." He was silent for a moment, considering, I imagined, whether he was obliged to repay the favour and tell me what had brought *him* to the library. "Do you know this publication?" he asked, carefully lifting one brick of his book wall and sliding it across the table. "Gordon Craig was a genius. He made this whole magazine himself. Wrote the articles, created the woodcuts to illustrate them, printed the thing. Some of it he did pseudonymously—to make it look like it was a team effort, I suppose. *The Mask*, he called it. Magnificent."

"Bea has mentioned him. Very avant-garde. Isn't he the one she is so fond of quoting about the difference between the actor and the *übermarionette*? Something about the body in trance, taking away personality and replacing it with divine fire?"

"You are a good listener, Libby. It is one of your great talents. Don't ever let anyone tell you that listening is not a talent."

"But at what point does being a good listener spoil one for being an original voice?" I meant it about myself, but he looked suddenly wounded. Henry is a famously good listener. "As a writer, I mean. How much reading is too much?"

Whether this appeased him or whether he was just quick to recover I could not tell, but his expression lightened. "You will discover that for yourself, Libby, I have no doubt. You are very talented. I think you will go a long way with your writing."

"Not as far as Frank or William with their art." I hesitated. Did Henry expect me to return his compliment? It would have been quite easy to add 'or you,' but I think we both knew his genius was for actual people, not portraits.

"Frank's is a solid talent, a reliable talent. William will go farther. You could go farther than either."

"Poetry doesn't sell like paintings."

"I am not talking about your poetry."

"I'm putting the sketches on hold," I said, a little angry that Suzanne—or was it William?—must have told him about them. I proceeded to babble about the complexities of the sestina I was working on at the moment. When his eyes looked sufficiently glazed, I excused myself to get on with it.

The table I chose to sit at was obscured from his by shelving, so I only caught a fleeting glimpse of him leaving the library. His fortification of bound copies of *The Mask*, I noticed, was still intact. He had made no effort to re-shelve them, which led me to wonder about the much slimmer volume that he did slide onto a shelf as he made his exit. Before I could get up from my seat to satisfy my curiosity, a beautiful young man who could not have been more than eighteen sidled by and plucked the volume from the shelf, settling himself immediately in behind Henry's wall.

As the morning wore on, I paid less and less attention to my poem and more to the elaborate dance going on around me in the reading room. Two more young men and one who must have been sixty repeated the pattern: retrieving the volume, settling in with it behind the fortress, and then casually slipping it back onto the shelf where they had found it. While it wasn't leaving the library, it was definitely setting circulation records.

There had been no action around the shelf for fifteen minutes when I sidled over and picked up the volume, imitating as closely as I could the gait of the first young man. I thought it might help to move like he did in order to feel like he did and understand his tastes. Back in my seat with the book open, I immediately wished I had imitated the entire ritual and retreated, as every other reader had, behind Henry's wall of books. It was not a library book at all, but a hardbound sketchbook of the kind I had seen William and Frank use. Large format. Every page was covered in drawings, some taking the entire sheet, some quite small and arranged in the manner of a storyboard. All of the figures were male. None was wearing a stitch. Actually, that is not true. Some were wearing masks. Every one of them was impossibly erect, although in some cases the viewer had to infer the erection because the actual member (that was what my mother had tried to teach me to call it, as if it were about being in a club) was buried in a pair of cherubic buttocks, or covered by the back of a curly head.

My cheeks burned but I continued leafing through. I was less interested in studying the new positions and methods each new page revealed than in trying to learn the draughtsman's own story. I had seen the consumers. I wanted to know the producer. There were no signatures, no initials; there was no if-found-please-return message in the front of the book. I dismissed the idea that the drawings were Henry's. Although he was the first person I saw with the book, why would he need to consult it in the library if it was his to begin with? He must just have been one in the line of users. (The word *users* seemed somehow right.) The drawings, however risqué they were, however dangerous, were undeniably good. Technique heightened the sizzle of the forbidden. They were definitely the work of a master technician, which narrowed it down considerably. I supposed I would eventually sort out whether William or Frank was the artist.

In the meantime I replaced the sketchbook on the shelf, praying that someone else would rescue it before the lovely lady at the circulation desk came across it.

___

The atmosphere in William's studio darkened in sympathy with the short winter days. Twice, I pleaded a sore throat so that I did not have to accompany Suzanne there. The bickering between them had erupted into outright sniping. Although I continued to take along my notebook to work while they worked, it was becoming harder to immerse myself, to shut out the quarrelling.

Perhaps worse, it was impossible to avoid transcribing some of it, and I worried that they might sometime look over my shoulder and see what I had written.

Most days, the unpleasantness started as soon as Suzanne emerged from behind the screen. Often, I had not even taken off my hat or pulled out my pencil. William would let out a great sigh and Suzanne would ask him what was on his mind as she passed him and mounted the throne. He wouldn't respond, and then she would start supplying possibilities. Was she getting fat? Was he tired of painting her? Had he slept? Had bad news? The more questions she asked on any given day, the deeper and longer the silence with which he responded. I asked her once on our walk to the studio whether she might try not taking any notice of the opening sigh, but she dismissed the suggestion as cowardly.

The stony silence, when it was finally broken, seemed cordial, in retrospect, compared to what followed. William's diatribes were always some variation on a set of themes, all of which concerned his prospects as an artist. The obstacles to his rosy future included the economy, the Upper Canadian art establishment, declining aesthetic standards, Frank Gray, inferior paints, and Suzanne. Most days, it was a combination of at least two of these. He was drinking more during the day, but never once did he mention the booze. That was normal in my experience.

On the worst day, I was afraid he might actually strike her. It had started as usual, with the sigh that greeted Suzanne's emergence from behind the screen. I thought about the henna surprise of my first day in William's studio and longed for those more innocent times.

"Why so down in the dumps?" Suzanne had chirped. "Try looking up at my bumps."

"You really are a shallow bitch, aren't you?" His reaction was so swift and so cutting I thought it must be a joke, flirtatious in the old bickering way. But then: "A fellow might be being eaten by acid and you'd not care as long as he was looking at you."

It was Suzanne's turn to be silent. She picked up a robe that was lying near the throne and shrugged it on.

"What the hell are you doing?"

"I think we should stop for today."

"Stop? We haven't started. Take that thing off."

"So you can paint me or fuck me? Are you really up to either?" She kept the robe tight around her shoulders. William looked over at me. I was trying to look engrossed in my notebook.

"Sorry, Libby," Suzanne muttered.

"You know what? Forget it. Get dressed. What's the point anyway? Nobody is buying. Almost nobody. The people who have any money to spend on paintings want landscapes. They're looking for portraits of mother nature to help them forget about *human* nature. And I'm out of burnt sienna, so there's your tits shot."

"How much have you had to drink today?"

It was the first time I had ever known her to mention his habit. When I had tried once to mention William's drinking to her, she had cut me off at the knees.

"Only puritans count a person's drinks," he snarled. "Only dried up old temperance biddies. Is that what you are?"

"You know I'm not, William."

"Prove it." He covered the six feet between them in two strides. His flask had appeared out of thin air and he was holding it to her lips. My legs turned to stone. I sat and watched as Suzanne took a long pull, then spit it in his face.

In reconstructing it afterwards, I was never sure whether it was the fact that she spat in his face or simply that she had wasted his precious liquor that made him raise his hand. I closed my eyes, so it was several seconds before I sensed the mood had changed.

They were laughing. When I opened my eyes and looked over, she was licking the booze from his face, depositing it on his lips. I didn't stay to watch any more.

Frank was so annoyed by the on-again-off-again nature of Reuben's marionette play that he threatened not to attend the opening. He had broken momentum on a series of portraits he was doing to start work on the marionettes. Then, when it looked as though the play would never be performed, he, in turn, suspended work on the marionettes and returned to what he had been doing. Finally, he had to drop the portraits in a hurry when it was suddenly decided that performances would start in two weeks. The final coat was barely dry for the last rehearsal. Why should he interrupt his work again just to attend the opening? I told him Reuben needed our support; and Bea did, Henry did. He asked (unfairly, I thought) when had they supported him. In the end, his curiosity about how an audience would react to his painted figures drove him to agree to come along. I should have known all along to appeal to his ego.

The proscenium opening for Henry's marionette stage was only about three feet by six or seven, which dictated all kinds of considerations about sightlines that ended up restricting the size of the audience. The structure that had always seemed exactly the right size in Henry's studio was dwarfed on the stage of the tiny Star Theatre, which they had finally settled on renting for the performances. Half a dozen seats on the ends of each row needed to be cordoned off as unusable. Movina had suggested selling them as obstructed views, insisting that they did that in New York all the time. But Henry argued that this was Saint John, and that any views from the ends of rows would be not so much obstructed as completely non-existent.

We were late arriving. Frank insisted there would be no trouble with seating, even with a reduced house capacity, but he had underestimated the draw. The entire Little Theatre group had turned up en masse, eager, I supposed, to assess the competition, to measure the threat to their live art from the little wooden figures. I waved to Suzanne across a sea of heads just before she took her seat. She had William in tow, the scowl on his face and slump in his shoulders indicating under what duress. There were also church groups of all persuasions, and a dozen or more students who must be from the vocational school—Henry's pupils, no doubt. The best Frank and I could do for two seats together, then, was the second-to-last row. At that distance, the tiny marionette stage appeared roughly the way the stage at the Capitol Theatre would if you were to view it from somebody's living room on Carmarthen Street, two blocks away. I was thankful that I had stuffed my opera glasses into my purse at the last minute.

I had dressed quite carefully for the occasion, cleverly walking a fine line, I thought, between actual elegance and an ironic imitation of it, not being certain of the correct code for marionette theatre openings. My long gloves were the same magenta as my hat (I would never get the dye out of the sink) and I had slung a strand of my aunt's pearls around my neck in a loop that aligned perfectly with the scooped neckline of my black gown. The silk stockings felt like a whisper compared to the growl of the lisle ones I had adopted since moving into the city, and getting the seams straight was an annoying and time-consuming ritual I had happily all but forgotten. Frank, whom I knew would dress himself smartly, said so many times how nice I looked that I began to resent it. Why should he be surprised? On the tram, though, he whispered that he was imagining me naked under it all. *As model or lover*, I wondered.

The house lighting was dim at The Star, probably in order to obscure the fading draperies and wallpaper, the threadbare carpet in the aisles. There was no printed program, so the light level didn't matter for reading, but even to make out familiar figures in the audience was a challenge. If I had not seen Suzanne and William before they sat down I might not have known they were in the second row from the front. I spotted Movina and Reuben only because she was windmilling her arms around to underline some point or other.

At five past eight, the feeble houselights went out completely and Henry stepped into a hard-edged spotlight trained on the apron of The Star's stage, just in front of the marionette theatre. He looked spectacular in evening dress. I felt good about having opted for my pearls.

"Thank you for coming," he began, launching into the usual litany of acknowledgements and caveats. What we were about to see could never have been made without etc. We got the potted speech about marionettes (they were not puppets) and about trends in contemporary theatre (agitprop, social realism). I was more interested in the conversation that seemed to be continuing between Reuben and Movina in the audience. It was interrupted briefly only when Henry asked the talented playwright to get up and wave. I couldn't hear them from where I sat, but I felt sorry for those who could, and wondered why they had not been shushed. I could only conclude that what they were saying was of more interest than the speech from the stage, which might not have been a very high standard to beat. Frank was watching them too, probably wishing as I did that we could somehow lip-read through the backs of heads. Movina's flapping arms were not much help as they were prone to flailing around even when she was talking about the price of eggs or which scarf to wear. Reuben's posture was more telling. He looked like a man defeated, rather than the triumphant poet-playwright at his world première. Was Movina trying to jolly him along? That seemed unlikely, given her usual catastrophic outlook on everything. Perhaps she was telling him how much worse *she* felt, whatever it was that he was feeling.

They made an interesting pair. I had had many opportunities to observe them in recent weeks at Henry's studio. What had been two solo acts had merged into a duo that was a surprisingly successful blend of their two previously disparate styles. Movina had always been the loudest and largest presence in any room, and that had not changed in its essentials, but now much of her energy was devoted to directing attention to Reuben, whose quiet, tortured brooding had not changed in its essentials either. In turn, Reuben's stormy silences seemed to beg for relief in the extravagant outpourings of Movina. Frank had wondered once, unkindly I thought, whether it had ever occurred to either of them that Movina's Slavic forebears might well have burned Reuben's ancestors out of their *shtetl*. I had replied, even more unkindly I suppose, that it wouldn't matter, since Movina reinvented herself and her story regularly.

The most obvious feature of her latest reinvention was her apparent shift of focus from all-about-herself to all-about-Reuben. Until you thought about it a bit more. Frank had put me straight. He pointed out that Movina's always evident proprietorship over Reuben made anything that *appeared* to be about him ultimately about *her*. Reuben's sufferings as a refugee were retailed by Movina, who always took her cut. Neither did she hesitate to remind her listeners that she herself was a refugee. If Reuben was a struggling artist who was often misunderstood (though there was no clear evidence of this), Movina assumed the same yoke as she ensured we all knew how difficult it had been for her to establish a ballet school in this rough port city.

Frank had developed a very funny routine in which he speculated on their sex life. It was full of exaggeratedly thick accents and stiff competition over whose post-coital *tristesse* was greater.

There was gentle applause—Henry had finished his introductory remarks. Movina turned herself away from Reuben to face the little marionette theatre. We all waited in silence (even Movina) for a full twenty-five seconds. And then the narrator began.

I tried to think about what it must be like for anyone who had not attended dozens of rehearsals to see the play with new eyes. When that task proved impossible, I shifted in my seat and bent to the left to try to get a line of sight on Suzanne and William. I wanted to see how close they were sitting to one another. I hadn't been back to the studio since the rye-spitting incident. I wanted to see if they were holding hands, but not even the opera glasses could help me; there were too many people in the way. Frank didn't appear to notice my awkward posture. I thought his eyes might be shut already.

Frank squeezed my knee. He was awake after all and leaned in to whisper in my ear. His breath ruffled the tiny hairs on my neck and I shivered. "Do you think it's right?"

The question was too vague. There must be more. I waited, although I wished he were finished. I hated it when people talked during a play, even if in this case there was no chance of the marionettes' hearing us and being put off their stride.

"Do you think it's right, making art out of other people's suffering?"

"What would Aristotle say?" If I was to be forced to talk during a play, what I had to say was going to be at least as clever as what was being said on stage.

"I mean, using atrocities that are going on halfway around the world to get an emotional reaction out of a Saint John audience."

"We need to know, don't we?"

"That's what newspapers are for. Terrible things are happening here too."

"Can we talk about this later?"

"Please do," said a fat bald man sitting on the far side of Frank. I thought how lucky the man was that he was next to Frank and not William. If William had been sitting next to this man, he would have kept talking just to gall him. I took Frank's hand and put it back on my knee, pulled it up the inside of my thigh.

Through my opera glasses I watched the evil prince winning the people over with his impassioned speeches. For a moment, I was drawn in completely. The peculiar little play became the whole world, focused through my binocular lenses. Then there was a disturbance at the edges of my circumscribed world. A figure had entered, a gigantic figure, eclipsing the marionette world momentarily. I dropped the glasses to try to make sense of the scene. There was no making sense of it, not then, not later. It was Reuben Weiss. He was holding a pair of tailor's shears. In five strokes he had cut every string in sight. Then he bolted from the theatre even before the houselights could be restored.

NINE

SPRING 1940

FRANK HAD NOT SPOKEN FOR TWENTY MINUTES. I COULDN'T stand the silence any longer. Silence is different when you don't have any clothes on. And different again when you are naked outdoors. I was not sure he understood those things.

"What am I today? Mainly geometry? Light and shadow?"

"Does it have to be one or the other?"

He had not gone deaf at least. And I was pleased that he had taken my question seriously, answered as if it were a legitimate thing to ask. From the first day he painted me nude, I had been a sponge for everything he could tell me about how he painted the figure, and he obviously had come to take it for granted that I had absorbed it all. Not that I had been remarkably quick on the uptake at first. My appreciation of what he told me had waxed and waned wildly several times as I tried to sort out the distinctions between the roles of lover and model.

His asking me to model without my clothes had been a significant hurdle for me to get over. What did it mean when the man who had told you that he never painted his lovers in the nude asked you to pose in the nude? Was the love affair over? Or was the "rule" just something he had said to get me into bed in the first place? I didn't ask. I had simply nodded and unbuttoned. And, right away, he began to explain to me how he worked.

Some women might have been horrified to hear how they were being seen so technically, reduced to planes and angles, light and shadow. I found it reassuring. When he looked at my body in the studio, he looked one way. In the bedroom, another. The two were different, I thought. Separate. Separable.

Over the weeks that followed, he continued his course of lectures on technique, sometimes demonstrating directly on my body a principle of composition or of colour theory, sometimes on the canvas. As he talked, I felt as though I had ascended out of my own flesh and could look at it objectively with him, dispassionately. I tried to reassure myself that there was a difference between observing dispassionately and unpassionately. I quickly found I was prepared to go to surprising lengths to keep his interest alive, to make him want to go on looking. I would guffaw at the demure poses he asked of me (poses I would have blushed to attempt only weeks before) and would suggest ever more adventuresome ones. Never pornographic, but bolder. If he suggested I sit turned three quarters away, I gave him crouched and three quarters on. When he asked for something reminiscent of Cranach, I gave him Ingres. I discovered that I loved being looked at.

In the bedroom, we continued to do things very much as we had that day that Suzanne had a cold. Frank saved his inventiveness for the studio. I came to be less afraid of losing him as a lover than of ceasing to be interesting to him as a model. Suzanne would sometimes ask me about sex with Frank. It was always just a pretext for her telling me about sex with William though: his whims, his fantasies, how he liked to have a mirror or would get her sometimes to put a barrette in her hair. If I had ever had to offer any information, it would have been that making love with

Frank was like the fade-out in a Hollywood movie. Everything went blurry and then the birds sang.

I began to sense a serious threat the day Frank asked to photograph me. We were taking a break and I had pulled on one of his old cardigan sweaters. It smelled of him and of linseed oil. He had made tea, which was unusual. He only ever made tea for me in his apartment. After sex.

"It would let me work when you're not here," was how he pitched the idea. "It's purely an *aide-mémoire*. The photograph would only be for my use in the studio." He misread the apprehension that must have been obvious in the way I held myself. He thought I was worried about naked photographs circulating. Of course I suppose I would have been, remembering that sketchbook in the library. But my real concern was something else. His request meant I could be reduced to two dimensions and a single moment in time. That was all he needed of me. Soon, it could be even less.

"I have all the time in the world. I can sit longer. You can work whenever you like. I have a funny thing about photographs, have I never told you? A kind of a silly superstition, really. Like the stories you hear about tribespeople who have never seen a camera. It's not my soul I'm afraid of losing, god knows. It's my youth." This was one of the most ridiculous stories I had ever let from my lips, but once it was out I shrugged my shoulders as if to say, 'What can you do? Shall we move on?'

But he had not been ready to move on. He had his tripod spread and was mounting the camera as though I had not spoken.

"Frank? I'd really rather not." It was the first time I had ever felt even a little bit unsafe in his presence.

"All I want is to capture the pose. It will free you from a lot of tedious standing. How is it different from—"

"I will be *absent*. Not here. Here, I can see you seeing me. That matters to me. I like it like that."

And so he let it drop, for a week. Then one day I sneezed and he asked what he was supposed to do if I got a cold. We could miss days in the studio, weeks. I thought about how Suzanne's cold had brought Frank and me together that day when she cancelled her sitting, and I relented and let him take a half a dozen photos—with the strict understanding that they be used only for a rainy day.

When he first suggested painting a kind of response to *Le Déjeuner sur l'herbe*, it took me several minutes to recover. Although I had myself been initiating studies in the studio that might reasonably be described as increasingly exhibitionistic, modeling *en plein air* had never occurred to me.

He assured me that Taylors Island would be deserted; he had selected the perfect spot. He would paint me recumbent on the cliff, with Manawagonish Island in the background. As near low tide as possible. When I asked who else would attend the little picnic, he smiled and said I would be dining alone. That made the whole thing more palatable.

The hired car smelled of cigars and smoked mackerel and growled threateningly all the way along Sand Cove Road, as though it upset its stomach to be playing a role in this sordid adventure. Along Saints Rest Beach, Frank kept two wheels on the marram grass for traction. I told him he had better not get us stuck since I was not about to get out and push. My shoes and dress were new, bought for the occasion. Bought for the occasion of taking them off on a Bay-of-Fundy cliff.... Frank was decent enough not to point out the irony.

In the end, we parked about three quarters of the way along the beach on a platform of smooth rocks, where he was confident we would be able to turn around for the journey back. He carried his gear along the rest of the beach and up the hill to the cliff face, and I toted the wicker basket with lunch. Or props. Both really.

The two bottles of wine made for a heavy load, but they clinked merrily, as if to assure me that everything would be all right.

"So, it's both light *and* geometry. Me and Manawagonish Island. And the waves in between, I suppose," I said, careful not to disturb my pose.

The hat Frank had given me to wear protected no more than my face. I could feel my shoulders starting to burn already, though I was less worried about them than the bits that had never seen the sun. The blanket was doing very little to cushion my bottom and I was hoping he would call a break. Perhaps we could start on one of the bottles of wine.

"Can I see?"

"Not yet."

I wanted to ask him why he hadn't settled for making some sketches here, even a photograph or two, and then finish the painting in the studio, but our squabble about the photographs was too fresh. And although he was mostly silent and the ground was hard, the sun hot, and I was beginning to worry about bugs, it was time spent together, time spent being looked at.

"More knife than brush?" I asked instead.

"How can you tell?" He knew that the pose he had me in meant I couldn't possibly see what he was doing.

"Hearing, partly. And trying to picture the composition, the subject. What would do it justice. Us justice. Me and the island. Oh, and the bay."

"You're quite a student. We've almost made a painter of you."

It may have been an innocent comment, just banter, but I heard something else in it. Something that might be saying, 'Get ready to fly away, little bird. I've nothing more to teach you.' I shivered, then assured him I was not cold. We reverted to silence. I thought about how different this all was from my picnic with Henry and the Bojilovs, and about Henry's lesson about balancing the order with the chaos, but I didn't raise any of that with Frank.

Lunch was delicious. He must have spent a fortune. There was bread and French cheese, even grapes. I couldn't remember when I had last had fruit that was not from a tin. There was something about the fresh air that made the wine work even faster. Although I gratefully put on my new clothes when he had called the break, I found I wished we were both naked, even if that broke the contract. I was about to suggest it when he leapt up and returned to his canvas. I was not sure what to do. Was lunch over? Were we going back to work? Uninvited, I joined him in front of the easel.

"Ah." It was the only word I could manage. Some writer I was.

If you didn't know I was there in the painting, you might mistake me for a rock (pinkish granite), or a trick of the light, a daub, nothing more than a tiny part of the landscape. The blanket, the basket, the bottles of wine— none of these things was there. This was his response to the great Manet. Worse, this was his response to me.

"We'll go back now, shall we?" I asked it as a question that had only one answer. He nodded and began to pack up his things. I don't think he looked at me once on the excruciating drive back uptown.

～～

People dropped in and out of William's and Frank's studios quite often while they were painting, but nobody I knew had ever witnessed Henry actually working on a canvas. We had all seen the telltale daubs of paint spilled on the floor of his studio, and we knew he guided the brushes of dozens of young painters in classes every week, but any canvases he might or might not produce remained secondary to the salons he held most evenings. I knew I should be flattered, then, when one night not long after my humiliation on Taylors Island, just as I was leaving his place, he invited me to come around in the morning. "Just the two of us," he said. "Bring your notebook, if you like. I should be painting. I usually paint early in the mornings."

It was not clear whether he planned to paint me. If so, I supposed it would be head and shoulders. But, just in case, at the last minute, I chose my nicest underwear and dragged the razor across my armpits and up shins and calves, wondering at the person I had become.

As I climbed the stairs, which were devoid now of any trace of the previous night's revelry (who cleaned it all up?), I thought about the last time I had been alone with him in the studio, and hoped I was not in for another lesson in the art of the marionette. It was a relief to open the door and find him apparently hard at work in front of an easel.

"Libby. Make yourself comfortable." He didn't look up.

Comfortable as a model or as a visitor? There did not appear to be anything resembling a throne set up that morning, so I ruled out the former and began shrugging off my coat, musing that the roles of model and of visitor both begin with disrobing.

"There is coffee, if you would like."

The cup beside him was empty and I wondered whether this was code for 'Would you get me some?' Retrieving the half-full pot from the corner that served as Henry's kitchen, I poured myself a cup of coffee and topped up his.

"Bless you," he purred, still intent on his canvas. "There were biscuits, but I think someone must have found them last night."

"Coffee is perfect for me," I said, although I was suddenly famished. I tried to remember when was the last time I saw anyone bring anything other than wine to Henry's. It had not occurred to me until then to wonder where all the food came from evening after evening. I wondered how he managed on the money he made from teaching, and promised myself I would contribute food to the next salon.

"How very accommodating."

I was not sure how to take this until he looked up with a smile. A compliment, then. Of sorts.

"What are you working on?"

"Just daubing, really. Trying to keep my wrist alive, my hand in, whatever metaphor you'd like for disproving the old adage."

"Remind me."

"Those who can, do; those who can't, teach."

I didn't know what to say. This was exactly what I had heard Frank say dozens of times. William, too, once.

"Did you bring your notebook?"

I wondered whether he was about to ask me to take dictation, but he read my mind.

"I hoped you might do a little writing here, while I paint. Sometimes it helps to know there is another artist producing in the same space. Don't you find?"

It was nothing more than I had been doing for months with William and Suzanne and, more lately, with Frank. But it seemed odd when Henry asked it. Forced, I thought. Studied. I supposed it was the teacher in him.

Did he sense my hesitation? In any case, he appeared to change the subject, carefully laying down his brush and taking up his coffee cup before he turned to face me, as though we were about to have a good gossip. "How is everything with you? Frank is well, I hope."

It dawned on me that the invitation was really for this after all. Henry was a famous meddler. Resistance, I had heard, was futile. But I didn't want to appear too easy.

"Frank is thriving," I reported. It was true. He was painting more furiously than ever. At what cost to me I did not mention.

"Painters are complicated brutes."

"Present company excepted."

Henry smiled. I expected him to say something self-deprecating about his not really being a painter. Instead, he said: "They're narcissists mainly. I don't mean that at all judgmentally. Just as a statement of fact. It is a necessary trait, really, if one is to make it as an artist."

"I don't think that Frank is…" I began. Then I realized that perhaps I did.

"It is what we require of them. Narcissism. Think about it, that old criticism you hear that so-and-so hasn't put enough of herself or himself onto the canvas. How is that a valid critique of a landscape or a portrait if we don't expect them to look at their subject and somehow see themselves?"

The argument may not have been strictly logical, but I was persuaded a little. "It has something to do with the difference between looking and seeing, doesn't it?" I asked. "Anybody can look, but a painter sees."

"And what they see is themselves."

"Not the model, anyway," I muttered before I could stop myself.

"Everything changes. That's the one thing you can rely on."

I wondered then how often Henry had been disappointed in love, but it appeared he meant something else.

"Art would be unnecessary otherwise, don't you agree? Impossible even. We try to do two irreconcilable things at once, most of us. To capture the moment, freeze it in time, fossilize it; and at the same time, suggest the moment that came before and the moment that will come after." He punctuated this series of pronouncements with several swigs of coffee. "Read your Lessing on *Laocoon*."

"Maybe that's true for visual artists." I was tired of hearing sweeping statements about the arts that really only pertained to painters and sculptors.

"I am thinking of your poetry, too. And fiction. The image must be perfect in itself, but at the same time it must demonstrate an attraction to the images before and the images after. A story does not work without desire, for the past and for the future. Every episode is both full and lacking at the same time. Part of the lack, and therefore the yearning, the attraction, is for other moments in time."

Whether it was the language he was using or the obvious passion with which he was speaking, for the first time, I had a sense of Henry as a sexual being and I worried briefly about what might happen next.

"Tell me what you are writing now."

For some writers, I knew, the question would be an aphrodisiac. For me, it nearly always had the opposite effect. I thought Henry knew that. And I remembered his response to the sonnets I had showed him. "Not very much, really. Some sketches, I suppose you would call them, word portraits. I think that Suzanne or William may have mentioned something to you about them already. Not really very interesting. I have no idea where they're going."

"That is hardly the language of a narcissist, is it?" When I didn't say anything, he went on. "Can you imagine Frank or William selling themselves so short? Even when they say they don't want to talk about what they are working on, you know they think it is the best thing ever painted. And they'd be crushed if you didn't ask."

And so I read him several pages from the notebook I had brought along. They were only the rough work for the pieces I typed up and shared with William, just fragments of conversations, miniatures of scenes at rehearsals, in studios, slightly cruel, over-done thumbnail portraits of Reuben and Movina and the Bojilovs.

"Bruegel," he said when I had finished.

"I beg your pardon."

"They remind me of Bruegel, these notes."

"Without the folk. Or the humour."

"They are drawn with a similar kind of care, your portraits. And with love, ultimately, I think. They remind me a little of those gargoyles at Chubb's Corner." He gestured vaguely in the direction of Princess and Prince William Streets. "They were all caricatures in stone of local celebrities at the time the building went up."

"Right. And nobody remembers anymore who they were. Isn't a lot of Bruegel quite grotesque?" I was thinking of a picture called *Dulle Griet* I remembered seeing reproduced somewhere: devils defecating, bums with faces, that sort of thing.

"That is a fine line you will have to discover for yourself."

"You think they are good, then, these bits?"

"I think you should keep on doing what you are doing, until the next thing comes along. And it will."

This appeared to be all the answer I was going to get. I offered then to do a little writing right there, keep him company while he painted, but Henry was already packing away his brushes. He had a class to teach and food to buy for this evening's salon.

TEN

SUMMER 1940

I BEGAN TO EXTEND MY CITY WALKS. I THINK INCREASING THE scale was a way of trying to comprehend Frank's shift in focus away from the figure toward something broader. Or maybe I simply needed new sights and more time on my own. The central peninsula of the city was suddenly no longer big enough, although I knew I had by no means finished collecting the stories it had to offer. The heights of the North End beckoned, and Mount Pleasant invited, but my favourite stroll quickly became the one across the bridge, over the Reversing Falls gorge. The walk had the advantage of incorporating the North End and Douglas Avenue, but it was the bridge itself that was the real draw. A bridge, I thought, is neither one place nor the other. It was its own sovereign territory, its own domain. I always stopped in the middle, judging as nearly as I could the spot that was exactly halfway across. The scene below was different every time. Sometimes the display at the rapids was spectacular; sometimes, disappointing. I did not plan my walks around the tide table. Taking what was presented at any given moment was part of the exercise. The river had its moods too.

Most days, I turned back after my pause in the middle of the bridge. The Lancaster side at its western end appeared to offer only the brush factory and what had recently been renamed the Provincial Hospital, the term 'insane asylum' having fallen out of favour. Neither seemed a likely source for inspiration. Not from the outside, at any rate. On one of the rare occasions that I did cross the entire length of the bridge and venture into Lancaster, I found William.

The brush factory, viewed from across the river and even from the bridge, was an impressive structure: a giant dress box with a water tower astride it proudly advertising SIMMS BRUSHES AND BROOMS. The building was mainly windows, each of which was divided into hundreds of panes, with transoms that seemed to be wide open in all seasons. I supposed it got stuffy on the shop floor, but at least it was light. Close up, the overall resemblance to a dress box was lost, of course, and one felt simply overwhelmed, dwarfed.

William looked tiny when I came upon him, standing about halfway along the street side of the enormous building, smoking a cigarette. I was suddenly reminded of that first night I saw him, at the Crosbys' party. How helpless he was as we led him out, how lost, the sick-sweet smell of booze and tobacco.

"Have you given up on the longshoremen?" I asked. It had been weeks since I last saw him. My visits to his studio with Suzanne had stopped altogether and she barely mentioned him anymore.

He took a long drag from his cigarette, held, and exhaled, then picked some shreds of tobacco off his tongue: a ritual I had seen repeated all over the city when I took my walks, but one that was most painstakingly performed on the docks by the longshoremen. William had learned it from the best, even if he had stopped painting them.

"What brings you to Lancaster?"

Not only was it not an answer to my question, but I couldn't tell whether it was itself really a question or simply some kind of coda to the cigarette performance, the obvious next line in an imaginary film in which he had cast us. Before I could make up my mind whether to answer directly, he went on.

"You're not coming for a stay across the road?" He gestured vaguely at the hospital glowering down on us from the hill opposite.

"Just gathering more material, I suppose, searching for inspiration." When he didn't respond I tried another tack. "Where's your sketchbook?"

"In the studio."

"You're working from memory?" Frank had told me once that nobody any good ever worked from memory. It was part of his ominous argument for making photographs of me. But Frank was a planner; his work was all about control. William had always been different. I meant to pay him a compliment with the question. Besides, I was often working from memory myself by then.

"Suzanne hasn't told you? I am working here."

"Oh, a commission? That's wonderful. Is it something large?" I remembered Suzanne's mentioning something about his wanting to go to Mexico to study with someone who was quite famous for painting walls in the United States.

"I work here on the line. I've just come off shift. The others clear out pretty quickly, go home to their families, or out for a beer. I like to have a smoke, then a nice slow walk across the bridge."

"You're making brushes?"

"Art Worker Takes Over Means of Production. It's not quite the headline Marx had in mind, but you can see how it fits."

"But why?"

"They pay cash. Every week. I was lucky to get the job. There are plenty without work, or maybe you hadn't heard."

"There's one that might not be out of work if you hadn't taken the position." It was mean, but I was sick of his putting me in the rich-girl box.

"Everybody's free to look for work. It's a competitive world. Who's to say I didn't need this job more than somebody else? I heard about the vacancy, and I applied."

Obviously he had been wrestling with this very question, then. "But what about your painting? You can't leave that."

"Can and have." His cigarette was burning dangerously close to his fingers. "I might dabble in the evenings, on weekends, but I doubt it. The lease on the studio runs just a few more months."

"And you can just walk away from it, from your life's work?"

"That's such an interesting phrase, don't you think, 'life's work'? It's equally imperceptive about both life and work. As if the one could ever define the other."

"Why not a longshoreman?"

"What?"

"If you wanted to become one of your subjects. Because that's what this must be, surely, a kind of field trip, a research exercise into what it feels like to be a labourer."

"I've stopped painting labourers. I told you: the transition is simple. Elegant. I have progressed from *using* brushes to *making* them. The bristles come from China, you know. Old Mr. Simms was very forward-thinking in that sense."

"Besides, you're not really built like a longshoreman, are you?" This was a risk. It would not be the first time I cracked a joke to end a serious discussion. And I probably should not have noticed how he was built. He was another woman's man, my friend's lover.

William laughed and crooked his right arm and rocked his shoulder up and down as if flexing his biceps under his baggy flannel shirt. Then he grabbed my elbow so hard it hurt, and said, "Let's walk."

We headed in the opposite direction from the bridge, passing window after window of the giant factory. Then, where the street made a bend so severe we could not see properly in either direction, he whisked me off the sidewalk into the road. A Ford that was driving too fast had to swerve and the driver laid on his horn, but William propelled us on. After dodging a truck coming the other way, we collapsed on the bank that rose up toward the hospital, puffing and laughing.

"We could have been killed," I panted, still clinging to him.

"And then what of our life's work?" When I just stared at him, he continued, "It's not really dangerous. Nobody is driving that fast. I wanted to show you something. You like to see new things, don't you?"

"I don't think we're allowed on the grounds. The inmates… you're not supposed to disturb them, are you?"

"We can stay outside the fence. It's a little steep in parts. Good thing you have on your walking shoes." He took my hand more gently than he had grabbed my elbow and led me through the grass, keeping the towering red-brick asylum on our right. "Sobering," he said after a minute of walking, "to think about it. How little separates us from them. Just those lawns and this fence."

"And our understanding of the world around us. They're in there for a reason. We're out here for a reason."

"I envy your certainty." He gave my hand a squeeze and dropped it. "'The lover, the poet, and the madman are all of imagination compact….' Isn't that a line from Shakespeare?"

"The lunatic, the lover, and the poet. Yes. But Duke Theseus is hardly an expert on the imagination."

"Here we are." He gestured like Satan from an illustrated Bible at the view from the hillside: the river, the harbour, and the distant city all lay spread out before us. "This is how they see it."

"The inmates?"

"The lunatics. This is how she sees it."

"She?"

"Suppose I told you I had a sister in there." Before I could come up with some lame expression of sympathy or ask for more details, he rested his hand on my forearm. "Let's just look at it all for a few minutes, shall we?"

We sat in silence. I scanned the skyline from left to right. That was the writer in me, I supposed, reading the landscape as if it were a page. I didn't know how he looked at it. Probably very differently. The spires of the cathedral and Trinity Church drew the eye, imparted some order to the composition, but the rest was a glorious free-for-all, climbing up one hill and down another to the harbour. At this distance, you couldn't see any people. It might as well have been unpopulated. Maybe the absence of human figures was what really interested him. I hoped not. Who knew what he was thinking?

When we got up to leave, I caught him stealing a glimpse back at the hospital. I allowed myself then to imagine a young woman with William's features and cropped black hair, her face pressed up to a high tower window, writing messages on the grimy pane. Halfway across the bridge, we both paused to look down into the gorge and I saw that face again, in the water, its mouth open, trying to say something to me.

Just before Labour Day, Bea and I travelled up the river to the Kingston Peninsula where the Bojilovs had their studio. They had promised Bea a series of pottery lessons back when they were working together on the Phaethon play, and she had finally decided to take them up on it. When she suggested bringing a friend, they were delighted. That's what she told me anyway. They usually seemed delighted. I had never known them to be anything less than cheerful, which made for a nice change from almost everyone else. Whether it was the fresh air on the peninsula or the simple fact that they were glad to be away from Finland, where it gets even darker in the winter than it does here, none of us knew, but we had all remarked on their seemingly irrepressible jolliness. William thought it had something to do with the fumes from the glazes they used for their pots, but the rest of us doubted that.

I was surprised when Bea asked me along. We had been seeing less of one another, although when we did meet up we kept planning to plan to get together—maybe to take another stab at automatic writing, we would laugh, although I was not sure it was a joke. I had heard that she and Suzanne had become quite friendly, though Suzanne never mentioned it herself.

Emil was very patient at first as Bea and I each tried to raise something on the wheel. He chirped encouragement and waved his arms like a symphony conductor. Marijke had prepared us with a speech about how you have to sense the spirit in the clay, to feel the form that is waiting to be released. Emil's approach was more technical. I was reminded of our picnic in St. Andrews, the differences in their approaches. Bea had trouble centring her pot, and I found I didn't have enough strength in my hands to raise the clay off the wheel. At one point, I thought I saw a cloud cross Emil's perpetual sunshine, but then Marijke rejoined us and suggested another approach.

Apparently, the wheel was only needed if you wanted to produce perfectly symmetrical objects. Mastering it was very difficult and could take a lot of time. There were other ways of shaping objects that were easier to learn, Marijke said, and faster. She told us all of this with a smile, but I detected a tiny waning of patience on her part too. Whatever the bond they had felt with Bea while working on the marionette play, its strength was being tested by our obvious lack of aptitude.

We both rejected her suggestion of coiling. It was too closely associated with the craft projects of our childhoods. I settled on making a pinch pot, and Bea was determined to make an animal, although she had not been able to narrow it down further. The Bojilovs set us up with tools and lots of clay at a table just outside the studio and then fled into the house. We were to call out when we had created the shapes we wanted them to fire for us.

After several minutes of working, Bea broke the silence: "I hear that Frank has a gallery in Toronto that's interested."

"He does. He's supposed to take the train up sometime next week."

"Will you go?"

"And leave this masterpiece unfinished?" I laughed, looking down at the lump of clay that was refusing to take any form at all. I probably would have gone along, if he had asked me. I was glad he hadn't. "You must be dreading the nursery school starting up in September."

"I love the children. And I've gotten a lot of writing done this summer. It will be time to change gears. I've asked Suzanne to come work with us. I thought she could do some dancing with them, put on little plays."

I knew she didn't need a second poet on the staff. If she had invited me, I would have said no, even though my nest egg was running out. But I was jealous anyway.

"Suzanne's having such a tough time right now. Well, you know how William can be. The moods. The drinking. You've spent so much time with them."

I thought if I pretended an interest in what Bea was doing with her clay, I could get her off the subjects of Frank and Suzanne and William. "That's a lot of balls," I said, instantly regretting the phrase.

"It's how Marijke makes her animals. She told me once. She thinks of them as a whole lot of separate volumes and then sticks them together. Isn't that a clever way to think of a creature, as a constellation of volumes jointed together? You score the clay and use some water to make the joins. See?"

"And what kind of an animal is it going to be?"

"I'm not sure."

"But you've made all the little balls."

"Sure. Four legs. I know that. And a head, and a body. And then all the other bits."

"So it could be a dog or it could be a rhinoceros."

"At this point, yes. I am waiting for the spirit in the clay to guide me." We both laughed. Fortunately. Then she asked, "What made you decide to make what you're making?"

"A bowl?" I was surprised to see that something like that was starting to emerge. A pinch pot, Marijke had called it.

"It's funny, isn't it, to think the clay is rock that has taken millions of years to decompose, and here we are trying to put it back together again. Pathetic." She paused to stub each of four squat legs onto the large ball that was destined to be her animal's torso. "When things fall apart, it's not that easy just to put them back together again."

"I think it will be a hippo," I said, refusing to play whatever game of oblique references and metaphors she had invented. "Those legs. Nothing could do anything other than lumber on those."

"Your bowl is turning into a vase."

I looked down to see that I had indeed pinched the clay up much higher. "An undetermined vessel," I said. "Like your undetermined animal. Maybe this clay has lost its spirit."

"Maybe we're better with words."

"I need a drink." I was by then regularly carrying a hip flask in my purse. Bea raised an eyebrow but accepted the offer. We both looked quickly back at the house as I wiped the clay fingerprints from the dull metal of the flask. Emil and Marijke were teetotal, another puzzling element in the mystery around their perpetual cheerfulness.

"Suzanne says William is drinking a lot. Too much."

I wondered what she thought that was supposed to have to do with me. "William seems to handle his liquor very well." I wasn't sure that was always true, but I hated the sudden moral superiority in her, wanted to take back the generous slug she had just helped herself to from my flask.

"I'm glad to hear it." She wasn't. She would much rather have had a good gossip about William's supposed blind drunken rages, or plotted with me how to find help for him. Or both.

My clay was becoming too friable. I had let my hands go dry. A piece broke off from my pot, just at the rim. I dropped the whole thing on the ground in frustration, and waited for Bea to make a comment about shattered vessels.

Instead, she picked up the fragments, held them at arm's length in her right hand, and intoned: "'Who canst thus express/ A flowery tale more sweetly than our rhyme: / What leaf-fring'd legend haunts about thy shape/ Of deities or mortals, or of both…?' Do you think Keats ever tried to *make* a Grecian urn?"

"Maybe I should try an animal after all." I could see Marijke peeking out the window, willing us to be gone. I took up a fresh lump of clay and began pulling off smaller pieces, rolling them between my palms to form a series of balls that I lined up on the table in front of me.

We worked then without speaking, the occasional thump of the clay saying all we needed to express.

"I think I have done what I can with this animal."

"Mine's done too," Bea sighed.

When we compared, the similarities were quite remarkable. We had both created something that was clearly half-human, half-animal. They weren't quite centaurs, but close. Creatures out of Ovid. And our deeper selves, I thought.

Bea called Marijke, who appeared so quickly she must have been waiting coiled just inside the door. "We're ready for firing," she reported.

"Have you hollowed them out, these creatures?" Marijke asked.

"Hollowed them?"

"They must be hollowed out, with an opening for the heat to get out. Otherwise they will never cook. And they might explode." She took a tool and deftly opened up a hole in the side of Bea's centaur figure. Handing her another tool, she instructed, "Now you must scoop out the insides very carefully. You can plaster over that hole and make another one to get at the rest. Keep going until it is all hollow. Emil will fire them tonight and you can come back to do the glazing another day." Before we could ask her any more, she vanished once again into the house.

Bea and I sat in silence as we used the tiny tools to drag the guts out of our creations so they were ready for the heat. I doubted that either of us cared enough to return up the river to reclaim them after the firing.

ELEVEN

FALL 1940

WILLIAM'S COMMISSION FOR THE POST OFFICE MURAL CAME IN late September 1940. That was two weeks after he and I had become lovers. We were still secretive at that point about what was happening between us. I liked to think that was out of our shared concern for the feelings of the other people involved, but it may only have been cowardice on my part and indifference on his.

My relationships with Frank, both as model and as lover, had been doomed the minute I became just another piece of the landscape on Taylors Island. I asked him to take more photographs of me after that. Being looked at through the lens was better than not being seen at all. Then he began setting the camera very close, framing portions of my body as topographical studies: hills and valleys and peaks and crevasses. My face did not appear. As I shrugged my dress on behind the screen one Friday when he had finished photographing me, he said we would pick up where we left off after the weekend. On the Monday, I simply failed to show up. There was no confrontation, no loud recriminations or remonstrations. He never admitted I had ceased to interest him as a subject, though that was clearly what had happened. I did not have to tell him how much it hurt because I found that it didn't anymore.

We continued to go out for meals and drinks, to appear regularly together at Henry's, even to sleep together, for several weeks. Neither of us mentioned that I had stopped modelling. It was as though we had only ever been lovers. The sex remained what I realized then it had always been: something two bodies did with one another out of habit and because they fit neatly together. When Frank seemed to start to lose interest in that, too, I let it go without comment. It had never been as important, as intense, for me as being looked at in the studio.

The end of William's involvement with Suzanne was considerably more dramatic. She treated me to detailed accounts every few days for nearly a month. I supposed she had been telling Bea the same stories. Modelling and painting had nothing to do with their problems. Suzanne had not lost William to a new subject the way I had lost Frank to landscape. William had pretty much put down his own brushes the day he went to work manufacturing them at Simms'. He had, however, begun to pick up the bottle more and more. One day, when Suzanne appeared at my apartment with a violet crescent under her right eye and a cut on her upper lip, I felt I had to ask her whether William had gotten drunk and done that to her. "If only," was her response. It seemed that alcohol never brought out the brute in William. She said she would almost prefer that to the sullen sot it did make of him. I told her I doubted that, and she took it back, though she then proceeded to describe the pits into which he regularly descended: the sobbing, the endless periods of silent sitting, the neglected state of his person and his apartment. I could almost understand why she longed for a burst of violence, of passion.

It was not more than a week after Suzanne had told me they were through that William and I became involved. I would say it began innocently if I didn't realize how ludicrous that would sound. Better to say it began without an agenda.

William's apartment door was ajar that evening, but there was no crack of light. I thought he must have forgotten to shut it, going or coming in a drunken haze. As I reached out for the knob to pull the door to, he barked out: "Leave it. Come in if you want."

So I did, and he poured me a tumbler of rye. We reminisced about that day I had found him sketching the longshoremen. And then we finished what we had not that afternoon. We had both changed, I thought. His seduction patter, far from improving, had simply ceased to exist. And I had learned from Frank that being looked *at* was not enough. William, I hoped, would give me something else.

The official commission from the postmaster was not a complete surprise when it arrived in the form of a registered letter, but we celebrated that day anyway. It was the first time I had drunk rye before noon.

"After the meeting yesterday, I wasn't certain they'd go ahead," William told me, for the third time, as I shrugged on my sweater and sat on the bed to put my stockings back on. He had reported the previous day's conversation with the postmaster word for word immediately after it took place. When I heard what he had said, I was convinced that there would be no commission, since William had brought up the issue of artistic freedom. He had, he said, told the story of Diego Rivera's Rockefeller Center commission a half a dozen years back. Rivera, it seems, liked to include famous faces in his murals. The Rockefellers objected to having Lenin featured in their picture and asked the artist to replace that likeness with another. When Rivera refused, they paid him, covered the work up with canvas, and, a couple of weeks later, broke it up and carted it off in wheelbarrows. William had insisted that he be allowed to depict whomever and whatever he wanted, and that he be given a guarantee that the work would be left intact for at least ten years. The latter had been a considerable compromise on his part; I knew he hoped it would be there forever.

"What will you tell everybody about Simms'?" I asked tentatively. He had been so adamant and vocal about giving up painting and sticking with the factory that it might be hard to backpedal with our friends.

"I never gave up on art. Just on art that is treated like a commodity, sold and bought and kept behind closed doors where nobody but its so-called owner can see it. Murals are different, you know."

I did know. He had rehearsed his lecture on public art on me daily, extolling the virtues of reaching the masses directly, the potential for displacing bourgeois notions of art making and art collecting. I had not raised the wallpaper argument with him. Perhaps it was not true anyway that people would simply become inured to the mural, eventually oblivious to its presence, twelve feet high on the wall of the post office lobby. The idea of truly reaching the masses had lifted him out of the pit. That and our developing affair, I liked to think.

The masses would have no trouble coping with the blow of his resignation from the brush factory. From what he told me and what I was able to observe, he had made no close friends on the shop floor. He ate his sandwich alone, smoked alone, walked alone daily to that spot just outside the fence of the Provincial Hospital. I never asked him about his isolation from his comrades, but I expected it was because, for all his wanting it, they nevertheless knew he was not truly one of them. And he knew it too.

The commission letter was accompanied by a bank draft. It was not a large amount, only ten percent of the promised fee, designed to help with the purchase of materials so the work could begin.

William had decided not to follow Rivera's lead exactly. Unlike his Mexican idol, he did not want to work in the old ways of pigment in plaster. Instead, he planned to work with encaustic paints, so his first expenditure was to buy beeswax and resin. For pigmentation he would use the tubes of oils he had not, after all, thrown out. From a building on Wellington Row that was being demolished we managed to salvage a segment of wall, three feet by three feet, to test with the encaustic paints. The two of us carefully sawed the lath and snipped the horsehair and then carried the whole thing like a critically wounded patient through the streets down to his studio.

I offered to help him with the conception, invited him to try out his ideas on me, but he insisted he must first be sure of the potentials of the paint. It sounded to me that he was saying 'I won't know what I want to say until I know how I can say it.' That approach would not have surprised me from Frank, whom I knew was obsessed with surfaces, but it seemed unlike William. I had always thought of him as trying to see more deeply. I let it go, though, for the time being, and settled for helping him to explore the medium. There might be something I could learn, too, from the careful sequence of melting, filtering, colouring, applying, and hardening that was encaustic painting.

Making the paint took up a whole day and tested the limitations of the studio. We had to borrow a hot plate to melt the beeswax and the resin crystals. Regulating the temperature to keep the wax from smoking was tricky, but the threat of being poisoned by the fumes turned out to be a good incentive to be careful. I developed a better sense than William for when to lift the pot from the element and when to put it back. For filtering, we first tried one of William's cambric handkerchiefs. He said they were gifts from his mother, and claimed never to use them. The weave was too fine, though. It did catch the bits of tree bark and bees' legs, but it also retained most of the liquid that we needed. In the end, we settled on one of my lisle stockings, which we slit up the side and cut up into six-inch segments so they could be draped in a funnel. The handkerchiefs turned out to be useful for leeching a little of the oil out of the pigment before it was added to the wax-and-resin mixture. Too much oil retarded the hardening of the wax. We made jokes about Icarus.

As the red began to solidify into a cake that could later be melted and applied to the square of plaster, William yanked off a piece, about the size of an egg, and began rolling it around between his palms.

"What are you making?" I asked.

"We'll see what comes. If anything. I like the feel of it. Knowing it could become anything. Or nothing. As long as I keep working it, it will take longer to harden, longer to become fixed in a single form. Longer to die, is what I suppose I am saying."

"Like not putting a name on something," I said, thinking that we must soon tell our friends how things were between us.

"Something like that." He leaned in to kiss me while his hands continued to worry at the wax.

I found the figure the next morning in my apartment, abandoned under the bed. I didn't know he had brought it home. It bore a remarkable likeness to a very sunburnt Venus of Willendorf.

In order to begin the actual painting on the plaster we needed to devise a hot palette. The borrowed hot plate had gone back and was anyway too small and too crude a device. We didn't want to be constantly lifting and lowering as we had had to for making the paints. We supported a large sheet of tin (also salvaged from Wellington Row) with bricks at each of its four corners, and then arranged a series of spirit lamps under it. Two of these William had on hand, and two I borrowed from my mother's trio of silver tea services. William was scathing about the fact that my mother owned three silver services, but let up when I reminded him we had struck a blow on the bourgeoisie by rendering two of them unusable.

"The tins are hot. Be careful." He held up his right hand like a traffic cop. I was annoyed that he was treating me like a neophyte. I had as much experience as he did with encaustics, had been there with him at each stage of his learning about them, so I was as familiar as he with both the process and its dangers.

"I've brought some clothespins. We can use them to move the tins around." I waited for him to make a quip about the domestic nature of my contribution, but instead he congratulated me on my ingenuity, taking the offered pins and wedging them on the tins as handles. The brushes were already racked on a bent coat hanger, their hog bristles (Simms' finest, from China) warming on the improvised palette.

He had transferred the outline of a streetscape from paper to our square of plaster using a spiked wheel. It was a technique I had read about but never seen, and I cringed with each bite of the wheel, imagining, irrationally I knew, tiny bubbles of blood appearing on its route. Then, as if ministering to the plaster's flesh wounds, he set to pouncing with a muslin bag of charcoal all along the perforations. The magical appearance of the drawing almost made the cruelty of the process acceptable, although I knew that the next step involved scalding hot wax.

We had set the palette up in the centre of the studio, while the square of plaster was propped upright against one wall. I suppose we had been so engrossed in preparing the medium that we hadn't thought ahead to how it would be applied. William had to stride halfway across the room each time to dip his brush, since moving the apparatus of bricks and lamps and sheet metal closer to the wall would have been too difficult—the whole thing would have had to cool down. Using the clothespins to remove a tin of paint from the heat even for a minute resulted in enough congealing to frustrate William. But the challenge imparted a vigour and urgency to his approach that I thought might shine through in the finished panel. He seemed to be enjoying the physicality of it, even improvising dance steps as he crossed the floor. I could not remember seeing him so happy.

He had borrowed a set of pottery tools from Emil Bojilov, and he reached for them every now and then to score or sculpt the waxy paint. Several times, he remarked how easily he could achieve texture without all the waiting that came with oil paints. It was only when he began to lay one coat of the encaustic over another that his enthusiasm flagged.

"How will I get them to bond properly?"

"What?"

"The layers of wax. How will I know they will stick to one another? I'd need another source of heat, something I could hold up to the wall panel. What time is it?"

He never wore a watch and refused to have a clock in his studio. I looked at my watch and realized he had been painting for three hours. When I told him, he dropped his brush on the palette.

"This will never work. Can you imagine trying to do a whole mural this way? Keeping the goddam paint hot, bonding the layers. It's not practical. I should have known. And this stuff would never hold up over time. It's all about surfaces. I'll have to try something else. Another way. Wet plaster, putting the paint right *into* the wall, like Rivera after all."

"Shall I snuff the lamps?"

"Leave them a bit."

"You're going to continue?"

"I have another idea."

I should have seen what was coming when he stripped off his shirt and reached for one of the tins of paint. He tested it first, just a couple of drips, on his palm. Then, swirling the tin, he lay down on the studio floor and began to pour the outline of a large red heart on his bare chest. I only saw him wince with the first few drops.

"Come lie with me. Bring the blue."

I suppose I did what he asked because it was so far from anything I had ever dreamed about. I wanted to try new things with him. The wax might burn me a little, but it would not be permanent.

TWELVE

WINTER 1941

IT WAS HARD TO IMAGINE WHAT THE LITTLE GIRLS IN TUTUS must have thought, must have felt, when they found Reuben. That is famously what suicides do not think about, or, if they do, what they decide not to care about: the people who find them. In this case, it was three little girls all under the age of ten. They had arrived a few minutes early for class. Movina said she would never forgive herself for not having been there already. I tried to inhabit the scene: the dispiriting church hall where the Little Theatre group rehearsed and Movina taught her classes, the grit underfoot on the scuffed hardwood floor, the faint tang of egg salad and armpits from a recent baptismal tea. I could even, without much effort, conjure up the frayed trouser cuffs and cracked leather shoes that would have been at the girls' eye level, the feet turning slowly, feeling out all points of the compass. The external features of the scene came quite easily. What I couldn't yet manage, though, no matter how hard I tried, was feeling how those little girls must have felt, or thinking what they must have thought.

Movina reported that when she found them they seemed perfectly composed, pointing dumbly, as if they had simply come upon yet another bizarre phenomenon of the adult world that they did not feel old enough to try to understand. All of the girls commented on how badly worn the man's shoes were. Movina was afraid to ask them whether they had looked up to see his face, or whether they smelled anything unpleasant. She bustled them into one of the Sunday school rooms as quickly as she could, locked the street doors, and went in search of the caretaker. He was in the church kitchen having his coffee and unhappy about being disturbed, receiving the report of a man hanging from the rafters as he might the news that a child had thrown up or that a toilet was clogged. No doubt he was used to Movina and, like most of us, discounted fifty percent of the drama from anything she had to say. When he had finished his coffee and rinsed out the cup, he did agree to accompany her to see what was what. And then he let himself into the rector's office and called the police.

Bea and I were having tea when we heard about it. We had been reading Auden's new collection, *Another Time*, and could not agree on the last two stanzas of the poem "September 1, 1939." Bea thought the phrase "We must love one another or die" was profound, while I had pronounced it banal, simplistic, cliché. She had retreated to the kitchen to make another pot, maybe also to escape for a moment from what she called my 'burgeoning cynicism.' There was a knock at Bea's door, just as there had been on the very date that lent its name to Auden's poem. And, just as on that day, it was Suzanne.

She and I had seen as little as possible of one another in the preceding weeks. Neither of us knew what to say about William. Seldom before at a loss for things to talk about, now that we had a lover in common (though not at the same time) things had changed between us. Bea thought Suzanne was jealous that I had William in the present, and that I was jealous of Suzanne's past with him. I thought it might be something else, something to do with each of us knowing William's every mole and wart, how he smelled in the morning, the things he did with his hands, his tongue, the names he liked to call out, the confined spaces he preferred.

"Libby. I didn't know you would be here."

"Bea and I—"

"Discuss poetry on Tuesdays. I know that. Of course. I should have thought."

"Who is that?" Bea called from the kitchen.

"Suzanne," we said in unison.

"I've just made a fresh pot. Of the stinky stuff. And we are definitely finished talking about poetry for now. Join us."

"We are not bad people, are we?" Suzanne asked as she took her cup. "We care about the right things. We are sympathetic when it's appropriate, understanding. There's nothing terrible about the way we live, the things we do?"

Bea reassured her that none of us was bad.

"Then why?"

We waited.

"Why would he do such a thing?" And she began to tell us about the little dancers finding Reuben.

I watched Bea closely, blaming Suzanne for not finding a gentler way to break the news, blaming her for breaking it at all. But Bea simply gasped in much the same way I did, and then her face became a mask. I thought about the grim fixed faces of the marionettes that Frank had painted. I thought about Reuben cutting their strings in the middle of the performance. And then I imagined the police cutting him down.

"Poor Movina." I meant it in that moment, both for what she had lost and for what she and her little dancers had found.

"Did he leave a note?" Bea's voice was tight.

"Not in the parish hall. But the police are sure he hanged himself. They don't suspect anyone else of—"

"Of course not," snapped Bea. "I didn't mean that. I only thought he would write something."

"He did. Henry has it. Well, the police have it now, but it was left for Henry. He copied it out before handing it over." Suzanne made a face as she tasted the lapsang souchong. "It's a kind of a poem, apparently. I suppose that makes sense, doesn't it? A last work of art?"

Bea's face was suddenly the colour of typewriter paper. I was afraid she was going to drop her teacup.

"I'm sorry, Bea. I didn't think you still had feelings for him," Suzanne said, several minutes too late. I wanted to remind her that Reuben was a human being, and that anyone would be saddened by the news. But I suspected that Bea had already figured out what poem it was that Reuben had left as his suicide note.

Suzanne had a Little Theatre rehearsal to attend. They had arranged for a different space for the time being, in the North End, so she raced off to catch a tram. Bea and I didn't have to discuss our next steps. We simply put on our things and headed to Henry's.

The studio was already crowded when we arrived. At first glimpse, it looked like any other early evening at Henry's. There was wine. There were knots of people in earnest discussion. Someone was picking out a tune on the piano. But I noticed that the marionette theatre was missing, and Henry, who was usually flitting from group to group, was nowhere to be seen. Bea and I agreed that it seemed callous to be drinking wine, but we both took a glass. There were so many people neither of us wanted to talk to that we stayed together, pretending to admire some new canvases Henry had hung since we were last there. They were by a student at the vocational school about whose talent Henry was very excited.

It was impossible not to overhear the various conversations, each debating an alternative theory for Reuben's final action. One group was interested in pursuing the he-was-inherently-troubled explanation. Two of them shared stories of occasions when Reuben's mood darkened the skies for all around him. From the moment he arrived in Saint John, they said, he was troubled, brooding. Even what they all agreed must be the exuberant lovemaking of Madame Sudorfsky had not seemed to lift him from his gloomy state. The third member of the group insisted there was a difference between being moody and being suicidal. While he agreed about Reuben's customary darkness, he could not accept that it necessarily would have led him to hang himself from the rafters of the church hall. A second group was rehearsing the disappointments Reuben must have felt in the Canadian government. Jews from Germany and the occupied countries were being denied entry as refugees because they were considered enemy aliens. Transit visas had recently been revoked, preventing them from even passing through. One senior government official was known to have made the bizarre statement that Canada would accept 'only Roman Catholic Jewish children seeking asylum.' The group was split, though, on whether disgust with government policy warranted suicide. Surely some kind of action to change the policy, half of them argued, was preferable to what amounted to a very selfish protest by Reuben, one that could obviously have no impact whatsoever in Ottawa.

A third group traced the act back to some criticism Reuben had received just before the début of his marionette play. Someone, they couldn't say who, had confronted him, asking why he didn't write about things that mattered closer to home, instead of trying to address events happening halfway around the world. This, they felt sure, had driven him to cut the strings on opening night, and to despair from there on.

Bea and I fell into speculative mode ourselves.

"There is a camp at Ripples. Did you know?" she asked.

"A camp?"

"Near Minto. An internment camp. It was built as something else, I think, in the mid-thirties, but now it's an internment camp."

I did know this, of course. My father had told me about it. B70 was its official name. But I waited for Bea to continue. When she didn't, I asked: "What has that to do—?"

"There are over seven hundred Jews there right now. Men and boys."

I knew this, too. They were refugees in England. Churchill was afraid there might be spies among them, so they had been sent to the deep woods of New Brunswick as if they were prisoners of war. "You don't think Reuben was afraid that he'd be rounded up, here?"

"It stands to reason, doesn't it? Well, it's the opposite of reason, actually, but you can see it happening. That the next step would be to intern people like Reuben, earlier refugees, in case they are some kind of fifth column—you know, like that Spanish Civil War general talked about. And the Hemingway play."

"Nobody could see Reuben as a German spy. Or as a fan of Hitler. He was a writer. Don't you think what he did to himself might have come out of some disappointment with his writing?"

If Bea had a response I missed hearing it because at that moment Henry swept into the room. We were suddenly in the read-us-the-will scene of a play or movie. The conversations stopped. All but one. Movina was telling a group of three young men how much she had loved Reuben, how much support she had given him, how she would have done anything, given up anything, for him. It was hard to tell whether she was assuaging guilt or whether she had already begun to appropriate Reuben's tragic death as she had so much of his life. *Pay attention to me*, she was saying, *the woman for whom a man died for love*.

Henry poured himself a glass of wine. It was the first time I had ever seen his hand shake. Bea kindly took the bottle and set it carefully down.

"Friends," Henry began as he fished for his reading glasses and then a folded sheet of paper from the inside breast pocket of his blazer. "We have lost a friend. We have lost a fellow artist, a poet, a playwright, someone who brought us news of the larger world and challenged us to respond to the dreadfulness of that news. I, for one, count myself blessed to have known Reuben Weiss. And I am honoured and moved that he chose me as the person to whom he sent his final work of art, or perhaps I should say, his penultimate work of art."

There was a small stirring in the crowd as two or three people muttered that they didn't think much of Henry's suggesting that suicide was a work of art.

"I believe that although he sent this to me, he would have wanted all of his friends, his fellow artists, to hear it."

Movina let out a theatrical sob and was immediately comforted by one of the young men to whom she had been declaring her undying love for the deceased. Bea scowled.

"The epigraph is from the Book of Job, chapter one, verse sixteen: 'The fire of God is fallen from heaven, and hath burned up the sheep, and the servants, and consumed them; and I only am escaped alone to tell thee.' The poem is in five parts. He has chosen to call them cantos."

When Henry loaned me the poem a week later so I could transcribe it, the lower left corner of each sheet of paper was still crumpled from his grip as he'd held it and read it to us that night.

Canto 1.

No port even in a storm
The St. Louis steams her zigzag line
From No to No and back again,
Her human cargo turned
Away at every turn by those who cannot see
My enemy's enemy is my friend.
A plant neglected on your mantelpiece
No sun no water
It pales and withers past hope, past care, past transplantation:
The Wandering Jew.

Canto 2.

I have seen what I should not.
No, not the goddess naked at her bath,
Nor the puppeteer behind the screen.
Instead:
Rocks heaved through windows
Hate scrawled across brick walls
Armbands worn before mourning
Smudged tears on orphaned faces.

Canto 3.

They told me: Pluck the string just so
And I would hear spheres' music
See the pure geometry of the dance
Speak with the tongues of angels.
They failed to note
That strings become entangled
Sometimes they snap
If the shears don't
Get them first.

Canto 4.

I have been a hunter
Of metaphor and image

Hot on the steaming trail of le mot juste
La vraie semblance
Lured from the troubles of the world
To a world whose chief trouble
Is how to re-present The World.
Words are big game, they give good chase
But they cannot warm or feed or clothe you
And may do worse.
Here I stand at the edge of the wood,
Set upon by my own hounds.

Canto 5.
The horror.

Nobody moved for a full minute after the reading finished. Then Henry raised his glass: "To Reuben."

The cheap wine burned my throat, but I drank every drop.

When I told William about it all later that evening, he steered me quickly past the story of the little girls discovering the hanging man, and he wasn't remotely interested in talking about what might have driven poor Reuben to kill himself. It was the poem he wanted to know about.

"Was it any good?"

If he had punched me I didn't think he could have surprised me more. "Good?"

"The poem. As a last work. Worth dying for? Will it change the world?"

He was drunk, I thought, must be drunk. Nobody could ask such an insensitive question sober.

"It makes you think, though, doesn't it? What would you want people to remember you by? What would I?"

I told him I was too tired, too sad, for this kind of discussion, and I went upstairs to my own apartment. When I couldn't sleep, I began scribbling notes about the little girls. I needed to understand from the inside. How might they have felt? What might they have thought?

⌒

Over the fall and early winter, William experimented eagerly with lime putty, water, and ground pigment until he was satisfied that the traditional fresco techniques were definitely the right approach for his mural. He tested his mixtures on a series of sacrificial segments of wall transported from the building on Wellington Row. I lost interest after a couple of weeks. Occasionally, he would paint a figure, but mostly it was abstract daubing, and he destroyed each panel as he went. There didn't seem to be any real progress.

He was able to persuade the post office to let him build a false wall as a substrate for the work, using galvanized metal lath. This, he told them, would prevent any condensation or leakage from the building's wall from ruining their investment. He didn't mention that it would also mean that the mural could be moved if necessary. He hired a plasterer to work with him. After the first day, William was already imitating the man's dress and mannerisms, pinching the way he delivered his *a*'s and dropping his *g*'s as if born to it. They started going for a beer after they finished each day. William would come back to his apartment tired and dirty, fingernails chipped, the wrinkles in his wrists caked in plaster. I teased him that he had finally achieved his dream of becoming one of the workers, although in my own work I was beginning to understand that imitating surfaces was not really enough. I was still struggling to find a way inside the hearts and minds of the little girls in tutus.

In the evenings, after I bullied him into bathing, we would talk about the message for the mural for a while, and then he would sit at the kitchen table, drafting. It would be in two panels, he was thinking: a kind of before-and-after presentation. The theme was the role of communications in improving society, with an emphasis on the worker: the postmen, the linesmen for the telephone company, the telephone and telegraph operators. The overall concept had been accepted by the postmaster, but the man had reserved final approval until he had had a chance to review William's cartoons.

"You will be careful with how you depict the bosses, won't you, William? They are paying your commission after all."

We were drinking rye from his usual filthy glasses. I knew it was risky to raise the subject at any time. When we were drinking was the worst time. We both tended to become a little more fixed in our opinions.

"I will only tell the truth. I told them that from the beginning. They still awarded me the commission."

"I know. I just think you will need to tread carefully." As if to show me how carefully he planned to tread, he stomped to the sink and dumped out the rest of his rye. I had never seen him waste booze like that before. It was certainly a signal that I should change the subject, and yet I blundered on. "Demonstrate the plight of the masses and the importance of the workers in addressing it, of course, but don't point the finger at the bosses. That's all I'm saying."

He spit in the sink, another habit he had picked up from his plasterer crony, I supposed.

"The main thing is to point the way forward, isn't it? Not to lay blame."

"I'm going out." He had already torn his jacket off its peg and was shrugging it on.

I knew this meant I should return to my own apartment, but I wanted to finish my rye, and there were dirty dishes in the sink I thought I should tackle, so I sat tight as though it was perfectly normal for him to leave me alone in his place. He hesitated only for a second and then was gone. I wondered whether he remembered that I didn't have a key. Half the time he didn't lock up anyway.

I poured another drink after I had washed the dishes, telling myself I would go upstairs after I finished it. It was the longest I had ever been alone in his apartment, I realized. For all the months and months of visits to his studio with Suzanne, for all the nights he and I had spent together since becoming lovers, I barely knew him. Frank had always maintained a carefully measured distance. It had not been possible to get any closer to him than the superficial intimacies we enjoyed in the bedroom and the studio. There were only certain parts of his life he was prepared to show me. I had come to accept that, even to wonder whether the parts I thought he was hiding actually existed, or whether his personhood was like his portraits: a few carefully chosen surface details that cleverly gave the illusion of depth. William, with those eyes that looked right through a person, I had hoped would be different.

The clutter of his apartment could be a gift, I thought, as I looked around. Evidence of who William really was might lurk anywhere, in any pile of books, any mound of dirty laundry, even in the way he did not organize his bathroom cabinet. But as I began to move through the rooms I had a particular object in mind. Months ago, when he had showed me the notes and sketches he had been making of the longshoremen, he had not handed over his whole notebook, just those few torn pages. It was that notebook, the one with the red cover, that I was determined to find. I had not seen him use it since that day on Long Wharf.

The bookcase yielded nothing, and neither did the mountains of books spilling from it over the floor. The kitchen drawers had only cooking things, and the dresser in his bedroom was altogether empty, the floor and chairs being the preferred places for storing clothes. The table beside the bed gave up a Bible. It was obviously well read, though whether by William or some previous owner, I could not tell. There was a palm cross (whose?) serving as a bookmark in Revelations. I didn't stop to read the particular verses on the page.

I found the notebook finally where I had heard men often hide pornographic pictures. The red cover was etched with the pattern of the bedsprings. My knuckle was bleeding, cut in the process of slipping the book out from under the mattress, so I went to the kitchen to wash my hand and pour myself another inch of rye. Then I returned to the bedroom. I felt I needed to devour the notebook there, exactly where William must look at it when he pulled it out. The sheets smelled of us, which gave me a moment's pause as I registered the betrayal I was about to commit. Then I dismissed that as ridiculous. I wanted to know what was in the book because I wanted to know him, wanted to get nearer to him. I lay on the bed as I imagined he might. I couldn't help thinking of the fortress of journals in the free public library, the sketchbook that circulated secretly there.

The opening pages offered half a dozen of the most delicate works I had ever seen by William. I concluded right away that they were old. They were graphite and had faded with the years. Each was a study of a young girl, who looked about thirteen or fourteen, although to call them studies would have been misleading. For all their delicacy and lightness on detail, they were obviously fully realized. What I was seeing was the final state of the work. The poses were all different, a kind of catalogue of the principal tropes I had learned while watching William and then Frank work: standing, recumbent, semi-recumbent, crouching, sitting. But the six pages were definitely conceived as a group.

That they involved a single model was actually the least of the elements of coherence—the manner of the drawing was what really pulled them together, the manner and the artist's obvious adoration of the subject. The model appeared completely at ease. In two of the pictures she seemed to be flirting, which set up a powerful tension with the impression of innocence evoked by the tiny breast buds and the mere wisp of hair at the base of the belly. I spent several minutes leafing back and forth through the sketches, jealous and aroused by turns. As I looked, I could hear the scratch of William's pencil disturbing the electric silence in the studio, or wherever the drawings were made. Words would have been unnecessary between them. Perhaps I was most jealous of that.

On the following dozen pages, the images were much darker. Some charcoal had been introduced, but the subjects themselves were more responsible than the medium for the shift in tone. Again, the depictions were all of a very young woman. Her face was turned away in all but one, but it was the same young woman in all of them, the same from the nude sketches. In these, she was clothed, but stiffly, awkwardly, a paper doll with cut-out frocks laid on and the tabs folded over. While the nudes had no context, these drawings all depicted the model in small rooms, tightly framed. The walls were all bisected by a hard horizontal line, clearly a paint line, not a chair rail. The setting was not a house. In one sketch, there were bars at a window. I recognized the shape of the window—I had seen it from the other side at the Provincial Hospital. Unable to bear looking back and forth through these as I had with the nudes, I focused on the one where the face was shown. She was not looking directly at the artist as in the earlier drawings. Her gaze was averted, downcast. I found it easy there to see the echo of William's nose, the shape of his eyes and mouth.

I knew I should stop. Put the notebook back under the mattress, leave the apartment, forget what I had seen and what I thought it meant. Knowing what you should do is not much help, though, in cases like this. After a long last look at the poor incarcerated woman, I turned the page to find the next several sheets covered with William's perfect handwriting. While I expected to find notes on visual details—elements of poses, colour, and light—these were quite different. They were literary notes. I can't think what else to call them: notes on readings William had done.

He had read Ford's *'Tis Pity She's a Whore*. I supposed at first he might have picked the play up for its title. But then I saw he had transcribed at length the speeches Giovanni makes to the friar and to his sister. There was no mistaking what interested him then.

There were notes on Ovid's *Metamorphoses*, beginning with the story of Myrrha's love for her father, but with most attention paid to the fraternal twins Byblis and Caunus. As with the Ford play, he had copied verbatim Byblis's reasoning with herself about her incestuous passion: *So long as I never attempt to commit such a sin in the daytime, it doesn't matter how often it happens at night in my dreams.* He had underlined her conclusion: *Rules are for prudish old men,* followed by portions of the fatal letter she writes to her beloved brother. Then William had written simply, *One-sided, unrequited. Lucky Caunus, or not?*

In his notes on Lot and his daughters, there were more questions. *Were the daughters who seduced Lot in the cave the same virginal ones he had offered to the threatening men at his door in Sodom? If so, was it only to preserve their father's seed that they acted as they did? Or was it more complicated? When was it ever simple?* And then: *Why are the daughters not given names?*

Finally, there was a page of notes devoted to the endlessly interesting question (his words) of the children of Adam and Eve.

How was the world populated if those siblings did not fuck one another?

Behind the cold logic of the notes, the careful rationalization of feelings the world would condemn if they were discovered, I thought I could read William's pain. But as I lay there on his bed, I felt even more strongly her longings. His sister's feelings and mine became one. I realized I did not know her name. Like Lot's daughters.

I turned to the last page before the gap left by the sheets he had torn out to show to me. It was a sketch of the Reversing Falls. In the rapids, or, rather, becoming the rapids, caught half-way between being human and being water, like one of Ovid's heroines, was the young woman of the first pages of the notebook, gloriously nude once again.

And just like that, I knew what I had to write about.

By the next evening, William appeared to have forgotten that he had stormed out on me. I told him I wanted to make dinner for him in my apartment. I didn't feel ready to be in his place again just yet, haunted as it now was for me by the tenderness of the notebook, its aching sadness. Nothing had changed for him, of course, and nothing would, unless he discovered that I had found his notebook and learned his secret.

"I bet even your damn cat doesn't eat better than this," he said as he finished his last bite of veal. I refused to rise to the bait. "We had sardines for lunch, John and I." John was the plasterer. "He calls them *sourdeens*. Eats a whole loaf of bread with them."

"That seems extravagant." I suppose I was rising to the bait after all.

"It's hard work, hungry work he does. You don't think he deserves a whole loaf of bread?"

"I don't know how he affords it. That's all." I began to remove our plates but he stopped me.

"I've been thinking about the mural. I have been busy building the wall, of course, but I've been thinking about the composition, the message to go on it."

I braced myself—*pleaded* with myself not to get into another squabble about the bosses.

"I want to do something bigger."

"More square footage?"

"Bigger in conception. Larger. Something that takes the theme in another direction."

"The theme."

"Communication. It's still communication, don't worry. But I want to say something more. To communicate more about myself, I suppose."

"And what would that be?" I knew I was supposed to ask this, although my head was still filled with the images he had made of his sister.

"Do you know the beginning of the Gospel of John?"

For a minute I thought he meant John the plasterer, but then I recovered. "In the beginning was the Word? That bit? You're going to put God in the mural?"

"Not necessarily God himself, not God the father, anyway, but maybe Jesus."

"Jesus. In a mural at the post office."

"And definitely some angels."

"Angels."

"Couriers of the divine. They speak every language in the world, did you know?"

"I didn't. William—"

"The trouble is, they aren't often seen these days. Sometimes they pull back the veil and reveal themselves directly. I can paint that, of course, but so often they communicate through signs. That's harder. That's the challenge, really, painting the signs, the things that aren't the thing but reveal the thing, the things that *point to* the angels' presence. You know?"

I wondered about trying to turn this into an academic discussion about representation. We could revisit the differences among metaphor, metonymy, and literal depiction. I had been thinking more and more about such things the longer I spent with painters. But he hurried on—possessed, I would almost have said.

"Goosebumps, for instance. They tell you that an angel is near, flapping his wings and making you chilly. Or finding a penny in the street. Left there for you by an angel. Or being itchy or sneezing without reason. That's from the feathers."

I began to think he was putting me on, but as I couldn't be sure I tried steering the conversation in another direction, sacrificing my former position on the bosses in the hope of returning to normality. "But the bosses will still be in there, in the flesh, blamed for their role in creating the current situation."

"I think so, yes. Only not so obviously. Now I see their sins as part of a larger design."

I didn't know whether to laugh or cry, so I poured us each an inch of rye from a bottle I had bought that morning.

"None for me," he said, too late. "I have work to do. Thanks for the supper."

And he was gone, down the stairs, back to his own apartment. He had given no sign that I should follow, so I stayed behind, washed the dishes, and drank both glasses of rye. Perhaps it was just as well. I wasn't feeling much like sex and I couldn't read him the latest entries in my notebook.

THIRTEEN

SPRING AND SUMMER 1941

NEWS OF MRS. WOOLF'S DEATH DID NOT REACH US UNTIL LATE in April. By then, she had been dead nearly a month.

William and I were in his studio when I read about it in the newspaper. He was working out a detail for a corner of the post office mural, which still existed only on paper and in his head. The false wall that he and his plasterer friend had finished constructing several weeks before remained utterly blank. Virginal, he liked to say. I had given up begging him to at least make a start.

I read the column through twice before laying the paper aside. "She is dead," I announced, thinking that saying the words might help me feel their weight.

"Who?"

"Virginia Woolf."

"Was she old?"

"Sixty, I suppose. She took her own life. Disappeared on the twenty-eighth of March. She left two notes. One for her husband and one for her sister. They found her body on the eighteenth of April. Imagine being that long in the water."

"The water?"

"She drowned herself, it says. Stones in her pockets."

"In the Thames?"

"In the Ouse."

"That takes real determination, drowning yourself."

"Doesn't suicide always?" I thought about poor Reuben, stringing himself up in the church hall.

"Oh."

"What?"

"An act of courage, you think? The received view is that suicide is pure cowardice."

"I know." I wanted to ask him when he had started caring about received views. "I met her once, did I tell you?"

"I don't remember."

"Then I didn't tell you. A school friend of mother's was related to them somehow. The Stephens. Cousin, I think. She arranged the introduction. Poor Mrs. Woolf. I suppose she was constantly being asked to talk to daughters of friends of third cousins, to encourage them to continue with their pathetic writing."

"She looked at your writing?"

"Of course not. I'm only saying that she must have had to put up with visits from hundreds of would-be writers."

"She could have said no."

"You haven't met mother's friend. It was only tea. I was too terrified to say a word, too much in awe. So the two of them prattled on about family. Mrs. Woolf was a great one for family."

"I wouldn't have thought she'd give a damn about family. Wasn't she what they used to call a bluestocking? And a bit of a believer in free love? Weren't they all, that Bloomsbury crowd?"

"Her own birth family. Her siblings. That family. They were everything to her." I stopped myself, afraid I might have touched a nerve. He appeared unbothered, though, so I blundered ahead.

"She loved her sister Vanessa. The painter, you know. Mother's friend told me the affection was unusually intense. People used to speculate."

"Speculate?"

"On just *how* intense. On how she might have acted on those feelings. Mother's friend used the word *sapphic*, which is wonderfully quaint, don't you think?"

"Nosy old prude."

"No. She was fascinated. Titillated."

"Exactly. Were any of the others mad?"

"Mad? Who?"

"The Stephens. Mrs. Woolf was obviously mad."

"Because she killed herself?"

"She was hospitalized a number of times. A rest cure, they called it."

"How do you know that?"

"I was interested, at one point, in that sort of thing. What runs in families and so forth."

"I'm not sure suicide runs in families. I would have thought it was more, well, more situational. A person finds herself in a place she must get out of."

"My mother committed suicide." He said it as if he were announcing we had run out of milk.

"I'm so sorry, William. I had no idea."

"Selfish bitch."

"Don't say that. She was your mother."

"Who has more right, then?"

"It must have been terrible for you, for the family." I thought about his sister, her nose pressed to the window of the Provincial Hospital.

"We should have a drink. Pour your Mrs. Woolf into the afterlife."

"It's not as though she was *my* Mrs. Woolf. I sat near her, a quivering wreck, and spilled some tea once, that's all." Still, I fetched the bottle and two jars.

We talked about the war and the weather, like two strangers who had met in a bar. Then we continued to sip in a companionable silence.

I didn't know what William was thinking about. I supposed his dead mother, his sister. My thoughts were all of Mrs. Woolf. I had lied to William. I *had* thought of her as mine since our brief encounter. He was the only person I had ever told how frightened I was, how silent, at tea that day. When I told the story to others it was of a quite different me. I would tell them how I had traded witticisms over sherry, about the books we found we liked in common, the plays and paintings. Harmless little fabrications the great writer would never be around to contradict. A bit pathetic, I suppose.

William broke the silence. "Do you think she felt in control, Mrs. Woolf, when she waded into the river?" So that was what he was thinking about.

"I suppose she did, yes. Perhaps for the first time in a while." I didn't know then exactly what I meant by that pronouncement, that sudden insight into the mind of the great Virginia Woolf, but I believed in it. William wasn't really listening anyway.

"Or was she simply being controlled?"

"By what?"

"Fate, destiny. Her family situation." He poured us each another drink.

"She was very happy with Leonard Woolf. That is what everyone said."

"The situation with the others. The Stephens."

"She and her sister got on very well, I believe." I tried to remember things I'd read, what I had heard in London. "In a guarded sort of way. I think there had been some strains long ago. They lost a brother to typhoid. There were some jealousies. Ordinary family things."

"The madness, then. Controlled by the madness?"

"I suppose that goes back to how one views suicide."

"Pulled about like a hinged wooden figure in one of those dreary plays Henry puts on."

Back in my apartment, when we put out the lights and went to bed, I could not interest him in sex. It might have been the rye, or all the talk of death.

What I had not told William, or anyone, not even mother's friend from school, were the eight words Mrs. Woolf had whispered to me just as we were leaving. We were in her garden by then. She was shaking my hand. Mother's friend had gone ahead. Mrs. Woolf fixed me with her sybil's stare and hissed: *To write about something is to kill it.* Then she smiled quite broadly and wished us a pleasant journey.

❧

Henry's class excursion to Saints Rest Beach was a highlight his students looked forward to all spring. They made a day of it, packing sandwiches to eat, blankets to lie on, and balls to throw. Nobody swam; few would brave the water even in August, and it was only June. Everyone painted, but not very much. It was understood that the air itself was the primary objective of the annual *plein air* session. Firmly under Henry's influence, almost every painting student at the vocational school was very interested in people and not much in scenery. Presented with the sweep of ocean and islands visible from Saints Rest, most would have had no idea where to begin.

When he invited me along to watch his students not paint, I hesitated. I was afraid the beach, with Taylors Island looming at its far end, might bring crashing back the blow to my ego delivered by Frank's *Le Déjeuner sur l'herbe* painting. I did need to talk to Henry, though, and I wanted it to be away from the rest of our friends, so the opportunity seemed too good to forego. I was hoping he might be able to help me with an ethical dilemma.

Those students who couldn't beg or buy a drive walked the full hour from Douglas Avenue to the end of Sand Cove Road. Henry offered me a lift. He said I would be doing him a favour. The car was packed with easels and brushes, paints and picnic paraphernalia, so that there would have been just room for one student; he would have had to choose which one if he hadn't promised the spot to me.

"Do you mind if we don't talk while I drive?" he asked as I climbed into the passenger seat at the agreed rendezvous point at the foot of Princess Street. "I'm actually frightfully uncoordinated behind the wheel and it takes every bit of attention not to end up in the ditch."

As we drove over the Reversing Falls and past the Provincial Hospital, I wondered whether, if he hadn't forbidden speech, I might have blurted a question or two about William's sister. I liked to believe I had the necessary self-control to keep William's secret, but found I was glad to have the ban on talking to deliver me from temptation.

A handful of students were already encamped on the beach when we arrived. They were mostly women, which, I suppose, should not have surprised me. Two quickly tore themselves away from the group when they saw Henry's car approaching. By the time he had cut the motor, they were opening his door and begging to help unload the easels. Henry's greeting of them was distant, professional. I wondered whether he was always like that or whether he was performing for my benefit. He apparently had no compunctions about loading down the willing horses.

Both girls staggered through the grasses to the beach under comically heavy loads.

"It will help dampen their high spirits, or whatever has gotten into them."

"Serious crushes on teacher, I would say." And I took his left arm. In his right was a large wicker hamper. I knew he couldn't have wine in it that day.

"I am a positive Svengali," he laughed. "A more kindly Svengali. That's what they are looking for: someone to tell them what to do, what to paint. Poor lasses, they haven't an ounce of creativity between them."

"That seems very harsh. Aren't you supposed to encourage them?"

"I do. I am only telling *you*." He set down the hamper about fifty yards from the students. "Everything they do is derivative."

I seized my opportunity. "Creativity is tricky, elusive, though. Originality, I suppose I mean. Everything we make is derivative of something, isn't it? The way we write it or paint it, not to mention what we paint or write about."

"We're not talking about my adoring students, are we?"

"Where do you draw the line? I wonder that sometimes, don't you? Between stealing and borrowing? And between borrowing and remaking?"

"Have you been showing your society sketches around?" He smiled, spreading a blanket for us to sit on. "Have you managed to get Movina's back up?"

"I have shared a few of them with Suzanne and William, as I think you know. I even read one to Movina a few weeks ago. None of them seems to mind being written about. Movina was a little bit flattered, I think. She recognized herself immediately. I wrote up something based on a few observations I made at Bea's nursery school, too. A kind of a playful allegory. She seemed to like it."

"So what's bothering you?"

"I guess it's a new wrinkle on the old question. What belongs to the model and what belongs to the artist? You see? Even my problems are derivative, second-hand."

"What would Frank say? Or William?"

"Frank claims that nothing belongs to anybody—except the buyer, once it's sold. He claims he doesn't care where his pictures end up, and that if *he* doesn't care then the mere *model* certainly shouldn't."

"He didn't say 'mere model.'"

"Not exactly, but I used to see him thinking it while he painted."

"And yet nobody beats Frank for technique. He takes more care making an image than anybody I've ever known. That shows a kind of responsibility to his subject, doesn't it? A form of homage. Respect, at least? And William?"

"He has some theory that the artist takes what the model gives, but somehow the model loses nothing in the transaction."

"I like that." Henry offered me an apple.

"It didn't work for him with the longshoremen. He said he couldn't allow himself to profit from their experience, their situation. Frank raised the same concern about Reuben's play—about making art from the suffering of others, come to think of it."

"The longshoremen didn't know William was painting them, did they? And Reuben didn't ask the victims of Hitler if he could write about them. Is that perhaps what's making the difference in those cases?"

"You're suggesting that it's only exploitation if you write about somebody's situation when they don't know you're doing it?" The apple was so tart my mouth dried the second I bit into it.

"Subjects have to come from somewhere, though. Stories."

"Exactly," I managed from between puckered lips. "And what if there are only so many stories out there? Just so many basic stories, and no more."

"There are people who say that, aren't there?"

"Then how is it stealing from an individual if you happen to reproduce his story? His story is already repeated all over the place, all over time."

"If you 'happen' to reproduce his story, or if you intentionally set out to?"

"Should you be supervising those students?"

The two girls had set up a line of easels facing out to sea and were trying to corral their classmates, who seemed more interested in an improvised game of volleyball. Henry rose from the blanket and clapped his hands three times as he strolled towards them. Everyone froze. Perhaps he *was* their Svengali. I propped myself on one elbow on the blanket to watch as he organized them and set them to work. It was impossible to make out his words at that distance, but I could imagine from the sweep of his arm and the way he turned his palm upwards that he was pointing out the line of a cliff on one of the islands and the play of light on the water. His students nodded slowly and leaned into their canvases.

I began to examine the small stones that dotted the sand at the edges of the blanket, relieved to have a few minutes to collect myself. Getting Henry's advice without telling him exactly what I was writing was going to be a challenge. I had expected that. But was it advice that I wanted, or simply his blessing? It was William's blessing I really needed.

"They're a pocket history of this beach over thousands of years, those stones." Henry was back sooner than I expected. Perhaps he felt that my need for guidance was greater than his students' need.

"I like the colours." I rolled four small stones in my closed hand and then threw them like dice.

"Sandstone, quartz, shale," he read the rocks. "And one with a granitic intrusion. That's what I mean. A history of the beach. And an example to us all. Slowly laid down layers at the surface, mixed with evidence of fire below. You're working on something new, aren't you?"

"That's the problem," I said, letting a handful of sand sift through my fingers. "I'm not sure I can."

"Because you don't know how, or because you don't think you should? What's the project?"

"The idea comes from someone I know, the inspiration." I didn't think that was giving too much away.

"How is that different from what you've done before?"

"They don't know I know this thing that I want to write about."

"Tell them."

"It's not that simple."

"Or don't tell them, and write something else."

"This is the only thing I want to write. It's a big story, a timeless one, I think. Finally, after a half a dozen false starts, I'm inspired by something that I feel I could make really great, but I am afraid it might come at a cost I am not sure I'm ready to pay."

"It's not a bloody newspaper article." Henry brushed some sand from the tops of his brogues.

"Meaning?"

"It will be fiction, what you write, won't it?"

"Of course."

"Then you know the usual formula. 'Any resemblance to any person, living or dead,' and so forth. Speaking of which, let's go see what kinds of resemblances my students are managing." He took my hand to help me up, waited while I brushed down my skirt, then offered me an arm.

The first half a dozen canvases we reviewed were earnest attempts to capture the scene from where the students stood, looking out across the water. Proportions, perspective, even colours, were identical, as if each was a print of the others. Henry made some gentle suggestions, but it was easy to tell that his heart was not in it any more than theirs were.

I was expecting more of the same when we approached the first of the easel-bearing girls, who had set herself off a little from the main group. Her ears burned red when Henry introduced her as Emily, one of his keenest students. I released Henry's arm, in deference to her crush, hoping she would look up so I could see her face properly. Then I realized that, far from hanging her head, she was actively staring at the beach, eyes riveted on her subject.

"You gave up on the great blue sea?" Henry asked.

"This fellow interested me more." She gestured to a crab shell at her feet. I followed her gaze as she lifted her eyes to her canvas where she had already roughed in a very convincing portrait of the creature.

"Emily was worried at first that it was dead." The second member of Henry's would-be *seraglio* had abandoned her own easel. "I dared her to peek inside. She said she wouldn't paint a dead thing. She looked and there was nobody home. It's just a cast-off."

"It's how they grow. I knew that," Emily quickly put in. "It's not linear, like us. They have to cast off their outsides when they are getting too big for them, and start all over again."

The other girl, whom Henry introduced as Gillian and whose ears turned exactly the shade Emily's had, was holding a second crab in her palm. "A day or two before they molt, they absorb a lot of water. That helps them expand enough to crack the old shell right along here." She ran a coral-coloured fingernail along a line on the underside of the shell. "Then they just start pulling themselves out, one leg at a time."

"Congratulations, girls." When Henry said it, they glowed so hot I thought they would both melt. "You've solved a problem Miss MacKinnon has been grappling with."

"Are you a painter, too?" Emily asked.

"A writer."

"Oh." She straightened her shoulders a little, no doubt lowering her estimate of how much of a threat I posed.

"Your crab shell is the perfect subject," Henry continued. "Just what Miss MacKinnon has been looking for. You can make its portrait while nobody's home. And if it ever complains that you didn't ask permission, you can say there was nobody around to ask. Because the insides have moved on, and this is just one of hundreds of crab shells along the beach. It could be anyone's. Its story is by no means unique."

Henry proceeded to offer Emily some suggestions for capturing the fine tracery of hairs at the tips of the crab's permanently bent legs. I was already planning the next steps in how I would write what I had decided both was and was not William's story.

❦

The Port Royal Pulp and Paper Company mill was only a few hundred yards from the Simms' brush factory. When William started work at the mill, he joked about its being a return to the scene of what he called his industrial beginnings. He also revived his stock lines about the artist finally controlling the means of production, neatly substituting paper this time for the brushes he had been making the last. There was not much humour in his voice when he said it, though; none of the satiric bite of the days he had worked at Simms'.

The decision to work on the line producing kraft paper must have been influenced by his recent experience with reams of the stuff. He had made enough brown-paper cartoons for the mural to cover the walls of every building on Prince William Street, inside and out. It wasn't that there was anything technically wrong with any of the sketches. Any of the first half-dozen he made could easily have satisfied the postmaster. But his conception of the work kept changing day by day, and so the imagery he wanted evolved. Evolved was perhaps not the right word, not in the Darwinian sense anyway, since the imagery was, in fact, increasingly and alarmingly religious. His fascination with angels seemed to grow by the day. At the same time, managing to represent them adequately, much like counting them on the heads of pins, I suppose, became a challenge he said he believed might be quite beyond him.

The postmaster was more than patient, although I never dared tell William I thought so. In the end, the blank substrate inside his building's grand entrance must have become an embarrassment to him. The official version was that the funds were no longer available. William received a two-page letter explaining the financial problems and apologizing profusely. William insisted, though, that it was censorship. Plain and simple.

"How could they censor what they haven't seen?" I asked him.

"It's what they do. Governments. They don't need to see."

"If anything, your original social critique has become less clear, less biting. How could they be threatened?" I wanted to say 'How could they be threatened by what nobody can even understand?' The imagery had become so arcane, the cartoons so cluttered.

"Think about that D. H. Lawrence you're always talking about. You don't think they actually read that book before they banned it."

I was quite sure I had never mentioned Lawrence, though I had read a smuggled copy of *Lady Chatterley's Lover* while I was in London.

"That was sex."

"There's sex in the mural."

"There's nudity in the mural. I'm not sure there is sex." As soon as I said it I knew it was exactly the wrong thing. It was the kind of thing I could have said to Frank. For him, the studio and the bedroom were divided by a clear line. For William, I had known since the first days of observing him and Suzanne in the studio, the drive to paint and the drive to fuck could not be as neatly divorced, much as they tried. "I mean, the sexual *energy* is there. But there is no *fornication*, no *fornication* depicted, that's what I meant to say. So the mural is not being suppressed as pornography."

"He who pays the piper calls the tune. And acts as censor."

"Unless there is nothing to pay the piper with. Read the letter again, William."

"They got to you, didn't they?"

"They?"

"You told them about the cartoons, what is in the cartoons."

"Jesus, William. No. How could you think that?"

"They pulled the plug."

"There is no money."

"Well, that's certainly true at this end now, anyway. I'll have to go back to work."

"Painting is your work."

"Labour. I'll have to go back to the factory."

And so he had signed on at the Port Royal mill.

Unlike when he had gone to work at the brush factory, this time William did not stop painting. If anything, he painted with more fervour and energy than ever before, early in the morning before he headed off to work, and in the evenings after we had our supper. The mural cartoons lay furled and abandoned, sloughed-off skin. He returned to painting portraits in oils.

Everyone knew he had continued right on painting but it was only Suzanne who had the nerve (and the history with William) to ask him one Sunday evening at Henry's what made this time different. He growled that the first time, he had taken a job because he was fed up with painting, depressed, blocked. This time, it was only about money.

After he started at Port Royal, we slipped quickly into a routine. He arrived at my apartment door at six o'clock exactly, reeking of the mill. The first evening, he cackled that he smelled like hell: rotten eggs mixed with the scent of a thousand heads of a thousand flaring matches. We traded lines about satanic mills. Then I filled the galvanized tub, as I came to do every night after that, and bathed him and dried him. We would move from spouting Blake's "Jerusalem" to crooning A. A. Milne (wasn't it fun in the bath tonight?). Then we would eat a cold supper and walk down the street to his studio, leaving the dirty dishes in the sink for me to tackle in the morning. He would paint and I would model, or, more often, write, until nearly midnight.

Occasionally, as he painted, he would ask me to read to him from those slightly blurry carbon-copied pages I had been feeding him for the past eighteen months. No matter which of the sketches I chose, his first response would be the same as it always had been. What a sharp eye I had, he would say, how good I was at portraying behaviours. Then he would set those eyes of his on me and tell me what he really thought. He was always very careful. He would lay the blame on the subject matter, say something scathing about the superficial lives the people in our crowd were leading, the tininess of the community, even the limitations of prose as a medium for representing human nature. I had enormous talent, he would say. He wondered what I might be able to do with it, given the right chance, a bigger story. He hoped I would find that chance. I wasn't ready to tell him I thought I already had.

One of the favourite topics of conversation at Henry's apartment during the summer was the question of National Art. Was such a label descriptive? And, if it was, was what it described desirable? Henry and Frank and William had all been founding members of the Maritime Art Association half a dozen years before, but had mainly lost interest since the association's founder and chief spokesman had moved west to Ottawa. Frank actively resisted the label of 'Maritime artist,' arguing that art, if it was to be effective, must be broadly human and readily transportable from its place of origin. William, largely to antagonize Frank, I think, said he could not turn his back on his roots, his people. He accused Frank of being embarrassed, of wanting to apologize for where he came from.

Neither of them, though, had any affection for the National Gallery. Although the MAA had been successful getting National Gallery exhibitions and lecturers to tour the Maritimes, that street had so far been entirely one-way: the gallery did not acquire a single piece of art from the Maritimes, and nobody from Saint John had ever been invited to lecture in Ottawa. William blamed the Carnegie Foundation. He said its goal from the beginning had been to homogenize Canadian art, centralizing and standardizing anything it might come across in the really interesting corners of the country. Frank blamed the Ontario art establishment, which he said championed the work of provincial hacks, educated at home in Upper Canada. He and William and Henry were all fiercely proud of the fact that their training, like the training of so many artists from Saint John, had been in the States. It made them more cosmopolitan, they argued, than their Toronto counterparts (they wouldn't allow the term *peer.*) They clubbed together to pronounce the Toronto crowd clannish and behind the times. Boston, New York, and Chicago were miles ahead. And with them, Saint John.

William, since going to work at the mill, had gone from mild disdain for the Group of Seven to vocal excoriation. Their control of people's thinking about how the northern landscape should be represented, he liked to say, was nothing less than artistic dictatorship. Henry usually leapt to their defence, reminding William of their role in awakening a national awareness. You cannot discount, he would say, their role in encouraging people to think of the scenery around them in this country as a valid subject for art. William loved to respond by intoning the title of an article he had read somewhere: "Come out from Behind that Pre-Cambrian Shield!" He repeated it three times. Then he invariably went on to how a nation is not its landscape but its people. Frank, who we all knew had made the switch to landscape painting, would look very uncomfortable, and Henry would cede the day.

So when Frank was invited to show with the Canadian Group of Painters in Toronto, the conversation became particularly heated. It was not Frank's first showing in Toronto—he had shown some watercolours a year or two before at the Picture Loan Society—but it would be his first showing of landscapes. William had still not forgiven Frank for abandoning the figure and devoting himself entirely to landscape. He had even suggested that Frank's next project should be painting the advertisements for tobacco and haulage that appeared on the brick walls of the buildings near their studios. But it was the word *Canadian* in the group's name that really set him off.

"Why don't you move right up there?" he asked Frank the minute Henry had announced the news. We were all eating *chili con carne* that Suzanne had made and tearing at a baguette that Henry swore he had baked himself. The wine was red and tasted like a barnyard. I think Frank pretended to have a mouthful to buy him some time to frame a response. This backfired, as William simply continued: "Pack up and move to Upper Canada.

That's the place to be *Canadian*." He spat the word as if it was a disease. "Only don't come back here when they chew you up and hawk you out. The road only goes one way, you know that. Look at the National Gallery—look at what Walter is trying to do to *Maritime Art*." The drift of the Maritime Art Association's magazine towards becoming a self-proclaimed national magazine had been a source of frustration for both William and Frank.

"Labels mean nothing," Frank muttered and quickly refilled his mouth with bread.

"Not up there, they don't. They call themselves Canadian but what they mean is Upper Canadian. For them, there is no difference. They think they own the whole goddamn country. And I think they're probably right."

William had been part of a four-person show at the Print Room of the Art Gallery of Toronto in 1938. The show had gotten good reviews, but his work was singled out as substandard. The reviewer went on for several paragraphs about William's failed promise and the inaccessibility of his work for a Toronto audience. Suzanne had told me all about it not long after I met him. I hoped that Frank would be sensitive enough to remember this. He wasn't.

"For them, the label Canadian means 'good enough to stand with artists from across the country.' I'm sorry if you have trouble with that, William."

"You all know what's wrong with culture these days, don't you?"

Everyone became very busy chewing.

"You'll tell us, no doubt," Frank sneered. He had the skin of a kidney bean stuck to his front tooth.

"The money and the leisure that goes with the money are all concentrated in a small industrial elite."

"The same elite that pays your salary at the pulp mill?"

"Exactly. The same elite that destroys the natural environment and ensures the development of a proletariat with no time for leisure and no consciousness that there might be alternatives to its mechanized drudgery."

"You are still painting, aren't you? Or don't you accept the label of proletarian?"

This stopped William cold for a second but then he continued. "The result is cultural institutions that favour private collecting by the rich."

"Like the Medici? You're right, William, it's an awful shame those Medici started collecting." Frank was shaking by then. Suzanne gently took his spoon from him but he had already managed to let some hamburger drop down the front of his shirt.

William would not let up. "The private collections form the basis of the museums. And the museums concentrate in large urban centres. They end up defining art, and the rest of us can go whistle."

"Museums pay artists," Henry interjected. "And they make art available to ordinary people."

"If they can afford the admission."

"So make admission free." Suzanne was trying to steer the conversation into calmer, more certain waters. "Lawren Harris has been talking about a people's national gallery, hasn't he? One where the art is sent out to all parts of the country and exhibited in art centres built by the government."

"It's still the wrong way around," William snapped. A fine spray of red sauce ended up on his knee. "It's still the centre telling the outposts what to think and feel. No. Art has to change. It has to stop being something we do to the people and become something they do for themselves."

"Within reason," said Frank, calmer then. "We still want to sell our paintings, don't we? I do."

"Perhaps Henry has had it right all along," muttered William.

"Don't stick me in the middle of this," Henry protested. And then: "I have? In what way?"

"You don't care about selling pictures."

"Well, I wouldn't say I don't care."

"You care more about teaching, about helping others find their talents. You avoid the problem altogether."

"I have my problems. What problem do I avoid?"

"The problem of labels," I said, catching up with William's train of thought. "You are neither Canadian nor Maritime. You are simply here. Quietly influencing all who come directly within your orbit."

"This get-together was supposed to be a celebration of Frank's achievement." Henry was obviously embarrassed by what I had said. "Not about me."

"I rest my case."

But the conversation never returned to Frank's upcoming show, and the party wrapped up as soon as the pot of chili was empty.

William's return to portraiture meant that he went back to painting me. I was happy that he had given up on the strange angelic figures he had planned for the mural, and I should have been glad that his gaze had returned to me. But whether I was deliberately sitting on the throne modelling for him or whether he was sketching or painting me as I went about my own work, writing longhand in a red bound notebook I'd bought, I had ceased to pay much attention to the canvases anyway. Suzanne had told me months before how it was for her, and I found myself understanding it finally. At first, she had said, you can't let go of the idea that you own your own image, whoever is reproducing it, and you want to see every version. After several dozen portraits, however, you cease to care. Or maybe you simply come to trust the artist, to know how he sees you. I thought that with William it was the latter, which explained why I was so horrified one particular night when he wandered down the hall from the studio for a pee and I happened to glance over and see the canvas he was working on.

The woman I saw had my hair, my eyes, what could have been my left breast but certainly could not be my right, my moles and freckles (although those could have just been spatter). But nothing was where it belonged. It was as if he had dismembered me and then hastily and ineptly put me back together. I thought about the utility knife I knew was in the drawer of the small table on which he kept his paints. I wished I could grab it and cut the thing apart and paste it together properly before he returned from the loo. Then I wondered whether that was what he hoped I might do. I suddenly worried that he had figured out that I had found his red notebook and this was revenge. But surely he would have confronted me.

"Interesting work," I said as flatly as I could manage when he sat back on his stool. "Very much on the cutting edge." I didn't say on the edge of insanity, although it was what I was beginning to fear, especially after what he had revealed to me about his family history.

"You had a look?" He said it so casually I knew he had left the room hoping that I would look.

"Just a peek. I'm in the middle of something here myself." I gestured at my red notebook, waved my chewed pencil, hoped he would let the matter drop.

"And?"

"And?"

"What did you think?"

"Fascinating." It was only a half a lie.

"I knew you'd get it. That you wouldn't mind how I represented you. You have no idea how liberating it is not to have to worry about sales, just to paint what you want, what you see and feel, not to think about decorating the walls of people's fucking living rooms."

I silently cursed the Port Royal Pulp and Paper Company and its damned paycheque. "Have you…is this how you have been painting for a while, then, like this?" I wanted to know how long he had been dismembering me.

"Like what?" he smiled and picked up his brush.

I pretended to write, moving my pencil from side to side of the page. And then, as often happened at that time, I started actually writing, the words about the two of them, their forbidden love, pouring out on the page in perfect rounded sentences, not a one out of place.

Two nights later, when he again went to the bathroom, I could not resist stealing a glimpse at what he was working on. I had steeled myself for the abstraction, persuaded myself that it didn't bother me. It was only another form of representation, after all. I had gone to the library and read a little about Cubism, if that's what it was. I knew I should be flattered he looked at me so closely. What I saw then ambushed me from a whole new direction.

This one, in pinks and oranges with peach-blushed flesh and an ethereal Pre-Raphaelite light, could almost have been a Rossetti, except for the violence. The wild imagery of the post office mural was back. My face appeared on every one of half a dozen angels grouped around a disembowelled prisoner. He lay, face turned away, on a beautifully worked Persian carpet, the cuts and bruises carved by his shackles a perfect tonal match for the knotted wool of the pattern. One of the angels stooped to touch the sausage-link guts that were pouring out of him, while the others looked on with a gleeful light in their eyes. If this was where his mural cartoons were headed, then I was glad the post office had run out of money.

What was more disturbing than the imagery was the fact that he did not mention the painting when he resumed his seat. I waited for him to ask me what I thought, but he just kept painting. Perhaps he was right, I thought. Perhaps talking about it was unnecessary.

He was cleaning and arranging his brushes and I was packing up my notebook when he asked me to read to him.

I was worried about his mental state, angry about how he was using my image, and sick of his habitual veiled criticisms of my subject matter. Perhaps the stupidest thing I could do was to read him what I had been writing since discovering his notebook, but that is what I did.

"It's a kind of a story, really, not at all like the random social sketches you don't seem to care for. It came to me nearly whole. Lots of it doesn't make any rational sense, like a dream, I suppose. It's not like anything I would write consciously."

"A good play needs no prologue. Isn't that your friend Shakespeare?"

I started reading before he could begin to criticize a piece he hadn't even heard yet. "They never knew anything but the island. The island and one another. From the time they were tiny, it had been only the two of them. And the island. It never occurred to them to need anything else, anyone else. Their island was fruitful, bountiful. Things to eat grew on the trees. There were fresh springs in the hills above the beach. They drew water from the springs and stored it in hollowed gourds: calabash, a name they thought they had invented. When the gourd was full or when the sea was calm, they could see their faces in the water. The water told them what they already knew: that their faces looked as like one another as two starfish."

"Do starfish look exactly alike? Or are they like snowflakes?"
It was not the interruption I had anticipated. I blundered on.

"The periods from sunrise to sundown were like one another too. Passed in swimming, foraging, eating, and playing their special games. But they did develop names for them, if only to recognize the changing state of the moon each night. This was her idea. She was fascinated by the moon, though she didn't call it that.

"One day, a day she calls Sliver, as they have finished their morning swim and are playing their morning game, he spies something in the mouth of the bay. Her displeasure at not having his undivided attention is quickly displaced by curiosity. They wait behind the trunk of an uprooted palm as the object gets closer and closer. It is like the split seedpods they like to float in the stream; only this is much larger and floats high in the water. And there is a creature in it: like them, but not exactly. He is larger. Hair covers his face and some kind of wrapping covers his body. In their hiding spot, the two look at each other and feel suddenly ashamed."

I looked over at William. His eyes were still shut, his face composed as if he was asleep, although I knew from his breathing that he wasn't. "Nevertheless, the girl rises up from behind the palm. The boy, seeing no alternative, stands up too. The stranger stands his ground but his face looks the way the pink flesh of fish does when they spear it. Finally, he extends a hand. First the girl and then the boy takes it. Within hours, they are showing him the best places on the island to find fruits and nuts and berries, and by the middle of the day they are all sitting down to eat together.

"After lunch, the girl and the boy resume their usual routine, playing their afternoon game while the stranger sleeps in the shade of a plantain. But the stranger awakes and shouts when he sees the children's game. They do not understand his words because they do not share his language, but his anger is clear. For a second time, they feel the unaccustomed emotion they felt on seeing the stranger's clothes. The girl flees east and the boy flees west. Even when she reaches the cliff at the farthest edge of the island, she keeps running. And as her feet leave the ground, she is transformed into a bird and she soars above the island and far away. Her brother's running feet are doubled and harden into hooves as he flees, though above he remains as he always was. When he returns to the beach, the stranger is gone and his sister is nowhere to be found. To console himself for her absence, he fills a calabash and looks long at his reflected features, until the light finally goes."

Any hopes I had that the fable might provoke a dramatic reaction had faded when his only interruption of my reading was to ask his question about starfish. But I needed him to say something, to tell me how he felt about what I was doing. He opened his eyes.

"You are becoming a surprising woman, Elizabeth MacKinnon, imagining your way into all kinds of unusual positions and situations. I am not sure I like that kind of fable very much. It reminds me a little of our dead Jewish friend. A little mannered. Not very direct. But I can see you are trying something interesting. Bigger, more timeless. That's good."

I wished he had exploded, accused me of spying, which he must have suspected I had. I wanted him to threaten me for stealing his secret and turning it into a story. Then, at least, I would know where we stood. Instead, he just suggested we go home.

Despite the fact that William seemed not at all upset, and despite the conclusion I had reached at the beach with Henry, I decided I owed William somehow, that I needed to make it up to him for taking something from him. The next night, as we finished our cold potatoes, I told him I would not take my notebook to the studio. I had been neglecting him, I said, not behaving like a proper model, not giving him enough. He nodded and smiled but said nothing.

When we got to the studio, I immediately went behind the screen. It was an important form of ritual. I knew he had watched me undress in his apartment or mine maybe a hundred times by then, although much less often recently. But undressing as a lover and undressing as a model were still two very different things for me. Frank had taught me that and I was still convinced he was right. I wanted it to be clear I was all model that night, all his to look at and to paint, to take what he wanted.

"You're losing weight."

It was true, although I was surprised he had noticed, surprised that that was what he had chosen to say. I didn't want a wolf whistle or even a sigh of appreciation, but I hoped he might at least allude to the fact that it had been ages since he had seen all of me. Maybe, I thought, the remark about the lost weight was his way of acknowledging how long it had been

He had me stand before a frame he had suspended from the ceiling. It was a stripped canvas stretcher, tattered fragments of cotton still stuck to it here and there. As he began to work, I felt myself relaxing. His brush was moving very fast across the canvas. He held the palette close to his chest to reduce the distance the brush had to travel as it flew back to load up. I was inspiring him after all, I thought. I hadn't felt happier in weeks.

It was well after midnight when he finally began to wipe off his brushes and nodded at me to dress. I went behind the screen, hesitated, and then emerged immediately.

"Maybe we could fuck," I started to say, using the verb I knew he would like. He was not looking at me, but staring at the canvas. I followed his gaze.

There I stood, my shoulders, breasts, and belly blue with the cold, seen through a barred window. Only the face that returned the viewer's gaze was not mine.

I went in search of Bea and Suzanne early the next morning. I needed to talk to another writer right away. And Suzanne had so much history with William. I hoped they could help me make sense of the ways he had responded to hearing my fable. I planned to talk in hypotheticals only. I wasn't going to betray William's secret, although I wanted to know whether Suzanne knew it.

The nursery school on Queen Square North was more obvious than on my first visit. Someone had taped the children's artwork in the basement windows, which looked out at street level. All of the paintings were of houses, and the effect was magical: a series of impossible reflections of unlikely buildings from across the square.

It took five rings of the bell before I heard footsteps hurrying on the slate floor, but it was neither Bea nor Suzanne who opened the door.

"Oh. Hello. It's Annie, isn't it? I'm Libby."

"I remember. Come in, if you like. I have to get back to the children."

I followed her, pausing first to lock the door behind me. Her shoulders seemed even more hunched than at my last visit. When I reached the schoolroom, the reason was obvious. There was no sign of Bea or Suzanne, and the children were climbing on the furniture and one another.

Annie clapped her hands and the mayhem decreased by half. Then she brandished a handful of paintbrushes. This reduced the noise enough for them to hear her offer.

"Not until you are completely silent. Then you may paint." Annie handed me a stack of paper. "Since you're here, you might as well help, make yourself busy." And I realized that was just what I needed to do.

"Where's Bea? And Suzanne?" I asked as we got the children set up.

"They didn't come in this morning." When I expressed concern she simply said, "It's something we have been trying. We spell each other off, usually just one at a time, though. It gives us some daytime hours to work on our art."

I knew the nursery school was a way for Bea to afford being a poet. I knew that it had started to serve a similar purpose for Suzanne's acting, as well as giving her some captive little dancers to work with. I should have suspected that Annie had a story too, things she wanted to do when she was not looking after children.

"Bea and Suzanne are working on a piece together right now. It's not ideal, but I'll have my turn."

I was not sure what to do while the children painted. It didn't feel right to take out my notebook the way I would have in Frank's or William's studios; and Annie did not seem disposed to further conversation, although she did whisper thanks when all the paper and paints and brushes and water jars were in place, adding that painting was the only sure way of settling them down a bit. I was about to ask her what I could do now when a very small boy answered my question.

"Miss?"

I didn't like the title, but I answered anyway. "Yes?"

"Will you come and look at mine?"

I recognized the look on the tiny face: the need for recognition, validation. The picture was more unformed than I expected, although the colours were vibrant. I was not sure whether to ask what it was. He saved me the trouble.

"It's my house." What was the fascination for houses, I wondered, in children's art? "Do you know my house?" I told him I didn't but I was sure this was a very good picture of it. He beamed.

"That don't look a bit like your house, Mikey. Wait a minute, yes it does. It's a mess and it's all falling down." This was the girl who had been a magnet for all the attention when I last visited. Myra. She was quickly joined by a boy and two other girls who began laughing with her at Mikey's painting. I looked across at Annie, who merely rolled her eyes as if to say 'The cruelty of critics.'

"Have you all painted houses? Let's see." If I couldn't comfort Mikey for the bad reviews, I could at least draw the attention elsewhere. Suddenly, every one of them wanted to show me their precious work. They pulled at my arms and pinched my legs. Annie clapped her hands, then put her fingers to her lips and whistled. I had obviously mistaken her for a retiring drudge, as well as failing to imagine she might be an artist.

"Back to your seats," she yelled. "Miss MacKinnon and I will come around to look, but not until everyone is seated." I was embarrassed that she knew my last name when I hadn't a clue about hers. Bea and Suzanne must talk about me. I liked that.

Finding something positive to say about every effort was surprisingly easy. Sometimes it was brushwork and sometimes choice of colour, made special always by their shining expectant faces. When I got back around to Mikey I found that he was crying, silently so none of the others would notice.

"They hated it."

"No."

"It doesn't look like they think it should look."

"Does it look like *you* think it should?" Contrary as this was to everything I believed about art, I didn't think there could be any harm in asking it of a child.

"Not really. I know what I want it to look like, but I can't make the paint cooperate."

"Cooperate is a nice word. It's hard to make the brush do what you want sometimes." I thought about my doomed experiments with automatic writing and was about to add that sometimes the brush surprises you and does more than you want. "Anyway, I like your painting. I think it may be my favourite."

"You can have it."

"I couldn't."

"It's for you. I can make lots more."

I admired how quickly he recovered from his hurt feelings.

Annie had the children pour out their water in the sink down the hall. They lined up with their little jars like a scene straight out of Dickens. Then the paintings, still wet, were tacked to the wall. There was some negotiation about whose should be next to whose. I thought about Frank's upcoming exhibit in Toronto. When the hanging was all settled, Annie announced it was story time.

"We want *her* to tell us the story," said the attention-seeking girl who was so nasty about Mikey's painting. The other children joined in a chorus of support. Annie shrugged her shoulders.

"Do they have a favourite book?" I asked.

"No, a mouth story. Not a book, a mouth story!" They were forming a ring around me and edging me toward the Windsor chair Annie had used to read *The Little Match Girl* on my last visit. I began madly flipping through my mind's files for something I could tell them. I thought about William, and I looked at little Mikey, and I decided.

"Children, this is the story of Pip and Grace." I didn't think Pygmalion and Galatea would be easy names for them. "Pip was a sculptor. Do you know what that is?"

"Sure, it's a statue," said Mikey who was sitting on my left foot.

"Well, close. A statue is a sculp*ture*. Or can be. A sculpt*or* is the person who makes it. Pip was a very good sculptor. Everyone liked his work. They admired its lifelikeness."

"Pip is a boy? Pip is a girl's name."

"This Pip is a boy." I realized I should have called him Paul. Or William. "Pip didn't like girls very much."

Annie stared at me, wondering, I suppose, where this was headed. The boys in the room nodded their heads, looking cautiously sideways at the girls.

"Pip decided he would have nothing more to do with girls, so he shut himself up in his studio, the place where he made his statues, and he worked and he worked on a special statue. Can you guess what it was?"

"A dragon?"

"An explorer?"

"Babe Ruth?" Babe Ruth's career had been over before these children were born. I marvelled at the mythological power of sport.

"It was of a girl. A woman. Pip worked and worked on his statue, day and night, night and day, smoothing the marble, adjusting the curve of her shoulder."

Annie was twirling her hands, signalling for me to move it along.

"Making her as beautiful as he could, as beautiful as the most beautiful woman he ever imagined."

"I thought you said he didn't like girls."

"He was disappointed in the girls he had met. That's a better way to describe it."

"Oh."

I was losing them.

"So perfect was his statue that he began to treat it like a real woman. He brought it things he thought a girl would like."

"Barley candy?"

"Spiders?"

"Shells and sweet things, so, yes, candy, and bracelets, and rings. He devoted all his days to thinking of ways to make the statue happy. And then one day there was a festival, a big party in his town." I paused, not sure how I would manage the appearance of Venus. I could tell from her expression that Annie was wondering too. "And there was a…a queen there, a magic queen with special powers."

"A witch?"

"A good witch, I suppose, yes."

"There are no good witches."

"In this story there are." I barrelled ahead: "The magic queen noticed that Pip was at the party all by himself and she thought that he seemed lonely, so she offered him a wish."

"When I'm lonely, nobody offers me a wish." Mikey said it without rancour, just as a matter of fact.

"This is a story, stupid."

Annie clapped her hands and the mean girl said, "Sorry, miss. This is a story, Mikey."

"And Pip wished for a girlfriend who would be as perfect as his statue. The queen said that was a tall order but she would see what she could do. Pip went home that night and hugged his statue as he did every night. The marble felt warm. Was that just the effect of the setting sun? But the marble felt somehow softer, too. Was he imagining it? He continued to let his hand, to let his hand play over her surfaces."

I could tell that Annie wished she had thrown me *The Little Match Girl*.

"He called his statue Grace. Did I mention that? Just like you might name your dolly or a teddy bear. As he hugged her he whispered her name over and over again. And sure enough, before the night was over, he heard a faint whisper from her stone lips. 'Pip,' she seemed to be saying. And then she began to hug him back."

"Ugh," said one little boy, but he was quickly silenced by the girls.

"Pip's beloved statue Grace came to life in his arms, and she loved him as much as he loved her, and so they were married at the magic queen's palace and they lived happily ever after."

"And then what?" asked the mean girl, Myra.

Exactly, I thought.

"What does it mean?"

"I beg your pardon?"

"What does your story mean?"

"Does it have to have a meaning?"

"Yes. The one about the little match girl has a meaning."

"Well, then. What does it mean to *you*?" I asked.

In retelling the old story, I had glimpsed something new about the relationship between William and his sister. What happened between them owed at least as much to their being artist and creation as it did to their being brother and sister. And suggesting that little Myra could interpret Pygmalion and Galatea for herself might be the beginning of an answer to my questions about William's puzzling responses to my own work.

FOURTEEN

LATE SUMMER 1941

WILLIAM HAD INSISTED HE WANTED NO FUSS MADE, SO I assumed the two of us would mark the day quietly alone together. More and more, as the summer came to an end, the two of us preferred one another's company to being with anyone else. Then, the night before his birthday, he handed me a formal written invitation while we were working in the studio. I thought it a little odd, but decided it was whimsy and told him of course I would be delighted to join him at his apartment at seven o'clock, and that I would comply with his underlined request not to bring a gift. He returned to his painting without another word, and I didn't think any more about it.

The door was locked when I arrived, but Bea opened it before I was finished knocking.

"Libby! How lovely. Welcome." She ushered me through the door.

I began to understand the written invitation then. William had invited others, too. It was a surprise party, but for me rather than him. I supposed it was a way of reminding me that I was not the only person in his life. "Bea. Where's the birthday boy?"

"Gone out for a bottle. He's left me in charge of the coats and everything. If there are coats." I looked around the apartment and wondered how long she had been there alone, and whether she was uncomfortable that William had so obviously cast her and not me as hostess.

"Is Suzanne not coming?" Bea and Suzanne had become inseparable. I had never mentioned trying to find them at the nursery school, but I was curious to know what project they could possibly be working on together.

"I don't know. Did William not show you his list?"

"He ran it by me," I lied. "I just can't recall everyone who was on it."

As if to help supply the missing information, the Bojilovs rolled through the open door, merry as ever. They were singing a ditty in what sounded like Old Norse. I assumed it was a birthday song.

"The man of the hour is not here right now," Bea said, and they stopped singing immediately, although the smiles stayed pasted on their faces.

I hadn't seen them for ages and was afraid they were going to ask when Bea and I would go back up the river to finish the clay animals we had started a whole year before, but they did not. Instead Emil brandished a bottle of sparkling wine they had brought. He apologized that it was not cold. Bea grabbed it from him and stuffed it into William's icebox. Hostess or not, she obviously didn't know how badly the thing worked.

"We really must get back to finish our creatures," she burbled. When the Bojilovs looked blank, she continued, "Those funny little centaurs or whatever they are that Libby and I made."

The smiles disappeared. I worried their feelings had been crushed by the delay. Then Emil said, "I am so sorry. They did not survive the firing."

"Bubbles," added Marijke. "There must have been air bubbles. They exploded."

After a completely disproportionate moment of silent mourning, Emil chortled, "So we have brought the bubbles in the wine!"

Sparkling wine always gave me a headache, and I knew it would take forever to reach a drinkable temperature in William's icebox, so I offered everyone rye from the bottle I had brought to share with William. Bea plonked on the counter four exquisite crystal glasses I had never seen, took the bottle, and poured generous dollops. Marijke sneezed the second her lips touched the rim. "Spirits," she said, meaning, I thought, the liquor and not ghosts. (William might have informed her an angel was nearby.) Then she downed the contents in one go. Just then, Movina burst through the door and knocked the glass from Marijke's hand. It spun end over end in the air and was caught by Emil as if the fielding of flying glassware were the Finnish national sport. Movina applauded, having freed her hands by neatly tucking the bottle of vodka she had brought under her armpit, as though that were the Russian national sport.

"Bravo," Henry shouted as he glided through the door. He had a box of shot glasses in hand. "We all know William's domestic arrangements," he apologized as he unpacked the box onto the table. "The state of his cupboards, I mean," he added after an uncomfortable silence during which he looked from me to Bea and nobody else seemed to know where to look.

Movina passed her bottle to Bea, who began filling the tiny glasses with vodka. "Where is Villiam?" she asked. "Ve should not start vitout him."

"He went out for a bottle," Suzanne announced as she breezed through the door. "I saw him on my way. He shouldn't be long."

"Nobody will go thirsty. Is there anything to eat?" Henry looked uncertainly from me to Bea and back again. William's casting coup was working.

"I brought peanuts," Suzanne said, fetching a bowl and emptying a large paper bag into it. I cringed, thinking of all the shells to be cleaned up tomorrow. "Frank said that was a crazy thing to bring, but William likes peanuts. I like peanuts."

"We all like peanuts," Henry reassured her. "Frank's not coming?" He asked it casually, careful of his tone, concerned, I supposed, that Movina or I might be upset that Frank and Suzanne had become a couple. Neither of us was.

"No. He says staying away is his present to William. You know how the two of them have been fighting. And he's been very busy getting ready for the show."

"Don't mention the show to William," I said.

"I wasn't going to bring Frank up at all," snapped Suzanne.

Movina surprised us all by raising a tiny shot glass and intoning: "To Frank!" She looked directly at me and rolled her eyes as she swallowed. Everyone murmured "To Frank" just in time for William's entrance.

"Am I interrupting something?" He asked it half laughing, but I could imagine how annoyed he must be.

"We hadn't finished the toast," Henry improvised. "Saint John's *second* most interesting painter…that was the rest of it."

"Flattery, and on my birthday, too. Or are you suggesting that you are the most interesting?" He pinched Henry's cheek and then embraced each of his guests, making jokes about getting shit-faced.

Emil retrieved the bottle of sparkling wine from the icebox and began the work of peeling foil and untwisting wire. In our household it had always been considered vulgar simply to let the cork fly. My father would coax it with his thumbs in a series of shimmies and twists that ended in a sigh with not a drop spilled.

Whether it was a cultural difference or the temperature of the wine, Emil's bottle let out a loud pop and the cork sailed across the room and hit the opposite wall.

"Apologies," he grinned at William who had leapt across the room to examine the dent left by the cork. "Think of it as a piece of art, sculpture, my friend. A small present for your birthday, although you said no gifts."

Suzanne, who knew as well as I how much value William invested in his pristine apartment walls, tried to elaborate. "You must name it, Emil. *In the Nick*, or something like that. Bea, you're clever with words. Help us out."

Bea was busy rinsing some of Henry's filthy glasses so that there were enough to go around. It was Henry who spoke: "Now that the subject has come up, I have always wondered about these walls, William. The bareness. *Barrenness* one might almost say. It's a little unusual, for an artist, isn't it? Not to have any pictures about the place."

"I have a studio full of pictures, Henry. In case you haven't noticed. You must come have another look."

"I know, I know, I just—"

"This is where I live. The studio is where I paint. I like to keep a boundary between them. I'm like a dog, not wanting to shit where I eat."

Suzanne and I looked at one another. William was exaggerating the separation. I wondered how Henry would respond, living as he did in his studio. William didn't give him a chance as he moved in for the *coup de grace*. "Great artists make boundaries, Henry."

Suzanne leapt to Henry's defence before any of the rest of us could. "Henry's life is his art. And the other way around."

Bea had poured shots all around. "To Henry!" she intoned. And everyone drank—even William, who might, from the toasts, have reasonably begun to wonder whose birthday it actually was.

"What a man hangs on his walls tells you something about who he is. Isn't that right, Henry?" There was a dangerous note in William's voice that I recognized. I tried to signal to Henry not to wade in.

"Well, yes, I rather think it does."

"Maybe that applies more to patrons than to artists," I ventured, but Henry was not for letting me save him.

"No, no, I believe it is a pretty general principle."

"Then let these walls tell you about me," muttered William. "They reflect my inner core at the present moment."

"What about the wall I just nicked?" asked Emil, trying to lighten the conversation. "It's an expression of…of what? Help me, Bea."

"It's a piece of aleatoric art," Bea pronounced. "Pure chance. Accident. Randomly created and only really given meaning in the reception, the way the viewer interprets it." It was as though she had swallowed an art book.

"And how is it to be interpreted?" asked William as Bea helped him to more of Movina's vodka.

"It is the tiniest imperfection on the pure wall. A *macula*, if you like. There's a nice word. A spot of sin." Bea was beaming as she put the bottle down.

"Very original," chirped Henry.

"The interpretation or the sin?" asked William.

"My father used to say that original sin is the gap between what we know we might have been and what we are." Suzanne looked at Bea for approval.

"I'm with Hamlet," said Bea. "I think it was Hamlet. There's nothing either good or bad but thinking makes it so. Isn't it something like that?"

"It's just a shitty bare wall, made even shittier by accident." William whispered it, but everyone heard.

"Accident is all we have, isn't it? As artists?" Bea would not let it alone. "Where would you be without accidents, William? Where would your art be? It's the people we run into by chance, the ones who cross our paths, that's who we end up painting or writing about. It's a cloud blocking the sun that suddenly lets us see an object or a person in a whole new…well…light. Without accident, there is no alchemy. There is no change, no… metamorphosis."

By now, Bea was actually standing on a chair, declaiming. I had never seen this group of people get so drunk so quickly. The party had become like some grotesque version of the social sketches I had stopped working on after I found William's note-book. I wanted nothing more then than to be far away from them all. I had to settle for one flight of stairs and my apartment. I said a quick good night, kissed William lightly on either cheek, a birthday kiss from a generic well-wisher, and fled upstairs.

I could hear the party going on far past midnight, and there was a series of drunken farewells in the stairwell, but I lost track as I sat at my desk and wrote well into the wee hours. I was still discovering the sister's voice, and it was going very well.

The next evening, William appeared at my door at exactly six o'clock, just like always. I expected him to look much the worse for wear after the night of drinking and a day in the mill, but he was surprisingly fresh. He even offered to help with the dishes before we repaired to his studio, but I declined. If it was his way of trying to restore our habitual domestic arrangement, I wanted nothing to do with it. His pushing me away the night before, casting Bea as hostess, pretending we were not a couple— that was his gift to me on his birthday, I decided. I thought the treatment might help me understand the sister better, and being pushed away had indeed freed me to write what I wanted. I wasn't looking for a return to the status quo.

Once in the studio, we settled quickly into our work, he with his easel and me with my red notebook. In the preceding week, we had fallen into a pattern of not talking at all while we worked, but I broke the silence after a few minutes by asking him a series of questions about the birthday night. How did so many people come to be invited? How much did they all drink? Who got the most drunk? Who was the last to leave?

The responses were brief. It just kind of happened. Lots. Not sure. Can't remember. And then: Why? Are you planning to write about it?

"I've stopped doing the social sketches," I said. It felt good to admit at least that much. We worked quietly for several more minutes.

"Would you put down your notebook and sit for me?" he asked.

"Shall I…?" I indicated the screen and touched the buttons on my blouse.

"Just as you are will be fine."

I crossed to the bedraggled throne and settled in.

"Without the notebook, please," he murmured, reaching out to take it from me.

"Where shall I look?"

"Out the window."

"As though I don't know anyone is looking at me."

"Exactly."

He had positioned his easel so I couldn't see him at all if I looked out the window as he instructed. I didn't like it, but I did as I was told.

After two or three minutes, I realized I was not hearing the expected sounds of brush on canvas. "Is something wrong?" I asked, starting to swivel on the chair.

"Please don't lose the pose."

"Are you painting?"

"I'm reading."

"What are you reading?" Then I realized. *Shit.* "William. That notebook is private. It's not for anyone but me. What I type up, that's what I want people to see."

"But since I figure so highly in it, don't you think I have a right to read this?"

"It's not about you."

"Isn't that what Frank always told you about his life drawing? That it wasn't about you? What a good little pupil you have been."

"You have both told me the portraits you make aren't about me. I've come to accept that." I needed him to believe that, even if I didn't completely yet.

"The first time I caught a glimpse of what you've written in this book, I thought it was just random notes. Research for who-knew-what. Maybe some kind of academic paper. The pages and pages on Lord Byron and his half-sister. The passages quoted from *Manfred*. That's all I saw. You had copied out two passages with a note they were from act two. I admired the way the line numbers of the original were so carefully recorded and the line breaks marked. Here they are."

I had turned around and could see he had the notebook open at a page about a quarter of the way through.

"Let me read this. 'She was like me in lineaments—her eyes,/ Her hair, her features, all, to the very tone/ Even of her voice, they said were like to mine.' And 'When we were in our youth, and had one heart,/ And loved each other as we should not love.'" He closed the notebook. "Then I got thinking about it. Why were you so interested in Lord Byron?"

"William, I can explain."

"Then I realized. The cover of this book. How could I have missed the symmetry? You had discovered my own red notebook. That is what happened, isn't it?"

There was no point denying it. I simply nodded, glad then to return to looking out the window.

"I won't ask you how you could go through my private notebook. It's so obvious."

"I shouldn't have."

"You couldn't help yourself. I can understand that, the inability to resist an urge. The need to feed your habit. The selfishness."

"You make me sound like—"

"An addict. Isn't that what you are? You have to watch. Watch and record. Sit on the sidelines of other people's dramas and report on them."

"That's not—"

"Even that I could forgive. From the beginning I have known you don't even know you are doing it half the time."

"Please let me have my notebook."

"I'm reading. I told you. Would you like to hear some more of it?"

"Stop now," I pleaded.

"Maintain the pose. I want to watch you as I read this page."

"It's fiction. It will be fiction, when I am finished."

He began to read a passage I wrote three weeks before. It was one of my first efforts at trying on the sister's voice. I hadn't gotten it quite right then. There was still too much of me, and not enough of her, but it had encouraged me to keep working.

William's voice was flat as he read the words back to me.

"When apart from him, I am only half myself. Breath comes shallow in scooped-out chest, half-made thoughts die lonely before they're fully born. Fingers tingle, go numb as they forget the forbidden touch of him. I count the hours to his return with marks on my thighs where none but he will see, tiny scarlet bubble lines in lily-white flesh that tell him how I miss him, how I miss my other self. I catch him in my mirror, pull my hair back off my face to make him come, but the cold glass only mocks: a blue-grey cloud on its surface where his warm breath should be. Father brings home suitors (does he know?) and mother bakes them cakes: a package deal, she seems to say, my daughter and my batter. For him they line up girls, choice heifers from the church, the school, the factory, begging him to take his pick, to carry on the family line in the time-honoured way. But we have found our way, a road less travelled, where every turn brings sweet release, a path just wide enough for two to move, breathe, think, feel, and sweat as one. He makes pictures of me, calls them maps for memory, says the time they rob from our precious stolen moments helps dull for him the ache of all the minutes we are apart. I feel his pencil on my hip, my breast, my cheek, the smudge of charcoal between my legs. Sheets of paper as softer sheets, inscribed with the love known only by us two."

He stopped there. I heard the notebook close with a snap. I could not turn to face him.

"You cannot know," he said. "How could you possibly understand?"

"I am trying to."

"The fucking presumption."

"William."

"To imagine you could get inside her head."

"I am a writer."

"To think that you could speak with her voice."

"It is a sketch. That is all. A way of working. And a way of trying to understand my characters from the inside, feeling what they feel. You can understand that."

"What if I do not want your understanding? Perhaps she doesn't need your understanding. She is not a character. I am not." A sharp crack of splintering wood followed. I cringed. He had snapped a paintbrush or stomped on a canvas stretcher.

"It would never see the light of day, what I wrote there. Names, places, everything will be changed by the time I'm through. It is a starting place for something else entirely. A novel. A bigger, older story."

"What right have you to use it as a starting place? Can't you leave her alone? How long have you been writing this?"

Somehow I found the courage to face him then, to get up from the throne and cross to where he sat at his easel, my notebook still in his hand. "I have never breathed a word of it to a living soul, in case you are worried about that. But this is something I am going to write."

"What if I don't want to see her suffer any more? She is not a subject to be rendered, not a starting point, a model, something to be reproduced in a fucking book!" He was waving the notebook furiously, as if to shake the life out of it. I was afraid he might be about to throw it out the window.

"The artist takes from the model, and yet the model loses nothing. You are the one who told me that."

As I took the notebook from his trembling hand, I glanced at the canvas and began to think I understood the source of his anger, the depth of the betrayal he had felt. She was there on his easel, an image that might have been lifted from the pages of his notebook: shyly naked, her face half turned away but still caught in a small mirror. Only the reflection was not hers but his.

He let me kiss his forehead. That, I thought, was something, a sign he might one day forgive me for the story I had taken from him and refused to give him back. I collected my things and left without a word. As I shut the door, I could see him playing with the single lay figure his studio possessed. It looked like he was posing it in front of the window, exactly as I had been a few minutes before.

Three days later, I heard that he had been accepted into the air force.

FIFTEEN

FALL 1941

THE LANDLORD IS WHISTLING WHILE HE REPAIRS THE splintered door casing of what used to be William's apartment. He can't be too upset by the damage. I mutter good morning and try to hurry past and down the stairs.

"Miss MacKinnon," he calls, breaking off in the middle of a pretty good rendition of "Elmer's Tune." His wife does all the paperwork, so I am impressed that he knows my name. Impressed and a little nervous. I turn to face him. "You're some kind of a writer, right? I've heard the typing."

"Yes."

"So you know something about the artistic temperament."

"I wouldn't say that."

"Painters, writers, dancers—you all live in a world the rest of us don't really understand."

I think that the separation of worlds he has just described is actually a sign of the failure of art to make a connection, but I nod and wait for him to go on.

"So tell me, please. Why does a fella do that? Why does somebody paint that filth all over the walls of his apartment? No, not *his* apartment. *My* apartment. What would possess him to do that?"

I find myself suddenly wanting to defend the mural. "I suppose…I suppose he had something he wanted to say."

"I guess he did. Plenty. Come in and take another look. That is, if you have time."

I can't, of course, tell him I have already studied the walls quite closely, can't admit that I helped Henry break the door so he could photograph every square foot that William painted. I say I have lots of time.

"Somebody busted this door in last night. Christ knows what they thought they'd find. The guy didn't have anything worth stealing. I wish they'd tried to lift the damn painting off the walls. They must have had some shock when they saw all that."

He puts down his tools and gestures for me to go through the door before him. I interpret it as chivalry and not just an excuse to get a look at my bum.

He makes a big production of turning on every lamp he can find, in addition to the overhead bulb, pausing every now and then to square a piece of furniture or straighten a lampshade. For a moment it feels like he may be trying to sell me on trading up to this apartment from my smaller one upstairs.

"I don't know how he got all these people in here in the first place. I would have thought I would have noticed the comings and goings. The missus should have noticed. There were parties, of course, we knew that, but that's different. Not that we encourage parties, you understand, but I'd much rather parties than whatever went on here to make this thing." He gestures at the walls without really looking at them.

"I don't think all the people would have been here at once. He would have painted it in sections. I think. It's not like a single picture. It's a series of images."

"Like a cartoon strip?"

"A little, only not as linear." I wonder about trying to explain to him the little I know about Medieval painting, how they tried to crowd everything in at once, regardless of timeframe or locale. Jesus's birth and his crucifixion, Adam and Eve and Noah and the Four Horsemen, all represented in one picture, the connections thematic rather than chronological. "He would have worked at it in smaller pieces. The pieces form a kind of network—a web, rather than a straight line. It's all connected, but it doesn't tell a single story in a typical way."

"With naked people posing. Here in my building, my wife's building." His face, already carnation, turns closer to eggplant. I wonder whether he has ever said the word *naked* in front of a young woman before today.

It's possible that understanding how William made the mural might make a difference in the man's decision about what to do with it, I realize, so I continue. "He would have worked from sketches, studies that he would have done somewhere else altogether. Even photographs."

"At Saints Rest Beach? Oh my God." He gestures to Suzanne as Daphne.

I am surprised I have not taken in her setting before. William was never very concerned with settings of any kind. He claimed they could seduce one into the cardinal sin of painting landscapes. But Taylors Island is clearly hinted at in the background. The army has taken over that area in the last few months, so I know the image must date from longer ago than that.

"He would have done the sketches in his studio, most likely, over time. He had a studio, I hear, on Prince William Street." I want to tell the man that sometimes people do model in the nude *en plein air*, but I am afraid I might then be the one to blush. "He would have made sketches of the model and sketches of the scene and worked from those. Sketches or memories.

But I expect he put the person and the place together here on the walls for the first time. Sometimes, he would have put the groupings together for the first time here too." I can't imagine William would ever have asked Suzanne and Frank to sit for him together.

"I don't know why he couldn't have kept it all in his studio down the street, then, the whole thing. Where it belonged."

He knows that I type in my apartment, so he knows the boundaries are not always so neat. "Have you decided what you are going to do with it?"

"You told me I can't just paint it over."

"Is that what you want to do?"

"I don't know yet. I guess what I want first is for somebody to explain it to me."

"Why he did it?"

"That would be nice, too, of course. You said he must have had something to say. So what was it?"

I have never felt so much pressure to explain a piece of art. Here is a man I had judged as a Philistine, someone who has given every indication of hating art and artists, or, if not of hating them, of finding them unfathomable, and he is asking me to interpret William's work for him. He seems to be suggesting that his understanding of the painting might help determine its ultimate fate. The choice can only be between painting over the walls and destroying them, though; I cannot imagine how he could rent the rooms with the mural in place.

"Let's try to figure it out together," I say. I think I am suggesting it more for my own reasons than for him.

"I wonder if there is any tea," he mutters, and immediately begins rummaging in the kitchen.

I let him find it for himself, just where William always kept it. I have to bite my tongue to keep from directing him to the chipped pot in the cupboard above the stove. He discovers it eventually and puts the kettle on. I wonder if I should offer to go upstairs to my place for biscuits.

"Do you know about *Metamorphoses*?" I hope the question will sound natural somehow if I ask it while he is fussing about making tea.

"Caterpillars into butterflies. That kind of thing?"

"Yes. Bodies transformed from one state to another. Ancient mythology is full of stories of transformations. A Roman poet, a man called Ovid, collected them all together, all the ones he knew, and made a book of them. Mr. Upham liked that book. Artists, lots of artists, like the book a great deal. It gives them ideas."

"Inspiration."

"Yes." I consider waiting for the tea, but I don't know what else we would talk about so I plunge ahead. "The woman there," I say, not willing to use Suzanne's name.

"The one whose arms are growing leaves?"

"Something about what is happening to her suggests to me the story of Daphne as Ovid tells it."

"And who is that next to her then?"

I am about to blurt out Frank's name but catch myself in time: "Apollo. God of…well, god of lots of things actually."

"Not gentlemanly behaviour, obviously. And not wine. That's someone else isn't it?"

"Dionysus."

"No."

"Bacchus."

"That's it."

"The story is that Daphne was not interested in Apollo's affections, his attentions."

"Even though he was a god. That's something."

"She fled from him as long as she could, and when she ran out of strength she begged the earth goddess and her father, who happened to be the river god, to transform the body that had brought her so much trouble."

"And they turned her into a tree?"

"A laurel."

"Why didn't the gods just smack Apollo?"

Why indeed? I remind him about the tea.

"So, you're saying that the painting is about people changing?" he asks after we are settled with our mugs. It's Red Rose, which I find comforting.

I blow the bubbles around on the surface while I think about his question, marvelling at its simple insight. For all of our careful study and discussion, our attempts to parse and to analyze, Henry and I have not been able to get to the heart of William's intent. I wonder whether we have been too concerned with who was who in the mural and not what was happening. "It's about a lot of things, I think, but, yes, I suppose it's partly about people changing."

Encouraged, he begins to move around the room, applying his idea to what he sees. "This one is turning to stone. There must be a story there. Who is she?"

"Niobe."

"She looks like someone I've seen in Saint John."

I will never dare to tell Suzanne that the man has recognized Movina but not her. "Really?"

"But what about this?" He has paused in front of Reuben-as-Actaeon. "How does this fit? It looks like a guy getting eaten by dogs. Where's the change in that? Apart from the obvious one from alive to dead."

"That's Actaeon. He came upon the goddess Diana in her bath. She was angry."

"So shouldn't she have turned him into something? Like the earth and the river did with the girl over there?"

"She made him look like a stag."

"I don't see it here."

"To his hounds. She made him look like a stag to his hounds. And they acted accordingly."

"Upham should have put some antlers on the guy."

"That would have been more consistent, you're right. He might have been trying to say something about how we all see things differently from one another."

"Do we?" He is standing now directly in front of Myrrha's bush, staring into its mysterious folds and foliage. I am afraid my mouthful of Red Rose is going to make its way out through my nose, but he is either too obtuse or too embarrassed to decode what is right in front of us. Instead, he points to Adonis. "That's him, isn't it? Upham."

"I think so, yes." Reflexively, I am still trying to maintain the fiction that I barely knew William.

"That's a funny thing to do, don't you think? To paint yourself? A little bit, you know—" I am about to supply the word *narcissistic* and go on to fill in the Ovid story about falling in the pool, but he goes on. "Vain. Still, it must be difficult, seeing yourself clearly enough to paint a likeness. It does look like him. I don't think I could do that. Even if I could paint. They say we look different to ourselves from how we look to other people. Have you heard that? But this definitely looks like him to me."

I think back to William's essays in self-portraiture, that day two years ago when Suzanne's emergency rehearsal of Coward left us alone in his studio—the hand mirror, the windowpane. I still have the sketch he made of himself from my description: 'my anatomization' of him, he called it later when I reminded him of it and showed it to him. It was true that that one didn't look a bit like him, but I later wrote a poem from it that did (I like to think) capture something about who he was.

"This is him, too, isn't it?"

I am relieved that we have moved away from the birth of Adonis and Myrrha's bush.

"As what-did-you-call-it. Bacchus, right?"

He is pointing to an epicene William, holding a bottle and a glass aloft as he oversees the destruction of Pentheus. Agave is turned away, playing out the story and ordering her bacchantes to tear her son apart. I sit up very straight in my chair, worried the landlord might otherwise recognize the curve of my shoulder in Agave. Pentheus's face is also hidden, so that I don't think the man will be able to tell that the back of his head is also William's.

"He was quite a drinker, Upham. I hate to see a man consumed by the booze like that. The wife thought he was getting it under control the last few months though."

I want to tell him some of what I think I have learned from William about people, that they move, metamorphose, defy labelling, but I am supposed to be nothing more than a fellow tenant. "I think I might know a couple of women who are looking for somewhere to rent. They might be interested in seeing this place," I say.

"You haven't told them about these walls, have you?"

"I can tell them you're going to do something about the walls. I'm sure it won't be important to them." Bea and Suzanne are never going to rent the apartment, of course. I just need them to see the mural, and this suddenly seems the easiest way of accomplishing that. "Is Tuesday night all right for them to have a look? That's the only time they're both free."

He hesitates, perhaps weighing whether a prospective tenancy is worth more than his weekly outing. "You know these women quite well? You can vouch for them?"

"I've known them for years."

"Would you mind showing them the place? Tuesday nights are hard for me and the wife. I could give you the key."

I tell Bea and Suzanne not to arrive before seven and that we will have to be out by ten. Bea is to bring wine and Suzanne has promised some food. They are not to mention the visit to anyone.

When they knock on my door, both are wearing large hats and have their coat collars turned up. "In case anyone sees us going into William's apartment," says Bea. "They'd never know who we are." It obviously hasn't occurred to them that their elaborate efforts at disguise might draw even more attention. They insist on tiptoeing down the stairs.

Suzanne says she still is not sure, and how odd this feels. She hasn't been inside William's apartment since the birthday party. She doesn't hesitate, however, to rush past me the minute I have unlocked the door. Bea is slower to cross the threshold. I have to guide her by the elbow so I can get in too and shut out the outside world. I turn on the light.

"My god," they say in unison.

"Didn't I tell you?"

"Words couldn't begin to describe it. Thanks, Libby. We definitely needed to see it." Suzanne has taken the wine bottle from Bea and is already fumbling with the cork.

"I forgot the glasses," Bea says, and then goes straight for the cupboard where William kept his, on those rare occasions when he actually put them away. She pulls down three jars and we all laugh.

"Fitting," says Suzanne, making sure to take the one that is least chipped, and pouring herself a healthy dose.

Bea fills the other two jars. "What did you bring us to eat?"

"Lobster sandwiches. I know a fellow. It ends up being cheaper than most things right now." Suzanne unwraps a tidy cube of stacked white bread with chunks of pink and white meat bulging out the seams. She knows where William kept his plates. "Isn't it odd that he didn't get rid of any of his things? He was giving up the apartment. He didn't owe anything on the rent. Why would he leave everything here? Why not store it all somewhere so it wouldn't be sold or thrown out? He might not be coming back to this place, but he is coming back."

We all know that William might not actually get back. Every day we hear news of men lost overseas, particularly fliers.

It takes Suzanne another minute to focus on the walls. "Jesus. What's happening to me there? I'm growing leaves. Is that what those are?"

"You're Daphne," Bea pronounces. "There's Frank, just over there. As Apollo, I think. The laurels. Obviously ironic. A bit mean of William, don't you think?" She has unpacked half a dozen brass candlesticks and candles and is arranging them around the room. "So we can turn out the lights," she explains. "Soften things a little."

I have to go upstairs to my apartment for matches. When I get back, Suzanne and Bea are examining William's depiction of Niobe.

"Poor Movina," says Suzanne. The reaction is all the more striking, given their history. "Oh my god. Poor, poor Reuben. That's the most grisly.... How could William?"

Bea has lit the candles and she switches off the overhead bulb. I wish Henry and I had thought of this, although his film would not have worked in light this low. The effect of the mural changes radically when lit from the side and below. The colours become richer and the mythological scenes come across as less awkward, less studied. It is as though the work was always intended to be seen in antique lighting. Maybe William produced it by candlelight.

"The candles help you understand the thing differently, don't you think?" Bea carefully douses the matches in the sink. "They relieve us of the impulse to read the piece too literally, help us see it in a different...well...light. It is mythology, after all."

I marvel at how quickly she seems to have worked all this out.

"I feel used. A little," moans Suzanne. "With William, I always knew what he was painting, how he saw me. It bothered him how I used to be able to tell what he was looking at, remember? But that was part of our arrangement, our understanding. I knew exactly what the world would see on the finished canvas. But this is different. A betrayal, almost. That's what it feels like. I didn't know he was painting me like that. I would never have agreed."

"He painted it from memory, evidently. And sketches." It is exactly what I told the landlord.

"Well, I don't like it. He should have asked."

"Frank would say we are all only instances anyway, instances of the ideal. We can't own our images. We can't control how others see us. You told me those things once."

"Yes, but to turn me into a fucking tree without asking. Daphne at least asked to be transformed, didn't she?"

"Her circumstances were different." Bea pours more wine into Suzanne's jar. "This is nice, the four of us together."

"Four?"

"I suppose I was thinking of William," she says, gesturing at the candles and the walls. "It feels like he's here too, doesn't it?"

"It sure helps that he didn't clear out any of his things," Suzanne begins.

"I mean something a little different. A little deeper." This is a more familiar Bea, dismissive of Suzanne, just this side of contemptuous.

Suzanne does not seem to notice, or, if she does, she doesn't seem to be perturbed. "You mean like a séance or something? But he's not dead." As if this last statement needs support, she adds: "I had a letter from him last week. A postcard."

This is the first I have heard about anyone having any communication from William. I suppose I have no right to be jealous, but I am. I don't want the others to see it, so I say: "He was always very fond of you. His best friend, isn't that what he called you, even when, even when...."

"Even when we were lovers. Yes. Thanks, Libby."

"He wasn't very good to you by the end." If Bea thinks this is pouring oil upon troubled waters, she is mistaken.

"William was complicated," Suzanne fires back. "People are. You can't just pick and choose the bits that suit you. He was... he is...."

"Please don't say 'a genius,' as if that makes everything all right," Bea snaps. "Being a genius shouldn't be an excuse for bad behaviour. It might be an excuse for never being on time, or not having clean shirts, or for humming in public, but it can't be used to forgive—"

"He never hit me."

Bea and I both look at her and then at one another.

"He had his moods, of course. I don't deny that. Black moods. Mostly when he was having trouble with his art, when it deserted him. Remember when he took the job at Simms'?"

We do.

"That was a particularly low period for him. He put on a brave front, you know, all that bullshit about getting in touch with the means of production or whatever it was he used to say, but in the evenings he was in terrible shape. He'd walk home across the bridge and stop for a drink at a couple of places in the North End. By the time I saw him he was usually cresting belligerence and starting down the slope of dully morose. Like a sad little boy. I would try to get him to talk but he never wanted to. Sometimes he'd lash out then. But it came from sadness, not from meanness. Libby, you must know what I'm talking about."

I am not about to compare notes. "Look at how many times William has put himself into the picture on these walls. What do you two make of that?"

"I think the Icarus manifestation is most interesting," says Bea. "Particularly in light of where he is now, what he is doing."

I had not noticed William as Icarus. He is tiny, falling into the sea in an upper corner of the west wall. Homage to his old idol Bruegel, of course. How had I missed it?

"What if it's not literally about flying, though? It doesn't have to be about flying." Suzanne is understandably upset by the idea of William blown out of his bomber's ball turret and plunging into the sea. "The Icarus story is really about overreaching in any form, isn't it? About being too clever for your own good? That's very William. And he became quite interested in angels, didn't he? Maybe it's not Icarus at all, but an angel. Swooping, not plummeting."

Bea and I hastily agree. For a moment, the only sound in the room is three women eating lobster sandwiches.

"Why do *you* think he joined up?" Suzanne directs the question at me.

"Why do you think it took him *so long*?" I let this sit for a minute. "He was packed and ready for the Spanish Civil War, remember? If that had lasted a month longer, he'd have been there. We all thought he'd sign up in the fall of thirty-nine. I guess things must have changed for him. He needed a new cause, perhaps." I can't, of course, claim to have been the reason for his staying out of the war at its beginning. In fact, I suspect that things I did may have nudged him into joining up when he did. But if there is any credit to be taken for his delay, it is mine rather than Suzanne's.

"Testosterone," says Bea.

"What?" I choke on a bit of shell in my sandwich.

"That's what made him enlist in the end. They can't help it, men. I'm not sure we would want them to, when it comes down to it."

I decide not to be shocked by this extraordinarily old-fashioned statement. Suzanne, who does not appear fazed, asks: "But why so suddenly? Two years go by and then suddenly his testosterone kicks in? Or does it build up if it doesn't have an outlet?"

This is clearly a dig at me. That I must not have been satisfying William as well as she did. That sexual frustration launched him into the arms of the air force.

"William seldom let anything build up, did he?" Bea asks it, but she obviously knows the answer. And that is when I first suspect that something happened between them. I should have seen it earlier, when she knew where the glasses were, and about lighting the mural with candles to get the best effect.

"Where are you in the mural, Bea?" I try to sound casual. It takes an enormous effort to keep my eyes from darting over to the birth of Adonis.

"Me? I was nobody to William. I don't suppose he took enough notice of me to include me in his masterwork."

Suzanne seems satisfied with this answer. I would suddenly bet my life it is a lie.

Three days go by before I can arrange to get Bea alone to find out what I want to know. I lure her by proposing another automatic writing session, this time at my apartment. My preparations are a good deal less elaborate than hers were, although I have lit candles. They have the added advantage of blurring over the piles of dirty laundry in the corners and making the dust bunnies do a magical disappearing act. I am hunched over my desk too much these days to keep the rest of the place in order.

She is late, flutters in with a murmured excuse about having been somewhere with Suzanne, which I know to be untrue because the Little Theatre group is deep into rehearsals. She wanted to keep me waiting. The wine she has brought has a good label. An expensive one at any rate. My palate grows duller every day. I pour us each a tumbler.

"There's no music. Sorry."

"We have the wind." She is right. It is howling between the buildings tonight. "I think the music last time might have been a mistake, a distraction. It garbled the messages."

I think of the phalanxes of hieroglyphs marching across the fields of paper Bea had laid out in front of her that night. So this is how she has explained that: not no message, just a garbled one.

"This way we can hear our own thoughts," I say, still not wanting to surrender my view of how this should all work as an expression of our inner selves. "Do you want a pencil as well, or is the pen all right?"

"The pen will be fine."

I wonder whether she actually has any intention of using it. Perhaps she knows this is really about clearing the air about William.

"It does work, you know, automatic writing. I...I actually had some luck later that night we tried it. Kind of unbidden, in fact. Well, I suppose that's the essential thing about it, isn't it?"

Bea takes a swig of wine and sits farther forward on her chair. "What was it like? What did you write?" This is exactly what I've hoped for.

"I could read it, if you like. I suppose. Maybe it would put us in the mood, open some channels, whatever."

"And it *is* in English, right? Not gibberish."

"You be the judge." I make a show of riffling through a pile of papers on my desk and then extract the sheaf I want from under a cushion on the couch where I placed it minutes before Bea's arrival. It is not, of course, the love letter I wrote to William that night after Bea scribbled her gibberish. I can still picture that paper crumpled in my wastebasket where it lay for weeks before I finally mustered the resolve to put it out with the trash. What I have decided to read her is, if anything, the opposite of automatic writing: the story of the children on the island that I wrote much later, under different inspiration and with much more labour. I need to know how much she understands about William and his sister—at least, to the extent that any true understanding of it is possible. I think the fable will be the best way of discovering how well she knew William without showing my hand entirely.

I read it to her just as I read it to William in his studio. When I have finished, I wait nearly a minute for Bea to say something.

"This all just poured out that night after you went home?" she asks.

"Just as I have read it," I lie.

"Where did it come from, do you think?"

"Where did it come from?" This is the moment I have been dreading.

"Spirits, or your inner self? Which inspired you?"

The old debate then, I think, relieved. Nothing more. She does not know, she cannot. Whatever her connection to William in his last days in Saint John—muse, student, lover—it was not as deep as what I had. She had not discovered as much. I pour us each a glass of wine.

"Well, shall we give this another try?"

I hold my pencil to the paper, but I know it will not move tonight.

With William gone, I find it increasingly difficult to inhabit my characters the way I want to. It is as though there was a fine thread running from his sister to him and, through him, to me. Looking at him, watching him, I felt I could see her. What he had sketched and written in the red notebook helped me understand what she must feel. So did the way he made me feel in the studio. And in the bedroom. And now that thread has snapped.

If I had his red notebook, I might stay connected to the story, but I know he will have taken that with him. My only hope, I decide, is the sister. If anyone knows about her it will be Suzanne. I corner her one evening at Henry's.

She wants to tell me all about her and Frank. She has graduated from the graphic tales of sexual experiments she used to tell me when she was with William. Either that or she and Frank have less sex. "He's going to paint the sets for the new play."

I have heard about the Little Theatre's latest venture: something about Madame LaTour, who was apparently one of the first European settlers in the city. Bea has written the script, with help from Suzanne. They are dedicating it to Reuben Weiss, although it sounds utterly unlike anything Reuben might have written: local, not international; history, not parable.

"The show in Toronto ended up being such a disappointment for poor Frank," Suzanne confides. "He needed a new project.

This seems ideal—a perfect extension of the work he's been doing in landscapes. He's abandoned human figures altogether. Did you know? The sets will be gigantic landscapes, the city imagined historically, long before it was a city."

I am not sure how that kind of imaginative leap will be achieved, but I don't say so. I need something else from her.

"Have you had any more postcards from William? Or maybe heard any news through the family?"

"Family? William had no family."

"His parents are dead, I know. I suppose I was thinking of the sister. Do you ever visit the sister?"

"He has a sister? He never mentioned a sister."

"Oh yes, he has a sister," I say, pleased to know something about him that she doesn't. I am not betraying his secret in the mere statement of fact.

"What went wrong between you two, anyway?"

I should blame the war, but I don't. "The old problem. Something about who was being looked at and who was doing the looking, I think." It feels dangerous to say even that much, but I don't think she knows enough to understand. "Here comes Bea. I wonder if Henry has any more wine."

The next day, I make the walk to Lancaster and the Provincial Hospital. I have no idea what the visiting policies are, or if visiting is even allowed. As I approach the front gate, I decide that brash self-confidence will be my best strategy.

"Good morning," I boom to the attendant. "I am here to see Miss Upham." I say the words briskly, trying to make it sound as if it is not my fault if he doesn't know her first name.

"Upham? Let me check."

I can't believe my luck. Apparently, it is as easy as appearing at the gate with a name. But then, why shouldn't it be?

"No Upham here, miss. Sorry."

Surely William would have said something if she had been released. I thank the man and make my way back past the Simms' factory. Halfway across the bridge, I stop.

Hard as I look, I cannot find her face in the swirling water below.

I am sitting at my desk, glaring at my silent typewriter, when Henry appears at my apartment door.

"Libby, you have to see this," he puffs, winded from the stairs. "It's remarkable. Changes everything."

I allow myself to be led down one flight to where the door of William's apartment stands open.

"The landlord called me. He got my name through the school, I think. Told them he needed an art person for some advice."

"You didn't tell him you'd already seen what William did to his walls?"

"He had no idea I knew who William was. He's much less interested in the mural than in the wall."

"He's going to smash it?"

"He was about to make a start when he discovered it didn't meet the mouldings quite right. That piqued his interest enough to pry away at one corner." Frank pushes me into the apartment and points to a bit of crumbled plaster where Daphne's roots used to be. "It's a false wall. William must have constructed it inside the apartment to paint the mural on."

I think back to how much William enjoyed working on the post office substrate with his plasterer friend, and I imagine the pleasure he would have taken in repeating the act at home.

"What are you smiling at?"

"Just a memory."

"Well what do you think it means?"

"Means?"

"The fact that he painted the mural on a false wall. It means he wanted it preserved, doesn't it? That he would want us to preserve it, to move it."

"Where?"

"Well, the logistics would have to be gone into, the practicalities. But I think the false wall sends a clear message. And those photographs I took will help us reassemble it."

"Perhaps he only wanted a pristine substrate to work on. Remember how upset he was when Emil's champagne cork took a bite out of the wall?"

"It makes sense of the fact that he left so many of his things behind in the apartment, too, doesn't it? He must have wanted it all saved, everything, until he comes back."

"Did he tell anyone that?"

"It's the obvious interpretation. It is a striking work after you get over all of the personal references. Even *with* them, it is an important record, I think." When I look at him with my best blank stare, he goes on. "Of us, of who we were, where we were. It's like what you were doing with those social sketches of yours, but put into a much larger context, a mythological context."

I look around at the walls and suddenly see something quite different. "What if the individual faces don't mean anything, Henry? What if they are just placeholders? Instances of the ideal? He had to give the figures faces of some kind. Faces are a necessary convenience. He told me that one time. But it's their bodies that tell the real stories, isn't it, the mythological stories? We know Daphne from her leaves and Niobe from her stones. It's not the individuals that matter. It's their attitudes, their poses.

"We've been looking at this the wrong way all along, trying to turn it into some kind of miserable allegory where

William is taking pot shots at each of us. But Reuben wasn't attacked. He killed himself. And Movina was not consumed with grief, and Frank is not a rapist. It doesn't work as an allegory."

"So maybe it reminds us how there are only so many stories. That all our little stories are retellings of older, much larger ones? Remember the cast-off crab shells?" I think Henry has forgotten that he is not represented in the mural. I don't think he has ever worked out where I am. "Surely that has some value too, some real merit. It's something worth preserving."

I look around at the multiple appearances of William's face in the mural. He is there as both Dionysus and Pentheus at once, and falling into the sea as wax-winged Icarus. My theory that the specific faces mean nothing does not seem to stand up here. I know he was trying to say something, with those multiple portraits, about himself. About his selves.

His use of my shoulders for Agave, too, means something. Possessed by William as Dionysus, I, as Agave, look on while Pentheus is torn to shreds, but the victim bears William's features, too. It is all very complicated, too complicated. I am trying too hard again. My eyes come to rest on the birth of Adonis. William again. Springing from Myrrha's incestuous bush. There can be no accident there. The intimacy of the rendition makes sense now. That is the part of the mural meant just for me. It puts the story of his incestuous love for his sister into a larger context. What happened between them is an instance of a much older story. The rest of the mural warns me to concentrate on the gesture, the ideal, and not to use his face, their faces, but the birth of Adonis gives me permission to write the story.

"I am sure William will be very pleased to know you want to save the painting," I murmur to Henry.

"And there is something more. The landlord found it in the corner, where he pulled away the wall, tucked down behind the mural."

It is the red notebook. I extend my right hand, hoping he will give it to me.

He begins leafing through the pages. "It's like meeting up with an old friend, seeing these early sketches of William's. I remember when he made these."

Nobody has any secrets from Henry.

"His sister," I murmur.

"What? God no. William doesn't have a sister. No, this was somebody we all drew. I can't remember her name. She was much older than she looked." He continues to turn the pages until he arrives at the darker pictures. "I've never seen these. They must have been done later. Not to my taste at all. And then all these notes. What a waste of a good un-ruled book. I wonder what he was thinking."

I think about how determined William was to show me the Provincial Hospital, how quickly he huffed out of his apartment to leave me alone, how easy it was for me to find the notebook under the mattress. I remember how he transposed her face onto my body. I begin to understand better his lukewarm reaction to my clumsy fable about the two children on the island, and the theatrical intensity of his anger at discovering the notes about incest and my character study of the sister he had, I realize now, invented for my benefit.

My sketches of our crowd were superficial exercises, surface tricks. William told me that often enough. He wanted me to go deeper, to wrestle with big, timeless issues—to try to understand things from a different point of view, to see myself in others and them in me. And this web of inviting lies was how he helped me do that.

"Would you like to have the notebook, Libby?" Henry holds it out.

"No. Thanks. I don't need it anymore."

I turn around slowly in the middle of the room, reacquainting myself with the figures on each wall as they play out the old stories, the old attitudes and poses, constant in their transformations. The year might as easily be 1441 as 1941, the place as easily Florence, or a cave in Lascaux, as an apartment in Saint John. And then I hurry up the stairs to my typewriter, eager to get back to work on the novel that William has given to me, because it was never really his to give.

AUTHOR'S NOTE

THE FORMAL RESEARCH FOR THIS BOOK STARTED IN THE course of an academic investigation of Saint John theatre between the wars. My immersion in Saint John newspapers of the period has been supplemented by nearly fifty years of walking its streets and imagining past scenes and lives. I am grateful to scholars and writers who have ably described and analyzed the city's arts scene of the late thirties and early forties, including Sandra Djwa, Costas Halavrezos, Karen Herring, Kirk Niergarth, Stuart Smith, and Jean Sweet. This book is a work of the imagination, though, an exercise in "what-if-ing," and I have chosen not to base my characters or their actions on any actual historical figures or events. Miller Brittain, Jack Humphrey, Ted Campbell, Kay Smith, P. K. Page, and others have nevertheless been on my mind from time to time.

ACKNOWLEDGEMENTS

A palette full of thanks to the team at Nimbus/Vagrant for the wonderful work they do to make the voices of Atlantic Canada heard. Special thanks to Whitney Moran, for believing in the book, and to Bethany Gibson for challenging and encouraging me to tighten its weft and be clear about what I really wanted to say, and to Kate Juniper for her painstaking attention to details large and small.

And, as always, to Sheila.

MICHAEL D. WENNBERG

MARK BLAGRAVE'S SHORT FICTION HAS APPEARED in several Canadian literary journals and in a collection of interlinked stories entitled *Salt in the Wounds* (2014). His novel *Silver Salts* (2008) was shortlisted for the Commonwealth First Novel Award (Canada and Caribbean) and for the John and Margaret Savage Award for First Novel. After a thirty-five-year teaching career in universities in New Brunswick and Ontario, Mark lives and writes in Saint Andrews, New Brunswick.